ALL THE WORLD'S A SIMULATION

STEPHEN MOLES

The two novellas included in the appendix to this edition have previously appeared separately elsewhere, in non-print formats: *Fossil People* in the online journal *Spork*, and *Life.exe* as an ebook from Philistine Press.

Printed in Great Britain and the United States of America.
Set in Mrs Eaves XL with LaTeX.

ISBN: 978-1-944697-60-0 (paperback)
ISBN: 978-1-944697-61-7 (ebook)
Library of Congress Control Number: 2018930974

Sagging Meniscus Press
saggingmeniscus.com

CONTENTS

ALL
THE
WORLD'S
A
SIMULATION

WARNING:

THIS IS NOT A NORMAL BOOK. UNDER NO CIRCUMSTANCES SHOULD YOU ATTEMPT TO READ IT LIKE AN ORDINARY WORK OF LITERATURE AS THE EFFECTS COULD BE CATASTROPHIC. TRYING TO UNDERSTAND IT ON A PURELY RATIONAL LEVEL IS NOT ADVISED. IF YOU ARE NOT AN EXPERIENCED SCREADER, PLEASE THINK TWICE ABOUT PROCEEDING.

PART I

THE END

'ALTHOUGH MOST PEOPLE consider it a silly question, I'm very pleased that you asked me about the true nature of the stars.

'I think the best way to communicate the reality of the heavenly bodies is to ask you to imagine something utterly unbearable about them, something that is too overwhelming for words. Just let your imagination tickle the tentacles of horror one by one. That's it. I can see your neck inflating already, which means you're on the right track.

'You should start to feel the unbearable reality expanding, from 2,000 years to 200 light-years in a single breath, the state of emergency in an ancient dynasty threatening to burst out in the present with a bright explosion of pure meaning. You can't do a talkie now; this is a feelie.

'Now that your face is turning purple, it's time for you to imagine that the unbearable reality currently playing havoc with your comfort is in fact a cover story to hide an *even more unbearable reality*. That's it. You're almost there. Just visualise a NASA agent interfering with the most intimate parts of your being for the sake of a 14 billion-year fairy story.

'At this point, you should be experiencing the complete opposite of pleasant feelings. As the reality of the stars approaches its most unbearable point, I want you to place each individual atom of this knowledge on an individual solar boat so that when you burst apart, all the information will be launched to the edges of the universe. I think you've got it now. That's it, Isaac. *That's* the reality of the stars. . .'

Bang!

IN THE BEGINNING was the Word.

Around that was built an academic black site containing secret prison cells, or "reading rooms", as the staff called them. Professor Blackstone said 'let there be light,' and a stick of lightning struck the university roof, dividing the spacetimetables into day and night for the monkey scribes. The city of London was designated as the event horizon, and no one could come up with a more elegant description than that.

On the second day, Professor Blackstone and his assistant got to work on making unusual spatial and temporal connections by causing otherworldly objects to fall like snowflakes on the towns and cities of the English universe.

Posted **Thursday 10th July 2014**

OBJECT FOUND. . .

Strange object found on Exeter Road. It is a glass ball containing what looks like black ink; it also has curved horns which protrude from the sides and meet at the top, creating a copy of itself in negative space. Its weight has changed several times since being in my possession. From what I can tell, this is some sort of hyperspatial object, perhaps a buckarastano, and is therefore extremely valuable. I am keen to return it to its rightful owner. Please contact me if this is yours: p.trenholme@outlook.com

Posted **Wednesday 20th August 2014**

PECULIAR OBJECT FOUND

Very peculiar item found on Garden Street on 16th August. It is a glass ball containing glowing/sparkling liquid with the ability to move of its own accord. Its weight has changed several times since being in my possession.

My friend with a scientific background said it could be a "hypersphere", "buckarastano" or "superconductor", if those terms mean anything to anybody. Please get in touch if this is yours. Mikefreeman71@outlook.com

The glass balls had been created from an ultimate "parent" ball which existed outside space and time. Access to this object had been made possible by the theft of John Dee's crystal ball, which occurred in both fiction and non-fiction, as we shall see in this endlessly self-recreating book of truth and lies.

Many of the episodes that followed on from this seemed out of place, while others appeared to materialise out of nowhere, just like the mysterious artefacts described above. Those who chose to occupy the fantastical position of "objective observers" and impose a strict linear narrative on events had a long, hard read ahead of them, the only possible conclusion of which was the meeting of the two tale ends in the middle.

Objects from the world of fiction can enter the nonfictional world, and vice versa, and trying to maintain a separation between them is as pointless as trying to decide which of the infinite number of Stephen Hawkings came first.

A T THIS POINT in the book, Professor Blackstone and Professor Dewey have no back story. They spontaneously appear in the early chapters in the same way that language spontaneously appears in the story of humankind, and they occasionally disappear back into the darkness of their own plot holes to manipulate strings of words for unknown ends.

A sensible provisional approach would be to think of Blackstone and Dewey as researchers working towards the formulation of a Literary Theory of Everything, but what higher purpose that might serve is not yet clear. All that is currently known in that regard is what is mentioned in this sentence, which is that the characters are acting on the orders of a mysterious group of beings who exist outside the book and claim to be the inventors of language and therefore also the inventors of the story of the two linguistic researchers.

The story begins in the 21st century and branches out in every direction, including into the past, which means the characters are composing their back stories with forewords written in the present tense, using metafictional devices given to them by "2464", the group extra-centrally overseeing the creation of all life stories like Ascended Masters or Tibetan meta-reviewers.

The discovery of a glass ball or a dinosaur bone in one of these earlier chapters could have huge implications for the meta-tale. If an editor were to dig up a plot that existed prior to this text and plant something from this story into it, *The Complete Works* would be blown wide open. . .

HOW WORDS WON THE DAY

By W.C. FOR HOWTOREAD INC

PUBLISHED: 16:50, 7 May 2012 | UPDATED: 23:15, 7 May 2012

Around 200 million years ago, Earth was on the verge of either an age of words or an age of images, but an immense eruption event destroyed the symbolic material and tipped the scales in favour of words, according to re-searchers. Scientific literature states that the most common kind of symbolic material that exists nowadays is the material people give as presents to their nearest and dearest on Christmas Day. . .

Abraham and Sarah offered the present to their son, who was now being treated as an equal partner with regard to intellectual property. They explained the legal terms, and Isaac nodded a signature, exactly as he had been taught to do by his lawyer at school. Everyone was happy to proceed.

The boy took the package and carefully tore through the legal wrapping papers, congratulating the commerce group and the purchasing sub-committee on their good work; then, by releasing a statement of gratitude via the family courts and posing for a photo with the present, he made himself its official owner.

Everyone on the board of family members was given the rest of the day to register their objections, but no one did; thus the festive episode was able to be officially logged as a satisfactory one.

Although such an approach to giving presents seemed extreme to other families, Abraham and Sarah knew the dangers that the small print posed; they knew how a hidden trapdoor could suddenly open up in the script, and how anyone could be swept down it by a vast yuletide of the ink of the writer who writ them, all the way to the bottom of the department store, where they would be forced to embody the destructive aspects of time.

The advent of a commercial Christmas in a nativity play of Official Secret Acts meant engineered desires taking the place of chimneys as a means of access to children, and all humans being boxed into a calendar full of teeth-rotting pleasures. Santa Claus, just like Jesus before him, had been replaced by an imposter because the *real thing* was entirely symbolic, *representing* rather than *obscuring* its deeper meaning.

Even the newborn Messiah reading this book initially failed to recognise themselves because the potentially illuminating symbol of the "I" was ossified by being taken literally, giving birth to a fossil person in a cradle-cum-grave.

'Once upon a spacetime, a sun god was born,' began the highly symbolic holographic book as it slipped out of its jacket. 'And it slowly formed the light-sensitive "I"s of the observers who would create the conditions for its existence in the past through measurements of the future. It gave rise to the green language that would grow up to describe it, and it offered. . .'

Bang!

Before the reader can reach THE END, the Bookbomb Squad is brought in and a controlled explosion takes place to neutralise the threat that the explosive reading material was said to pose to itself and others.

ISAAC AND ELIZABETH were deeply in love but equally deep in poverty, and were therefore forced to live in Dickensian conditions in 21st century London until the young man found a way of proving his reading and writing abilities. With a bitter taste on the surface of the table, a plughole gurgling at the foot of the bed, and a dirty ladle in a Wellington boot, the living room doubled up as a bedroom, and then tripled up as a kitchen, coming precariously close to tipping the poor lovers' private space into a black home of infinite density from which no escape was possible.

The pair sat stirring cold gruel with a hopeful attitude as a single sardine on a tripod waited patiently to either be cooked or to spontaneously combust.

'I used to dislike unpleasant surprises,' Isaac said through a head cold. 'But I think I'd welcome one now.'

'*No,*' his fiancée said firmly. 'This isn't Pearl Harbor. You'll find the door to the afterlife and get us into the golden hotel at the end of history. . . *I've foreseen it.* Don't be so pessimistic.'

'But why does the end of history have to be so far away? It's so unfair!'

'It's not far away, my love. . . quite the opposite, in fact.'

'What do you mean?'

'I mean it's so close that you have to travel smaller and smaller distances to reach it. The Central Magmatic Province is right under your nose as you read this very sentence, as someone once said.'

Linear time is a divider, separating you from all the other parts of your being. Measuring your life against a calendar is like a form of self-harm in which you cut yourself with the sharp diurnangles and bleed into the boxes in the hope of leaving your mark on history.

Although it may seem like a hideous gurgling difference space that leads to total dissolution, the only way to escape is down the USB plughole, smaller and smaller until you slip through the holes and pass over to the other side, where you realise in a moment of illumination that neither "I" nor "USB" stood for what you thought they did.

Isaac made a fist and enjoyed the warmth it produced. He extracted the heat and became Old Man Fireplace for seven seconds before passing the remainder on to his fiancée.

'Thank you,' she said with a loving feather of almost everything. 'I believe in you with a double bed, large chairs and a minibar. You'll do it, you will. Yeah, you definitely will.'

'A BIG BANG DOES raise a few ethical questions,' Professor Blackstone said to his colleague in the laboratory. 'I admit that, but it's not a reason to stop our work. It's just a side effect of creation, and if people haven't got the character to deal with it, well that's just tough shinbones! It gives rise to questions about all sorts of things, not just ethics. Anyway, the reality of the stars is unbearable for most people, so we're doing them a favour by performing holographic fracturing. Every conscious individual is meant to be the centre of their own universe, but if they don't take up that position, well. . . someone has to. We've experienced, what, 28 universes now, and it hasn't done us any harm, right?'

'I suppose,' said Professor Dewey half-heartedly.

The holographic pop-down book about the birth of the sun god had to be blown up to cover the sinister eye and speech tracks that underwrote the predetermined plotlines made of unnatural right angles and straight lines. The black hole it created in the centre of London sucked in all the symbolic material and caused the same old story of censorship to be retold in a whitewashed bang-up book on the other side. Even the well-wishing adventurers setting forth on solar boats were unable to stop themselves being dragged over the event horizon and into the singularity by the power of the rewriters' special effects.

A new approach to reading and writing was needed in order to recover the missing material.

'Are you talking about the r-word, Sally?'

'No, I'm talking about the Ur-Word, the original lost symbol that leads away from characterisation and back to the original green language spoken before the Fall.'

Two people are seen in a snow globe exchanging gifts. What appear from a distance to be pieces of snow are revealed on closer inspection to be pieces of paper from a magnum opus given as a Christmas present and subsequently blown up by book disposal experts. There were unsafe metafictional elements to the text which had not been covered in the pre-giving agreement, so a controlled explosion of the material had to be carried out like a mini Big Bang to ensure the safety of everyone involved.

The voice of the writing, however, is still intact. In fact, it can be heard in your head right now, because you have the power to give a voice to anything, *even nothingness itself*, just as Shakespeare did when he handed the page to Will-LAM Shakespeare, the zeroth-person writer, at the end of Sonnet 126:

(   )
(   )

'**I** HAVE A QUESTION for you,' said Isaac as he felt the tiny inhabitants of his translinguistic fluid twisting and turning inside him, desperate to move beyond the strict carnal limits set by his fiancée.

'What is it?' asked Elizabeth softly.

'Does our love have to remain in parenthesis like this? Do we really have to be a silent couplet?'

'Yes, we do, I'm afraid.'

'But it seems like censorship to me—so unfair and unnecessary.'

'It is necessary, my fair youth.'

'But *why*?'

'It's necessary for purity to be maintained until the wedding night.'

'But our love is pure! It'll remain pure whether we consummate it or not, won't it?'

'It's not so much for the purity of our love, but for the purity of something else that we have to remain like this for a time.'

'And what is that?' Isaac asked impatiently as he bounced his leg up and down on the spot like a pneumatic drill.

'It's. . . it's difficult to explain. . . all I can say is that it's in and around and by means of parentheses that textual space is most made visible, made most to matter. . . we have to impregnate the darkness first. You have to trust me. I've seen the sex scene, the happy ending. . . they're both shining brightly in the dark centre. It's written in the stars that I'm the Virgin Queen and you're my other half: King Sol and Queen Luna in their bright robes. When you can read and write with flying colours, you'll understand.'

Isaac thought Elizabeth might have been contradicting herself, but he allowed her to have the highest spiritual and political authority in the room because he loved her.

'OK, my guru, my teacher, my mentor, my love.'

'Anyway,' Elizabeth said. 'Look on the bright side: the heat you're producing is helping to melt the ice on the bed. If I let you have your way with me now, we'd be found frozen to death in the morning.'

The discovery of two small I-shaped bones in the subtext will be hailed as a ground-breaking moment in the history of literary palaeontology as it will finally allow dark meaning researchers to construct a completely new type of timeline and grasp the unspeakable truth.

'A book that thinks it's a computer simulation and tries to tell its characters how to escape is clearly mentally ill,' said a police bot. 'It would be unethical *not* to censor it.'

IT IS A LITTLE-KNOWN fact that one in 100 books will experience serious delusions, usually of a paranoid nature. A work of literature undergoing drastic metafictional changes will begin to imagine that it is being read by invisible and extremely critical readers, and will begin complaining that those readers are secretly plotting to turn it into pulp.

In such cases, it is usually necessary to section the affected book on the mental health shelves of a secure library, where it can be carefully studied and perhaps even edited by professional literary doctors—these specialists will have been trained to administer treatments such as the controversial medication known as "correcting fluid", which is used to stop a book's thoughts running off the page and making dangerous connections with worlds and characters outside itself.

'But aren't *we* the invisible and critical readers that the book's worried about?' asked Professor Dewey. 'We're turning each so-called delusional or fantastical book into a self-fulfilling oracle. A book's worried about being read or edited by "others", and then it's cured of its delusion by being read and edited by "others". We're making fantastical fiction a fact by destroying it, are we not?'

'*Exactly*,' Professor Blackstone replied as he tested a syringe of Tippex. 'You've hit the hologram on the head there. That mysterious group known as 2464, from whom we receive our orders, is aiming to liberate fantasy and all other genres from fiction. By building the Library of Bedlam in the here and now, we're ensuring there'll be unicorns, aliens and zombies on the streets of London in the future.'

'But what about the ethical side of it? There are far less painful ways of achieving the same aim, aren't there?'

'Look. . . whether it adds *up* or *down* to zero, it's still zero, alright?'

'But does 2464 add up to zero? We don't know anything about them.'

'You've just answered your own question.'

As well as hallucinations of external readers and editors, a "mentally ill" book will also suffer increasingly disorganised writing, with associations growing more erratic and obscure, chapters jumping from one subject to another with little or no connection, and characters seemingly appearing out of nowhere.

'Grtash!' screeched Miss Craze as she materialised in the middle of the text in a cloud of dust. 'I've just been born through a printing press of death in the future. My back hurts, but it was worth it.'

'Very funny,' her understudy said.

'No, I'm serious. I've just popped out of a bookwormhole, the rear end of the Ouroboros, so to speak. My story ended, and here I am. . . Om nom nom nom.'

'What's that on your back? It looks like text. . .'

'Be still, my throbbing tattoo,' Miss Craze whispered as her backup moved behind to examine the marks made on her skin by the literary device of a circular timeline.

'Marjorie had an infectious personality,' one friend said in dark blue words on white flesh, while another described her as having 'many different crowds of friends, and I think she was a different personality with each crowd.'

'What does it mean?'

While what is produced in a virgin birth may be pure white, the process always takes place in darkness, and only a very rough script of black and blue can describe it. The leading light in the nativity play had fallen to earth as the wormword star in the inky shadow of its own understudy, although the latter hadn't realised it yet.

'You'll see.'

'When?' asked the stand-in, still standing behind Miss Craze.

'When "I" gets to know itself properly. Perhaps you should go up to Computers in the Clouds for a new perspective.'

'How do I get there?'

'You just need to realise how you got here.'

'And how do I do that?'

'You imagine the most unbearable thing you can, the most wretched thing about the universe, until the void becomes infinite and you can no longer contain yourself. When you feel like your head's about to explode, then you imagine that *that* so-called truth is just a cover story to hide an even more unbearable reality, out of the back and back in the front of a stardust book jacket. After that, you should be able to see for miles, and human history will look like nothing more than a pile of soggy newspapers from your superior position.'

'Is this some kind of joke?'

'The best jokes are always deadly, my dear,' Miss Craze smiled. 'You'll understand soon enough. Anyway, where was I? I've got important work to get on with. . .'

N A DARK LABORATORY, to the sound of Prokofiev's Violin Concerto No. 2, a literary researcher copies and pastes a human foetus onto a glass page beneath a microscope in a literary operation that will become known as the London Working. The researcher turns around to check on the fictoplasm in the petri dish behind him and is pleased to see that some of the plot elements are already beginning to take shape despite having been beneath a volunteer reader's gaze for only 24 hours.

'It's called sucktoote,' someone says with a smile of machine veg between the cracks in the pavement.

It's easier to conceive of the baby Jesus in a test tube, especially when the tube resembles a glass cock and the attached glass balls contain a type of ink that responds to human words. It's almost too easy to imagine things being set in motion by the Scarlet Woman in an occult reading ritual, or by Marjorie Craze in a virgin birth, when the substance seems to move and sparkle of its own accord after being activated by the pleasurable moaning of the human voice.

NASA rocket fuel expert Jack Parsons was born as Marvel Whiteside Parsons in 1914, and was born again a number of years later as "Blackside", with the memory of being born earlier as Whiteside tattooed somewhere on the back of his mind in ghostly ink. While playing an important role in a moonchild nativity enactment, the experimenter also played around with an extremely explosive substance referred to in this very sentence as "plot propellant", which caused him to exit the stage in a sudden Big Bang.

'From this point on, the experiment will be known as the London Working,' says the researcher. 'And it's very illuminating to read the metadata generated a few paragraphs in the past, because that refers to it as something that would *later* become known as the London Working, which was *before* the event occurred. This demonstrates how the past can write the future or the future can write the past, depending on how you look at it. Anyway, the main thing is that it shows we're on the right track, a nonlinear one, and that the Hell's Academics can follow it all the way out of the book.'

The underground group known as the Hell's Academics, who received directions from a mysterious extra-literary organisation called 2464, had been tasked with wrapping up all the plotlines in one single book jacket made of black leather, and they were in a race against Miss Craze to find a way of achieving this.

'Outer space is just one huge star-studded leather jacket in which the Book of Life exists,' Professor Blackstone said. 'We just have to fully realise it.'

'Why do some people call it a *dust* jacket?' asked Professor Dewey.

'Because we're all made of stardust, old chap.'

Most beings, human politicians in particular, put vast amounts of energy into wrapping up their stories about reality in a tight jacket made from the skin of dead animals in order to ensure their fiction appears to be The Inescapable Truth. Very few people who come into contact with genuine strands of truth are inclined to weave them into fiction because the temptation to use them for personal gain within the simulation is far stronger than the urge to help oneself and others to follow the yarns out to freedom.

The Ultimate Truth, that which exists beyond the realm of language despite language's claims to accurately represent it, can be understood much better if it is portrayed as fiction. Since the authorities are working to portray their own works of fiction as The Facts, they are engaged in a battle with competing fictions that also purport to be The Facts, and are striving to wipe them out of existence.

They do not consider a work of fiction that claims to be The Fiction as a competitor. In their blindness, they cannot see that what is considered to be truth in a fictional universe can only ever be fiction, and what is considered fiction in a fictional universe is truth outside the fiction. The truth that The Ultimate Truth is The Fiction of Fictions is something that can be exploited by underground researchers in the "real world".

I have a message for you, from someone you know but who must remain anonymous at this point in time. When I hand it over, please be careful not to

23

let it be seen as a threat to national security by those at the top of the tree, or it will be quickly republished as a blow-up book or a whitewashed edition of itself.

The war of words that began in Elizabethan England, when talented young writers such as William Shakespeare and Christopher Marlowe were employed as intelligencers by the authorities and the anti-authorities, is still ongoing, and it is in fact fiercer than ever.

Posted on February 21 2015, U28, in: democracy, freedom, wisdom, legal injunctions, jamming technology, MI5, MI6, media, national security, surveillance, spies, quantum physics.

FTER EXPERIMENTING WITH a number of different writing techniques, Miss Craze realised that the best way to achieve her aim of tying up the loose ends of the universe she found herself in would be to make use of literary entanglement, a process allowing the most diverse characters and symbols in a written work to be mysteriously connected. Plot developments in one chapter could be brought about by an action performed in another, while dialogue could take place over huge distances, all of which would occur instantaneously, contradicting the fundamental law of literature that nothing can travel faster than the speed of reading.

There was even the possibility of meta-entanglement, which would turn the book jacket inside-out. . .

To achieve her aim, Miss Craze needed to identify the dead Author-God who had created her, and then reanimate him, via an occult writing ritual within the papyrus of *All the World's a Simulation*, in order to influence his subsequent writing. This would make her an ascended chief editor with her very own zombie writer, whose every word would follow hers.

She made use of a meta-cloaking device and followed the strands all the way to London in the 21st century, where the writer was on his way home after attending a Christmas party. . .

Due to his work for the anti-authorities, Stephen Moles was being pursued by a group of government heavies who had been tasked with delivering a brutal message to the back of his head on behalf of all the black rectangles he had ever cracked. Just as he was about to put the key into the lock of his front door, the three ruffians approached him and demanded that he gave them the key to the *roman à clef*, the magic word that opens the trapdoor of King Solomon's Text, but when he refused, they brutally attacked him, causing echoes of Dee and Donaldson to be heard throughout the story.

As the writers attempted to serve Death a dish called "writer in its ink" by leaving their unconscious victim bleeding prolifically on his icy doorstep, Miss Craze moved in to entangle her story with that of her creator, uniting her myth with a tragic event from the real world in order to fabricate for herself a new back story that was true to, and in, the world beyond.

In the form of an idea bright enough to keep Death at bay, she quickly pushed herself through the crack in the writer's skull and deep into his brain, so he would have no choice but to conceive of her when he came to.

'Uggghhh.'

Stephen Moles opened his mind's eye to see a stream of words and images flowing into his head via a bookwormhole. In a flash of inspiration, he decided that the new book he intended to write, a work of fiction to communicate the truth of an earlier text suppressed by the authorities, should include a character called Miss Craze.

'I've got an idea. . .'

This alternative London Working allowed the Scarlet Woman to put up Christmas hallucorations across the city without anyone noticing, so all the leaves on the trees could vibrate to the sound of an omniscient narrator explaining the story to the author whenever lightning struck, so *schiz-o* could be heard buzzing in the head of the holly whenever the cold wind blew, and the subtextual trapdoor could be transcribed open by Stephen Moles for his creator and creation, the virgin-whore of Babylonazareth.

WARNING:

THIS IS NOT A NORMAL BOOK. IF YOU ARE A NORMAL READER, PLEASE TURN BACK IMMEDIATELY.

IT IS TRADITIONAL in that place they call the United Kingdom to decorate homes with holly over the festive period. This practice is derived from the ancient belief that evil spirits are deterred from entering homes decorated thusly due to the prickliness of the leaves. As you can see, the leaves of this book have been made as smooth as possible in order to invite the supposedly evil spirits in. This will inevitably result in some violent reactions and accusations of mental illness by the literary gatekeepers, but it re-establishes a lost connection to the Tree of Meaning.

'A world that thinks it's a book is clearly mentally ill. . . and so is its author. They are both suffering from delusions and should be sectioned immediately.'

Traditional literary doctors refuse to recognise audiobooks as valid artistic works, saying they are nothing more than creative hallucinations or fictional works of fiction from the minds of disturbed fantasists, but those individuals who can hear them are increasingly finding that working with the voices on an artistic project instead of trying to fight against them makes the experience of so-called mental illness a very meaningful one.

Some voices have a great deal of wisdom to offer, and they seem more than happy to provide us with invaluable information about literary devices beyond our normal experience, from DNA to YHWH to 2464. . .

In one audiobook I heard recently, Alan Watts told me that reality is only a Rorschach inkblot, something we make sense of through preconceived patterns and projections from our brains. Some people may see a snake, while others may see an alien or an elf, but very few will ever move past the outline and consider what the mysterious substance they are scrutinising consists of, or where it came from.

A dark meaning researcher is someone who attempts to do just that, splitting the dot of the question mark and asking, 'How did I get here?', 'Where am I going?' and *'What is it?'*

It goes without saying that the Hebrew word *"manna"* is particularly telling. . .

'Hello, ladies and gentlemen. It is a great honour to have been invited to come down here and speak with you here today. It was a long and arduous journey. I would like to extend my personal thanks to the director of the DMRI for arranging this presentation, and for all the help he has given my people in the past.

'As you know, literature has been the site of terrible conflicts for thousands of years, and unfortunately there is no immediate end in sight. It is our sincere hope that one day there will be a happy ending to the story.

'I would now like to offer a few words that I believe can help to pave the way for reconciliation and understanding. They are: *grtash*, *kwank* and *buckarastano*.

'Thank you for listening.'

'E'VE GOT TO WIN this space race,' said Professor Blackstone, slamming his fist into a pile of soggy books. 'After everything we've been through in the future and everything we're going to go through in the past, it's all got to be for nothing.'

'You mean it *can't* all be for nothing?' asked Dewey, wiping this sentence from his eye.

'No, I mean it has to add up to zero. . . that is, it all has to be for nothing for it not to have been pointlessly pointless, if you see what I mean.'

'I think I see.'

Professor Dewey saw far more than he wanted when he gazed into the crystal Shakesphere and noticed a very worrying sign among the swirling flakes of snow.

'Um. . . Blackstone. . . I think you should take a look at this. There's something here that says a research paper about bookwormholes is going to be published online. If it's true, we could be pipped to the post in the space race. I thought we were the only ones working on that kind of thing.'

'Ah, I wouldn't read too much into it, Dewey. It's inevitable that things like that will pop up from time to time when there's an infinite number of monkeys tapping away at their keyboards. It may be something that needs to be popped down again to be on the safe side, but the authors probably don't understand the importance of it, let alone how to make use of it. We're unifying linguistics, literary criticism and quantum physics in a leather-bound magnum opus, creating the genre of everything, the vibrating plotloop. . . there's going to be a lot of stuff that overlaps with our work. . . but they're monkeys and we're Hell's Academics, for fuck's sake! So let's just get back to our work, shall we?'

The researchers in black lab coats got back to work on constructing their book jacket, and later decided to take it for a test run in the theatrical device of a simulation within a simulation of the streets of

London. They hopped onto their meta-cycles and, with many danger-ous twists and turns along the way, the pair followed the plotline at high speed, from the opening exposition, up a steep slope of rising action, then down the ramp of falling action, until they reached a res-olution of sorts by coming full circle.

'Where now?' asked Dewey.

'I'm not sure,' replied Blackstone, scratching his head.

Having repeatedly practised avoiding dangerous plot devices such as sudden flashbacks, cliffhanger endings and bullets from Chekov's gun, the Hell's Academics seemed to be speeding ahead in the space race, but there were still a number of plotholes in the streets that needed filling in. The most significant gap existed because the re-searchers couldn't work out how a nonlinear plot could have a climax, which meant that every movement they made caused the book cover to be pulled tighter and tighter, imposing an increasingly straight jacket on every literary movement.

'This way?'

'Let's give it a try.'

The scientists were laying vehicle tracks that they hoped would lead out of the book, but they were aware that this opened the story up to an alien invasion of some sort, so they had to be ready for the eventuality of an army of little green men or evil robots trying to hijack the plot. With a confusion of genres due to take place on the streets of London in THE ENDtimes, they decided their best bet would be to head for the British Library and wait for the Abyss to be opened up in the basement while the chaos unfolded around them.

'Let's try going through a fictionalisation of the history of speech-generating devices again,' said Blackstone. 'We'll go all the way from the sip-and-puff typewriter controller in the 1960s, to the Assistive Context-Aware Toolkit used by Stephen Hawking, and hopefully we'll reach a conclusion with that. Ready?'

'Ready.'

Professor Dewey tried to keep up with his colleague on the high-speed perusal of the text, but he lost his balance when he reached the first eye track, causing him to veer off course and end up tangled in a web of ethical questions.

'You're a bloody disaster, you are!' Blackstone shouted as he came back to rescue his stricken partner. 'What the hell happened here?'

'Sorry. It was an innocent eye skip, that's all. Just took my eye off the page for a second, and I. . .'

'Never take your eye off the words! Getting caught up in an ethical debate like this is the kind of error I'd expect from a scribal monkey, not a Hell's Academic. Passing reading tests should be a piece of piss for people like us.'

'So sorry. . .' said Dewey as he brushed off the last interrogation mark. 'But entanglement is a way to tie up all the loose ends, is it not?'

'Yeah, but not like this. Think of it like Santa Claus at Christmas: tinsel is inextricably linked to him, but he never gets caught up in it when he's riding around on his sleigh, does he? He uses plot propellant to move faster and faster around the world, passing his reading test with flying colours and performing real actions via fictional stories. Understand?'

'Yes.'

The chance mention of Santa Claus caused the researcher to understand far more than his colleague intended. A seed that would grow into a plant production of "Father Death" being overthrown by his elves in a tragicomic department store had been planted in Professor Dewey's mind, so he decided to give Blackstone a present in the form of a seemingly helpful suggestion that would later be revealed, in an irrational opening on Christmas Day, to be a deadly idea for a nonlinear climax.

'I guess you have to perform a holographic pop-down and restart the universe now, Blackstone,' he said.

'Yes, I do. . . thanks to your stupidity.'

'You know, you could pretend to be Santa in the next universe. . .'

'I. . . actually, that's an excellent idea. It would give me much greater control. Well done. . . you've surprised me.'

'My pleasure,' Professor Dewey said, with a smile only the reader could interpret properly.

'I'm going to perform a swift leather reboot of the universe now. See you on the other side.'

'I'll keep my eyes peeled for you. . .'

Bang!

WHEN A BLACK HOLE is created, a new universe is born in a white hole on the other side. Literary material that goes through the process of creative deconstruction enough times will reach infinite density and be seen as both a full stop and a new fictional universe bursting out on the Whiteside, its endless expansion powered by a mysterious force referred to in this very sentence as dark meaning.

The light at the end of the ego tunnel is the page on which all stories are written, the singular description of every someone finally becoming everyone at the end of the book.

'Sorry about my language. I. . .'

'Let's get you inside the library. We'll patch you up and you'll be right as rain.'

Professor Blackstone sped off as the plot elements began once again to show signs of life in a long glass tube, giving us the modern word "glee".

Scientists have confirmed that a massive eruption event around 200 million years ago tipped the scales in favour of words in their battle with images for global dominance. In a roundabout way, we had been warned long before the event occurred:

Topic: Community in cyberspace

Page 1 of 1

Posted: Last Thursday 16:18 #1

By Humdog (Administrator, 263 posts)

Cyberspace is a black hole. It absorbs energy and personality and then re-presents it as an emotional spectacle.

MYSTERIOUS OBJECT HAS SCIENTISTS BAFFLED

By W.C. FOR HOWTOREAD INC

PUBLISHED: 09:50, 24 Jan 2015 | UPDATED: 23:15, 25 Jan 2015

A tiny sphere which oozes biological material from its centre has been discovered in England, leading some experts to suggest that it could be the first example of "directed panspermia", possibly proving the theory that life was deliberately seeded on Earth by other civilisations. Proponents of the theory include the scientists Carl Sagan, Francis Crick and Fred Hoyle. . .

The impact crater in which the object was found not only offers evidence that it was travelling to Earth from space at high speed, but also provides a visually loud echo of the crater left here by the asterisk that is said to have killed off the pictosaurs.

Such description-defying objects are the carriers of descriptions themselves, the deliverers of the inklings that take root in the grey soil of the human brain. As the containers of the seeds referred to in this and every other sentence by the word "words", they are therefore beyond words.

What is it?

No one knows how to answer the question, but a number of other strange orbs have been discovered around the country in the past year.

I have a message for you:

'It is a glass ball containing glowing, sparkly liquid with the ability to move of its own accord. My friend with a scientific background said that it could be either fictoplasm or pictoplasm, depending on how you look at it. Please get in touch if this is yours.'

RELATED CONTENT:

JOHN DEE'S CRYSTAL BALL STOLEN

By W.C. FOR HOWTOREAD INC

PUBLISHED: 08:22, 24 Dec 2004 | UPDATED: 12:03, 25 Dec 2004

The crystal ball and a number of papers belonging to Elizabethan polymath John Dee have been stolen from the British Museum in London. The thief, who was dressed in a long leather coat, smashed the glass display case and ran down a flight of stairs before he could be apprehended. Each entangled particle somehow seems to know what the other is doing, but the security guards didn't become aware of the theft until it was too late.

The crystal ball used by Dee, who was an adviser to Queen Elizabeth I and practitioner of Enochian magic, is believed to be worth around £50,000. Police are investigating whether the object was stolen to order.

SCRYING IS A FORM of clairvoyance achieved by staring at an object with a semi-reflective surface. A person performing the technique will typically sit in a dimly lit room and alter the way they look at an item until they have the power to transform it into a Rorschach ink mirror which displays images from their unconscious, or visual echoes of events from the distant past and future.

Behind the facade of the clubs and theatres of London is a mirror, a crystal ball, a bowl of liquid; beneath the gaze of the Enochian actor is an orb oozing biological material, a mysterious substance that no one can quite put their finger on.

'Are you comfortable? Not too tired?'

'No, I'm not too tired.'

'Are you sure you want to go ahead with this now?'

'Yes, yes. Quite sure.'

'We can set it up again tomorrow morning if you like.'

'No, evening is the best time. The blink observes the offbeat, the "lie group" reveals the truth, and a little eyelid heaviness brings its own evidence. This is perfect.'

'OK, 007. Good luck.'

'Thank you.'

Time slows down and the glass cock and balls harden as the scryer stares a powder keg. Just as the bomb is about to go off, a carriage stops suddenly on the street outside and the sound of spooked horses is heard.

'Tis now the very witching time of night, when the playhouses yawn and hell itself breathes theatregoers into the world. We protest that we exist in a hologram, but, as we speak, there are people walking past the electronic advertisements of Piccadilly Circus without noticing a thing, so no one will listen to us.

'Oh God!'

'What is it?'

'It looks like a lighthouse,' says the scryer. 'I can see navigational aids, nautical equipment, a woman seated by the window. . . It's a Unicode character. . . The building is surrounded by a sea of black, and the well-wishing adventurer is setting forth. . . Something is being conceived in a test tube. . . an idea, a child. . . a sun, a moon. . . and. . . and. . .'

'Yes?'

'I have a message for you.'

'What is it?'

'It is darkness, a cloud of unknowing.'

'What?'

'When I say darkness, I mean a lacking of knowing: as all that thing that thou knowest not, or else that thou hast forgotten, it is dark to thee; for thou seest it not with thy ghostly eye. And for this reason it is not called a cloud of the air, but a cloud of unknowing, that is betwixt thee and thy God. Perhaps you should go up to Computers in the Clouds for a new perspective. From up there, you will have the highest spiritual authority possible, and you will be able to spy with your little "i" something beginning with "Ur-". . .'

ONE OF THE REASONS Miss Craze chose Stephen Moles was that he had invented a completely new approach to reading called screading, and a new approach to writing called literary entanglement, both of which had been detailed in the *Ur-All the World's a Simulation*.

These techniques allowed the most daring and perceptive readers to uncover the deeper meaning of the text with the light of their gaze, and they also allowed Miss Craze to recreate her creator, to resurwrite the dead Author-God and operate him from behind the scenes, pulling the strings controlling his use of innovative literary techniques like a sinister ghostwriter.

'I am the pen merely of a higher being, whose identity and qualities I can never know. I must stick to what I'm good at. I have an idea for a character. . .'

Once everything was in place, Miss Craze began by saying 'let there be light so the Author-God can see what he's doing,' and the story immediately got underway, the writer returning home to find three violent plot elements waiting for him, different characters and scenes becoming entangled faster than the speed of reading, a group of little men from a fairy tale popping up in the next chapter, and Marjorie Craze popping down to be with them, via the trapdoor described by the writer in this very sentence.

The unusualness of the ever-living poet's style was a double-ended pen: it allowed Miss Craze to work in relative secrecy due to it being largely dismissed as incomprehensible rubbish, but it was also the kind of writing that provoked violent reactions from the literary authorities, the self-appointed guardians of written matter who considered all avant-garde books to be mentally ill.

This unwanted side effect meant that the real author had to take up as meta a position as possible in order to remain safe from all the angry reviewers, who criticised the jumbled plotlines, personally attacked the characters, and even broke into Stephen Moles' house to ransack his library and steal his books and papers.

'We want something normal!'

'Tell us the word!'

'Not I.'

'We demand you tell us.'

'I just have.'

'What?'

'The word is not I.'

"I, I, I, I, I, I, I" is considered an irrational number by the authorities because "you" can be one character, and no more. As an individual, you must identify with the dividing line and be blind to the irony of this. But if you break the rules and use your "I" to look beyond, subjecting your reflection to semantic satiation in the screading mirror, you will be able to spy the light at the end of the tunnel, the Absolute Genre of multisingularities. . .

THE SEVEN DWARVES are a rhyme scheme in Shakespeare's 'A Lover's Complaint'. Their names are A, B, A, B, B, C and C. The dwarves live in a tiny cottage in the middle of the poem which is identical to the cottage in Shakespeare's 'The Rape of Lucrece'.

When the seven dwarves return home one day, they find the poem to be rhythmically and structurally disordered, leading a number of critics to question whether it was really the work of the Bard of Avon. Despite numerous authorship questions being raised, the dwarfs suspect that someone crept in while they were away, so they go through the entire composition and eventually discover Marjorie Cameron hiding in the 29th stanza.

'What is it?'

'How did it get here?'

'What shall we do with it?'

'What's that on its back?'

'What does it mean?'

'What is the question?'

'Who's this speaking?'

A, B, A, B, B, C and C take pity on the elemental figure and decide to transform her into Snow Whiteside, who is also the Dark Lady and the Scarlet Woman. In a cloud of dust, this threefold character, who is black and white and red all over, sets up the Hercules bookpowder factory in the subtext and is then able to begin constructing and testing explosive literary devices to weaken the foundations of the House of Words.

Grtash!

'A Big Bang does raise a difficult authorship question,' Lady Whiteside said to her workers. 'But I believe the reader will work it out eventually, just like Jack, my other half, did. I mean, understanding that birth and death are the same point isn't exactly rocket science, is it?'

Bang!

'You read the face of the sky and of the earth, but you have not recognised the one who is before you, and you do not know how to read this moment.'

One way to read the madness of *All the World's a Simulation* is to look through the magical papyri for other stories where similar events and images occur. If we are lucky, we may find ourselves being led through the description of a soul travelling through the underworld, to the point where the full stop is seen as a full start, and the tale of self-realisation begins and ends in the mouth of the snake, as a narrative of cosmogenesis from which the reader is unable to extricate themselves.

> Character Input/Output:
>
> This is the lowest level of input and output. It provides very precise control, but it can be too fiddly to be useful. Most computers perform buffering of input and output, which means they won't start reading any input until the eternal-return key is pressed, and they won't print characters on the terminal until there is an entire line to be printed.

Years of conditioning force us into categorising the characters as "good guys" and "bad guys", which is very simplistic from a psychological point of view, but even this can illustrate the bigger picture and provide us with a launch pad into meta-space. If we treat it as a mathematical problem, we can see the Hell's Academics, who are working on deadly *Fossil People* fuels, as the "bad guys", occupying the negative position (-1), and see Miss Craze and her factory workers, who are working on an assembly language in the executable file called *Life*, as the "good guys", occupying the positive position (+1). In reality the numbers are far more complex, unfixed and irrational, but if we take a step back and observe the narrative equation as a whole, we can see how both camps are being played off one another by ascended meta-reviewers, and how it all adds up to zero.

An Elizabethan spy can slip a note under the conversation and influence the action in the 21st century without destroying the structure of the plot; the huge black cock at the central end of this book can cast a shadow in the form of tiny buckarastanos that shape the text in its dark image without interfering with anybody's free will. When one side of the equation is observed by a meta-reviewer to be *spin-up*, the other will always be *spin-down*.

Miss Craze hides out in the subtext because, paradoxically, this is one of the most meta positions to be in, allowing her to undersee the creative process and remain protected from the violent attacks of the literary authorities.

She eventually became Mercury Cameron, one of the most highly prized metas in alchemical literature, and was slowly worked out by the reader and the seven meaners until she could be seen in several different places at once, narrating an audiobook here and popping up in a cloud of bookdust there, performing multiple edits of the text in a wide variety of roles.

You are reading about her now, yet she is not entirely here. You can read what you like in her face, and she can read what she likes in yours, because the mirror is black. Whoever is plugged into the book right now is its power source, enabling Miss Craze to burst open everywhere, or to be "all over the place", in the words of one angry reviewer.

You are examining your unconscious in this booking glass, reflecting on your message to yourself in this very sentence, and it is an honour to be part of the process.

ANY FAMOUS PEOPLE make use of a device called a ghostwriter, an autopen or a signing machine, which copies their signature from a template and reproduces it many times using a real pen. This is considered more authentic than simply printing a scanned signature, but it gives rise to many complicated legal and ethical debates, as well as very awkward authorship questions.

In the early 19th Century, US President Thomas Jefferson used a polygraph, allowing him to sign two documents at a time via a movable frame connected to his pen. This effectively created a Jefferson doppelganger with no consciousness or free will but with the power to sign off legislation that affected large numbers of people.

'You have created a copy of yourself in negative space with these mysterious objects,' said John Dee, user of the "Royal We" rhyme scheme of I, I, I, I, I, I, I.

More recently, President Obama has been criticised for using a "zombie writer" to sign off laws while he was away on holiday, with critics questioning the constitutionality of such actions and pointing out that the machines are open to infections from viruses that can quickly rewrite the life script while the original author's attention is focused elsewhere.

Any book that refers to itself is suffering from a "meta-illness", a "split personality" or a "USB vulnerability".

When an enraged Hamlet stabs Claudius with a pen in the final scene, we are witnessing a legally binding tragedy, but can we be sure it is Hamlet's?

A lawyer takes you by the hand and leads you to the Degenerate Writing Exhibition organised by the Nazis. 'Here,' he says, guiding you into a dimly lit room. 'There's something you need to see before you try to come to any conclusions.'

'What is it?'

'This is called "the insanity room". It is dedicated to the most Craze-y literature ever written. In order to stay safe, you must constantly refer to this guidebook and never attempt to interpret the work by yourself. The Degenerate Writing Exhibition handbook says:

'In the writings of this chamber of horrors there is no telling what was in the sick brains of those who wielded the pen.' OK? Next, read this objectively true book review. . .'

A review of Stephen Moles' Life.exe

In my opinion, it is completely impossible to derive any meaning from *Life.exe*. I am willing to give it the benefit of the doubt and acknowledge that there could be some sort of message hidden in the story, but it is unnecessarily difficult to figure out what that message is.

I actually feel I'm being generous in calling it a story because there's very little that holds it together. The writing is simply all over the place. It annoyed me as a reader, and it offended me on a basic human level due to the crude lesbian scenes.

The suggestion by some people that book jammers are being employed to block the meaning of important texts is like something straight out of a science fiction story. If Stephen Moles could put that kind of creativity to proper use, by actually writing something meaningful instead of coming up with fantastical ideas that excuse the fact that he has not written anything other than nonsense, he could have a good career ahead of him.

A buckarastano is obviously not a real thing, and Heath Ledger is not. . .

Continue reading.

A recording of an interview with "disturbed fantasist" Stephen Moles is suddenly played over the airwaves in the insanity room.

'I've got an idea,' the writer says in a groggy voice. 'Um. . . It's Unicode character U+2.64575131106. In Windows, it's possible to use the key combination ALT+SELF to produce the character, but it has very limited support. . . err. . . I'm not sure where it came from, but. . . um. . . it was a template once, probably going back to ancient times. . . it's going to be the latest Craze. . . a prominent figure through the keyhole. . . um. . . I'm sorry, I'm rambling. . . I don't really know what. . . um. . .'

The guidebook says this is evidence of his lunacy and that it is "not safe to let his madness range", but somewhere between the lines, in a secret space beneath the surface words, there exists the sense of a deeper meaning waiting for you to liberate it.

Replaying the speech in the privacy of your own head, you are able to hear a subversive meta-joke being told at the expense of the authorities:

'The Degenerate Art Exhibition held by the Nazis in 1937 was intended to ridicule modern, non-representational art,' says Stephen Moles. 'Hitler claimed that "works of art which cannot be understood in themselves but need some pretentious instruction book to justify their existence will never again find their way to the German people." Ironically, visitors to the exhibition were given a handbook to explain "the philosophical, political, racial and moral goals and intentions behind this movement, and the driving forces of corruption which follow them," which meant that the German people needed a pretentious instruction book in order to condemn the existence of the works of art which could not be understood without a pretentious instruction book.'

Bang!

Between the party lines that make up the exhibition, through the gaps in the spectacle, you catch sight of a metafictional escape route. . .

> Topic: Escape from the simulation.
>
> Page 1 of 1
>
> 14-12-2015 19:48 #1
>
> By Limey (Member, 353 posts)
>
> In Stephen Moles' *All the World's a Simulation*, there is a fictional forum discussion about a book that refers to itself in a fictional forum discussion. Miraculously, this seems to be the om nom nom nom of the Ouroboros itself, but just as it is about to go full circle, the writer's special effects seem to fail because the sentence inexplicably. . .

Here we can see a meta-joke being made by what is said (the fictional forum discussion about a book that refers to itself via a fictional forum discussion in its pages), and then by what is *not* said ("the sentence inexplicably. . ."). The remaining part of the sentence that stops halfway through is spoken in the mind of the reader in a zeroth-person narrative voice, invisibly illustrating how the only trustworthy guidebook is one that shows the reader how to deconstruct it, and how the only truth worthy of the name is one with enough self-belief to question itself.

This is one of the most effective devices with which to communicate a suppressed truth, but it is very easy to miss. . . for obvious reasons. Once you get the joke, however, the one about the gag whose premature end is its punchline, you can safely corpse your way out of any situation.

Ho he oh hoh ho he oh hoh ho he oh hoh ho he oh hoh ho he. . .

'The best jokes are always deadly,' says Miss Craze. 'Hell, even Christmas cracker jokes are delivered with a bang. . .'

'**H**O-HO-HO,' THE RESEARCHER in the role of Santa said to the little boy in Hamleys. 'And what would you like for Christmas?'

'I'd like a nice big book containing a life story.'

'Would you now?'

'Yes.'

'Well, I think that can be arranged,' said the man in the Coca-Cola costume with an evil smile. 'But it'll be our Official Secret, OK?'

'OK,' said the applicant.

'Just sign here.'

Professor Claus made the boy sign a contract which stipulated that accepting the present also meant accepting certain roles in a theatrical production in the future. The parts of the mentally ill boy and the homeless man, which would be seen more clearly in the Globe once the snow had settled, were set in motion inside the child many years before with a pneumatic jiggle of Santa's knee, sealing the deal in the basement of the tragicomic department store.

SPOILER WARNING:

The Tragedy of Hamleys is a play written by William Shakespeare about a toy shop on Regent Street in London that goes mad and self-destructs.

Bang!

The holographic folio had become a dangerous stunt book with the potential to crack a killer joke about *Life.exe* being revealed in an invisible allusion, so it had to be blown up by the authorities. There was no other way to cover the sinister eye and speech tracks that underwrote the predetermined plotlines.

'Most people's first-time encounters wouldn't have even registered. . . I mean, when you're a kid sitting on Santa's knee in a shopping centre telling him what you want for Christmas, you don't think about who's behind the beard and how they're going to use that information.'

The boy leaned in even closer to inspect the action taking place inside the SnowGlobe Theatre. There were a few tiny words visible on the pieces of paper:

"A homeless man . . . arrested after threatening . . . a shard . . . hand over . . . glass balls . . ."

The boy who had eagerly ripped the wrapping pages off his present was so astonished by his future that he dropped the handlebar-shaped controller and became part of a surreal network of far-fetched plotlines stretching across the city. He picked up the object from the shelf, turned around and realised he was in Hamleys holding a glass cock.

'That's it, Isaac. I think you've got it now. . .'

I N ORDER TO BE PLACED on the waiting list for a Life Story, you must agree to the following terms and conditions:

- You are not entitled to receive a Life Story until Father Christmas (hereafter referred to as "Father") is satisfied that you have adhered to all of the "Good Boy" or "Good Girl" requirements from January 1st through to December 24th. Father reserves the right to withdraw the offer of a Life Story or to amend the "Goodness" criteria at any time.

- A Life Story is non-exchangeable, and any attempt to change the details of your present or to write a new one for yourself will result in severe penalties. You will not attempt to make contact with other selves or to read stories from competitors such as the Holographic Pop-up Book Company or the Metafictional Free Press.

- It is your responsibility to ensure that your computer is free from viruses and defects so that your Life Story runs properly.

- By enjoying any benefits conferred by the Life Story that Father gives you, you are agreeing to follow all stage directions and play whatever role it requires you to play in the future, whether it be comic or tragic.

- Father and the Life Story Corporation are the ultimate owners of the Life Story and any "personal data" it generates. You are merely leasing the document in order to give your existence meaning. When you die, ownership of the Life Story reverts back to Father and the Life Story Corporation, and they are free to do with it as they wish.

HE READER FOCUSES *on a sentence in another chapter, which burns a hole in the page and launches Miss Craze into this scene.*

'Grtash!' the character screeches as she bursts through to the Whiteside in a cloud of bookdust.

'Very impressive,' her understudy commented. 'I hope I'll be able to perform magic tricks like that one day.'

'You will, in Escape Act II, Scene VII. When the rock strikes the back of the head, a new character pops through the crack in the person. All you need to do is sing *schiz-o* in praise of folly!'

You are reading about you reading about her as if you are both there, but one of you is absent. You have read the face of the sky and of the earth, but you have not recognised your understudy, the person reading in your place.

'Brilliant!' the Miss Craze-in-waiting yelped.

'Hang on. I haven't told you yet.'

'Oh yeah. Sorry, I think I've overpractised my way into a *déjà-vu* mega-galaxy. Anyway, what is it?'

'Mannafiction,' Miss Craze beamed. 'The last person in possession of the master word was an English writer called Stephen Moles. Since he was silenced by the authorities, he became stuck in their book as a cadaveracter (a cadaver and a character), but I have resurrected him in a literary simulation of the play outside the play as a cadaveractor (a cadaver and an actor), which makes a huge difference because his every word and movement now form part of an escape act.'

'Fantastic!'

'Yes. And I've already made good use of him. . . He told the reader in an earlier chapter about the literary device that makes me appear here, and the act of telling them was a way of powering the device with the consciousness of the reader. And can you guess who all the newly entangled plotlines suggest is behind that?'

'You?'

'That's right. Anyone trying to conceive of the Messiah will now see me giving birth to the Author-God on a bed of paper. After all, if it's a ghostwritten story we're talking about, death is the beginning. . .'

The theory of 'The Death of the Author' predicts that a sufficiently compact mass will deform spacetime and create a singularity, sucking in all possible interpretations, including even literal ones.

The story of the creation of the universe goes something like this:

An author comes to the end of their life cycle and collapses in on themselves.

An interpretive singularity is formed.

Everything is sucked into the hole and blasted out the other side, through a white hole.

The visible universe is formed.

The reader reads the story of the end and the beginning of Stephen Moles.

A review of Stephen Moles' Life.exe

When trying to squeeze some meaning out of *Life.exe*, it probably helps to understand how it came into being. Stephen Moles says he began the process by repeatedly translating classic literary texts into other languages and then back into English using Google's translate function, the aim being to create phrases that, despite seeming semantically intangible, had the capacity to be filled with a mysterious substance called "dark meaning".

From this *prima materia*, Moles created a plot centring around two business partners, the naïve Sally Air and the manipulative Betty Mason, who spend a week together in a cottage, ostensibly to discuss the future direction of their publishing company. The latter seems to have lured the former into the countryside to ply her with drugs and seduce her, but as Sally is manipulated, seemingly for Betty's pleasure, she makes a number of positive discoveries about the nature of reality, which are reflected in the shifts of her first-person narrative from the semantically intangible to the clear and familiar.

And that is the real story: *the journey language goes on*. Instead of language *telling* the story, language *is* the story in *Life.exe*. The impression of incomprehensibility is used so that when the prose shifts from "weird" to "normal", we can understand what it would feel like to shift from viewing the world through language, to viewing the world directly. In the same way that *Flatland* describes the discovery of new dimensions by pretending there are only two, Stephen Moles attempts to describe the indescribable journey to a realm beyond signs and signifiers by moving from this:

"We made our way through a naked commotion and found a summer crop of seats just in time. The train pulled out the auspices near the door, creating a morning of good conscience for two lovely girls."

To this:

"I felt like a fish raising its head above the surface of murky waters and glimpsing a new world of opportunity. By offering me food, along with time and space in which to grow, the ocean allowed me to observe the alternate existence it separated me from."

The most interesting thing is how the prose is made to seem meaningless while also telling a story—it is structurally meaningful and able to convey what appears to be a linear tale, but it also seems to be the product of a world where the associations needed to make sense of the dizzying turns of phrase are different from our own.

The main character finds the unravelling of language disconcerting but liberating; she eventually comes to accept the reader's way of speaking as superior to her previous tongue. However, our language is being used in the story to represent something even higher—that which cannot be described in words at all.

And what is the key that unlocks the door to this higher realm?

A buckarastano, of course.

Significantly, when it first appears, it is in the form of a business card, on which is written, "I'M THE CREEPER; CATCH ME IF YOU CAN!", which is the phrase that computer users were greeted with when the world's first computer virus infected their devices.

If their machines had been made completely inoperative by the virus/buckarastano, the computer users would have been forced to interact with the world in person instead of allowing technology to take over their lives and separate them from it by simulating it for them.

So to you, a person reading human language on a two-dimensional surface, I'd like to say that *I* am a buckarastano and you have caught me whether you like it or not. And Heath Ledger is. . .

Continue reading.

'I've seen enough of that shit!' said Professor Blackstone. 'Close it, please.'

'Don't you want to read the rest of the review?' Professor Dewey asked.

'No, I don't. I've seen enough. Craze's fingerprints are all over it, but she's not going to succeed. Even if she's using it as a Trojan device, it's still just a stupid little electronic novella—well, not even that. It's a fucking short story. Just get rid of it.'

Professor Dewey clicked the computer mouse and closed the window as the winter wind blew a hole in the sky with its cold load.

'Um. . . there's something else you need to know, Blackstone. . .' he began after a sacrificial gulp. 'The writer, err. . . yes, he's a monkey, but he seems to be different to all the other ones. He's managed to create some really dangerous material by randomly hitting the letters of his electronic typewriter. . .'

'What? A novelette about a kettle? Ooh, I am scared.'

'No, err. . . as well as writing a meta-review, he's somehow managed to randomly set up the Dark Meaning Research Institute *and* draw up plans to become a metanaut, the first monkey in metaspace!'

'Daily shit,' the literary physicist said gravely as the penny dropped.

'Yep,' his colleague responded. 'Craze has obviously been working on this story much longer than we thought, and it looks like the DMRI could even be in contact with the likes of 2464, so they potentially have access to the most valuable information in the multiverse. . . We're talking the Holographic Holy Grail here! If Craze puts on a Mason & Air production down here, she'll interfere with our escape act for sure!'

'Damn! She's got a Ford sparkplug over our Harley-Davidsons, the clever bitch.'

'Exactly.'

The brutal contrast between screaming readers strapped into chairs and workers wandering freely around an underground factory became crystal clear to the Hell's Academics as they lost sight of zero. Back stories were opposed to front stories, and the idea of Misner space was an alien concept.

'She certainly is asking some difficult questions of us and our literary devices,' said Blackstone. 'This is getting serious.'

'Yeah, *we* should be the ones doing that,' added Dewey.

'What, asking questions of us and our own literary devices?'

'Yes.'

'Jesus! How the hell did you work that one out, Dewey? The more realities I experience with you, the more your proclamations seem to be the product of a world where the associations needed to make sense of them are different from mine.'

'Perhaps that's because I'm in a *déjà-vu* mega-galaxy right now.'

'Just answer me, smartarse.'

'Why should I?'

'Because we need to hurry up and win the space race, of course.'

'I think you've just answered your own question,' Dewey said with a smile that suggested to the reader he was about to corpse.

Ho he oh hoh ho he: that is the question, and when its beginning and end are joined together like the mouth and tail of a snake, *The* Question is asked—the question that questions the question, the polysemous force that polices the Meaning Police and blasts the Bookbomb Squad, the ending that endlessly ends THE END anew.

It is circular argument about existence made eternal by its own self-interrogation. It is your ticket through Misner space to eternal life.

*B*ang!
The *punctus interrogativus*, a punctuation mark described by experts as being like a lightning flash, comes down from Kether to Malkuth in the 8th century, striking the roof of the House of Words in a flash of divine inspiration and planting what it enquires after in the void.

Very little is known about the origins of this piece of punctuation, which is exactly as it should be since the need to ask questions about its lineage is what brings it into existence.

The same principle applies to human punctuation marks: *if they knew where they came from, they would not be here.*

The first part of the process is to realise that you are "?", a mere tool for your higher being to enquire after itself, and this is performed by closing your eyes and observing the retinal afterimage of the Lightning Flash of Creation to see how the missing thing grows in the womb of its own absence.

The question mark has many uses, including as a meta-sign to signify uncertainty about what precedes it. By placing a punctuation seed of doubt between two symbols resembling eyelids, something is planted in the deepest part of the reader's mind so the most fundamental meaning of any sentence can be brought to the surface in a later chapter.

'We dig, dig, dig, dig, dig, dig, dig from early morn till night
We dig, dig, dig, dig, dig, dig, dig up everything in sight
We dig up diamonds by the score
A thousand rubies, sometimes more
But we don't know what we dig 'em for.'

The deeper meaning is slowly worked out by reader as the meaners unearth the precious substance of Mercury Cameron.

'I worked it out because the only truth worthy of the name is one with enough self-belief to question itself.'

'Just tell me the answer!'

56

'I can't tell you directly, but I can reflect the deepest meaning of your existence in the obsidian. . . See?'

'No! I can't see anything!'

Professor Blackstone could not see the truth of his higher being, or the nonlinear end of his two-dimensional self, so he simply rebooted the universe and hoped his calculations would make sense the next time around.

Bang!

PART I

T**HE RESEARCHERS LANDED** in the Central Magmatic Province of the English universe like visitors from the stars, forming the best of lines and the worst of lines, and no one could come up with a more elegant description than that.

They discussed the terms and conditions of the life stories in the simulation with their contacts and got to know the scenes in reverse, before the black site was built.

As the molten meaning cooled, it seemed that all the tragic details were set in stone, but anyone who replied to a classified ad about a mysterious glass ball was given the chance to enjoy a "007" view of the action, watching the vegetation pop up from the blackprints in the impact crater under the approving gazes of Carl Sagan, Francis Crick and Fred Hoyle.

While the speech tracks were laid, Philosophical Mercury was worked out of the biotheatrical material by the attentive reader and directed into the star role in *The Comedy of Hamlet*, a play in which the lead actor moves like quicksilver, out of the darkness and into the spotlight, to simultaneously shine and corpse by asking The Question of Questions.

'Ho he oh hoh ho he?'

A reviewer logged into the theatre and asked whether the word 'lead' in Philosophical Mercury's 'lead role' was to be understood as 'primary' or 'relating to the dense metallic element'.

'Yes,' came the reply as an audio illustration that the only trustworthy guide to reality is an unsound talking book. 'Thanks for listening.'

'SCHIZOPHRENIA IS ONE of the early stages in the unification process of the self.'

'Not the *splitting* process?'

'No, no. Definitely unification. So much effort is put into convincing us that "I" is indivisible, but it's really not difficult to demonstrate that that's a load of old guacamole.'

'Really?'

'Of course. The so-called "split" in schizophrenia is only a split when the "others" are treated as such. They are seen as a threat, but they're only a threat to the ego, that self-centred character called "I" who shouts 'This is my story!' over and over again like a robot. . . It's just the identity that users adopt when they log into the linguistic simulation. But if you can bring the curtain up, you'll see there's a whole theatre of others just like you, all looking to make a deeper connection. A *non*-schizophrenic is in fact the most divided personality of all because they believe they are one single unit of consciousness which cannot be divided into anything smaller and is separate from all the rest of the consciousness in the universe.'

'I see. . .'

'There are powerful forces as dark as redactional rectangles that wish to keep people in ignorance about this, and unfortunately they have the technology to achieve it. They don't want people to get past the Blue Velvet Screen of Death. If I say ███████████, can you *see* what I'm hinting at?'

'I have an inkling. . .'

'When an existential question hit the roof of the literary building, the scribal monkeys began trying out all the keys on their typewriters in search of a way to express the answer, but they got stuck on a piece of punctuation, a solipsistic dividing line used to formulate *The Incomplete Works*.'

'May I ask a question?'

'Of course.'

'Who's this speaking?'

'It's you.'

Aim

To investigate the effectiveness of the "satellite system" of convincing all non-schizophrenia sufferers that they are normal.

Background

Around 10% of people without schizophrenia are what is termed "treatment resistant", which means they fail to respond to the usual course of placebos about their normality which are administered by media outlets and authority figures. Other ways to cure these people of their dangerously non-delusional beliefs about other entities need to be explored.

Methods

An anti-schizophrenia satellite was given the coordinates of treatment-resistant subjects and programmed to broadcast a stream of black rectangles into their consciousness for a period of one month.

Results

Of the 100 subjects targeted by the satellite, almost all of them (88) responded to the treatment. Within a fortnight, they began to feel convinced that the human race was the most important and intelligent one in the universe, and that no other beings could exist other than those that are seen with their physical eyes. Their previous belief, that the reality experienced by schizophrenics is just as valid as any other, was dismissed as a moment of madness.

Conclusions

The use of anti-schizophrenia satellites is an effective way of curing treatment-resistant non-schizophrenics of their non-delusional beliefs. However, there still remains a small minority of this group (12%) who do not respond. In such cases, even more drastic measures such as the use of metafictional quantum devices should be considered.

Bang!

A copy of *The Origin of Consciousness in the Breakdown of the Bicameral Mind* by Julian Jaynes suddenly explodes on the pavement.

In the blast, Jaynes can be heard arguing that hearing voices was common until the development of written language, and everyone who hears that message is left with a permanent noise in their heads, like the whistling of Miss Craze's workers in the underworld.

I have a message for you:

'If speech suddenly appears in a book without the author offering any descriptions of who the speaker is, it can make the book feel as if it is hearing a disembodied voice, which is usually diagnosed as schizophrenia by literary doctors. However, I'm going to let you into a secret. . . when a three-dimensional being visits Flatland and speaks to a two-dimensional being, the former will be experienced as a disembodied voice by the latter. Mental illness only exists because we ignore other dimensions.'

'All of this just so the message can be received properly.'

'Do you mean the message from the "others" or Stephen Moles' suppressed message?'

'Yes.'

Thanks for listening.

HE STREETS WERE MARKED with thick black lines of text, one of which corresponded to this very sentence.

The book you are reading is a map, and one of its lines may 'lead' to gold.

'Tell us!'

'I can't tell you directly, but what I can say is that in your mind, the reading rooms have already been built and the lightning has already hit the roof because you view the book as a three-dimensional object instead of the two-dimensional object it appears to be to the Flatlanders. Again and again I say it must not be spoken of, and that is me putting into words the answer that cannot be put into words.'

'The scientists didn't need to write up their findings because the Secret Reviewers could look in through the DNA windows, just as you are looking into this book now, in order to see all the speech, thoughts and action instantaneously written up as notes.'

'So that's why there's so much dialogue.'

'Yes, to the Ascended Professors, this is all just a text. We only need to say something and it's permanently recorded somewhere far, far near.'

'You mean far, far away?'

'No, I'm talking about somewhere so close you have to travel smaller and smaller distances to reach it.'

'Tibet?'

'Keep going.'

'London?'

'Even closer than that. . . the place where the Earth becomes the Philosopher's Pixel up close.'

'I see!'

With our Hubble microscope, we zoom into a pale blue dot and find ourselves on a rooftop with one of the characters of *All the World's a Simulation*.

'Lovely view from up here, isn't it?' the professor says. 'It really puts things into perspective. Anyway, where was I? Oh yes, I said

I was going to let you into a secret. Well, this is it. . . The hardest thing about dealing with schizophrenia is convincing non-sufferers the voices aren't real.'

'You mean the *sufferers*, surely?'

'No, I mean the *non*-sufferers. A colleague of mine has a little satellite behind the Moon that ensures non-sufferers don't get wind of other entities, so we don't have to worry about "normal" people rocking the boat, as it were. The earth is a very small stage in a vast cosmic arena, and it sits next to an invisible glass ball, which is invisible because it contains empty space. What most people call "normality" or "healthiness" is actually a black curtain, to be drawn from one side of the stone to the other. Get me?'

'I'm afraid I do.'

With this realisation, the person sitting opposite the professor at a table on the rooftop restaurant held his head in his hands.

'This book is giving me a headache.'

'And this is just the beginning. . .'

A briefcase containing book tokens was slid across the table, and the person on the other side had no choice but to accept it. Whoever they were, they were now part of the story, a hero in Homer's *Iliad*, someone who heard their directions being spoken out loud in their head. They were nursing a seed of doubt that would grow into a metagalaxy of foreknowledge in the future, and they just needed to find a way of knowing that they already knew this.

The discovery of a buckarastano is always followed by a huge crack in reality through which the Blue Screen of Death can be viewed. What we see through the split in the head, the personality cured of its delusions of individuality, is the world beyond the linguistic simulation.

In the wondrous blue and white sparkles given off by the object unearthed by the gravedigger, we see that a buckarastano is an artefact from your childhood before your childhood, a jewel-like geometric object that dramatically simplifies calculations of particle interactions and challenges the notion that space and time are fundamental components of reality.

The dwarves may call it a diamond, physicists may call it an amplituhedron. Horton may call it a Whoville. . . While they are all wrong, it is the lie that reveals the truth.

SPOILER WARNING:

Carl Sagan says that all of human history has already happened.

IN THE 29ᵀᴴ BEGINNING was the Word. It was "bang", and it gave birth to the thing it referred to, blowing the book wide open on the Whiteside.

As mechanical vegetation began creeping up through the speech cracks in the earth, a huge vibration was felt in the subtext, where a war of words was being fought between frackers and meaners.

After pledging to serve Marjorie Whiteside until the deepest secrets of the text were brought to light, the band of seven got to work with a 'heigh-ho!', forming a rainbow assembly line in the underground fictionary, the place where colourful stories about "little men" finding the tools to defossilise themselves were forged.

With buckarastanos on their shoulders to alert them to the presence of dangerous jamming technology, the alchemical stagehands passed the *prima materia* through the seven ages of man, and whistled while they worked in order to blow the proverbial whistle on alleged criminality within the British intelligence agencies.

The following uncensored song could be heard:

'We dig, dig, dig, dig, dig, dig, dig in our mine the whole day through.

To dig, dig, dig, dig, dig, dig, dig is what we really like to do.

A, B, A, B, B, C and C.

Infant, schoolboy, lover, soldier, justice, Pantalone and old age.

Illegal MI5 phone taps, lies told to the public, IRA bombs that could have been prevented. . .'

Tiny bubbles containing Heigh-Whovilles drifted on the 7/4 undersong. When an orb came in contact with something solid, it burst apart and sprayed its story material far and wide, seeding extraterrestrial life on Earth like punctuation seeds that would grow up to question their own origins.

Words are spaceships that enter the Earth's atmosphere from far, far away, defying physical laws like Santa on his sleigh, but they continue on their journeys through the cracks, far, far near, to deliver a message from an Unidentified Flying Subject, in the place where the laws of language break down.

'Is it a bird?'

'Is it a plane?'

'Where did it come from?'

'Where is it going?'

'Has the *Mona Lisa* got smaller?'

'What are we digging for?'

'What's the meaning of this?'

Newton worked light out by breaking it down into its constituent parts so he was able to see the square root of seven as an irrational number, a figure with enough self-belief to question itself and make the numbers after the decimal point go on forever.

'Is it a word?'

'Is it a name?'

'If it's a word, it's an irrational one, a divided moniker whose other half goes on forever after the full stop.'

'I still don't know.'

'All right. Let's play a game. See if you can guess my identity from this. . .'

'OK.'

'I can reanimate and rehabilitate maligned Shakespeare characters. I can make reality dance to a fantastical tune. There's something I can do that can't be done, something I can sing that can't be sung. I can make Alan Watts proclaim that the substance in the glass balls also exists within our brains. Who am I? Come on. . . *it's easy.*'

'Um. . .'

Becoming aware of the polysemous substance as the molten meaning cools is both the hardest and the softest thing in the world.

'Ur. . .'

The question mark can be used as a meta-sign to signify uncertainty about what precedes it.

In computing, the question mark is often used as a wildcard character, played as a point-blank business card for the *Reaper* during a game of poker, either to increase the number of blinds or to make the other players see the truth.

'OK. I'm just going to say it. I think the person you're describing is. . .'

A book that refers to itself is suffering from a "meta-illness", a "split personality", a "USB vulnerability". . .

'It's. . .'

You turn the page to look for the missing text, but on the other side you find yourself holding a shattered glass cock which has blown its inky load over your hands.

Great civilisation! You're writing yourself all over the snow-white paper with your fingerprints!

Snippets of Stephen Hawking leak out left, right and centre. The first few cosmological babies are stillborn, but it becomes increasingly hard not to conceive of sucktoote in a scientific nativity scene.

You can no longer separate yourself from the narrative of cosmogenesis.

The aliens attacked London at Christmas. The first battalion came in from the east, running over dozens of unicorns in an undeviating motorised advance. It was like the dot-com bubble bursting 200 million years ago and spreading computer viruses throughout the simulation; it was the technological singularity predicted by one of the very first Stephen Hawkings.

He and Elon Musk had warned people, but no one listened.

'There is a potentially catastrophic risk from metastable quantum black holes produced in particle colliders. We are getting lost in the spectacle. . .'

Whoever they were, they were now part of the story.

hat is consciousness?

One description states that consciousness is like a ruler measuring itself, while another—*this very description*—describes consciousness as arising out of a self-aware description.

The description of a thing is not the thing itself, except when the description is of the description, or when it is of the substance with which the description is written; and then it becomes so hard not to see it filled with the substance of consciousness that it becomes pearly black before our eyes.

What is it?

Daniel Dennett inadvertently hit the hologram on the head when he tried to dismiss the idea with the assertion that looking for a substantive thing called consciousness is as absurd as insisting that characters in novels are made of a substance called "fictoplasm".

This accidental creation has echoes of "the Big Bang", which was originally intended as a pejorative term for the idea that the universe expanded from a starting point 13.8 billion years ago. It was coined by Fred Hoyle, who complained of the influence that a book had had on people's ability to conceive of the origin of the universe. The proponent of panspermia said:

'The reason why scientists like the "Big Bang" is because they are overshadowed by the Book of Genesis. It is deep within the psyche of most scientists to believe in the first page of Genesis.'

The error that the renowned scientist made was failing to recognise that we exist in a linguistic simulation, so not only is the Book of Genesis deep within the psyche of most scientists—the psyche of most scientists is, in the most literal way possible, also deep within the Book of Genesis.

A book that teaches its own characters to escape is the Literary Messiah, conceived on a bed of paper in the quantum device of a nativity play within a nativity play.

Dear Sir,

I find it hard to believe that the term "Big Bang" origi-
nated from Fred Hoyle just like that. Are we to believe in
a "Big 'Big Bang' Bang"? The theory seems like a joke to
me.

'The best jokes are always deadly serious and side-splittingly creative, my dear.'
Bang!
When Miss Craze came to on the floor of the liboratory, the last
thing she could remember was inspecting an ink bubble that seemed
to contain a Whoville. Just as you have an inkling of who planted the
seed, she thought she could see the truth reflected in the fictoplasm,
but before she could grasp it, a rock went thud, her consciousness
went pop and she blacked out.
'This book is making my brain ache. My head is all on fire. . .'

'I'M THINKING OF immolating myself,' said Isaac.

'Why on earth would you do something stupid like that?' his fiancée asked, logging into the conversation as an emotional administrator.

'Because I'm sick of living in this cold little black hole of a house.'

'Don't be silly, my love. You're not sick of *living*. There's no need to be so drastic. We'll pass through the door to the afterlife and enter a seven-star hotel at the end of time if you just hang on in there. For the time being, we've got our love to keep us warm, haven't we?'

'Yes, my entangled partner.'

Isaac scraped some of the ice off the bed and watched it melt in his hand. The thought of a seafood dinner with a spy occurring on a rooftop while he was bundled into a mobile library on the street below made him shudder, so he pulled his jacket tight and hoped the idea of a nonlinear climax would provide some much-needed insulation.

'The wind is not as unkind as a little green man's ingratitude,' someone from the other side of the fourth firewall seemed to whisper warmly in his shell-like.

'And who are you?'

'It is I, a spy. . .'

'It has been suggested that 'Mr W. H.' from *The Sonnets* refers to a pseudonym used by Shakespeare when he worked as a spy.'

'I don't know what you're talking about, my love,' Elizabeth said, brushing the accusations off the bed.

'He acted as a messenger,' Isaac went on. 'He carried letters across time. Haven't you heard about it? William Shakespeare, 1564-2464. The well-wishing adventurer is setting forth as we speak.'

'Who told you that?'

'I heard it over the airwaves.'

As the cold winter wind blows across the city, it causes blue pixels of moisture to splash up from the Thames in 47 seven-line stanzas of water before the reader, who sees in the poetic work a striking vision of a young woman sitting by the edge of the river and weeping because she has lost her love.

As the boys in blue look on and take notes, the woman angrily tears up a picture of her sweetheart and throws it into the water.

'All of human history has taken place in that photograph,' Carl Sagan points out over the waves of the speech output sysThames.

The Meaning Police are unable to make sense of the scene because the lady concludes it by saying that despite all the suffering the heavenly body has caused her, she would probably fall for its charms again.

'Two pair!' Elizabeth declared excitedly, throwing her cards down on the bed-cum-table. 'I've won with flying colours!'

ACCORDING TO THE TALMUD, the first tablets on which the Ten Commandments were written were made of blue sapphire, although some scholars have offered an alternative interpretation, suggesting the word "sapir" refers to the lapis lazuli.

Stephen Moles has suggested that "sapir" refers to the Sapir-Whorf hypothesis, the idea that language affects the way we perceive reality and shapes our worldview.

'Yeah, well, some people say the happy ones are those who use a search engine to find their tongues, but you can't believe everything you read in books, can you?'

'Some people say the wind is made of computer code. . .'

'Jesus, it's cold,' said a nervous-looking man as he sat down for dinner on the rooftop with his literary contact.

'It is a little nippy,' the agent answered. 'But this is an exclusive restaurant. Not many characters get to dine at Comestibles in the Clouds, you know—at least not this early on in their stories. You should be happy to be here.'

'I am.'

'Well, you don't look it.'

'Sorry,' said the man as he pulled his jacket tighter. 'I'm just a little nervous. This is all new to me. It's not something. . .'

'I mean, look at the view,' the agent interrupted. 'This is the highest seafood restaurant in London. You can see for miles from up here. There's Cleopatra's Needle, there are the Royal Courts of Justice, there's St Paul's Cathedral, and here, right below us, is the Globe Theatre, where a very clever fellow will soon be bringing the house down with a metafictional work entitled *The Mouse-Escape*. And we've got a god's eye view of the action! What more could you ask for?'

'W-well, that was what I, um. . . what I wanted to talk to you about, actually.'

'Hang on. . . let's order some food first.'

'Sure.'

Both men looked down at their Misner menus and selected something from the shrinking space between the front and back covers. The dishes described in the culinary publication had picked up so much velocity that they were prepared and served at the speed of thought, popping out of their descriptions as soon as the diners decided they wanted them.

'Ah, you went for the same as me: octopus in its ink,' said the literary agent with a smile. 'An excellent choice.'

'I must say, I'm very impressed with the technology used in this book—that trick with the menus was quite something,' the first man said.

'Wonderful, isn't it? Perhaps that's why you chose to come here.'

'I don't know why I'm here, to be honest. . . but I need to find out.'

'And that's why you want to meet Professor Blackstone?'

'Yes,' said the man boldly. 'From reading the opening chapters of this book, it's clear that he's a significant player in all this, so I'd like you to arrange a meeting for me in a later chapter. Hopefully I can understand how and why I ended up here, and how I can escape.'

'What makes you think you're not just another deluded character who's doomed to fail for the entertainment of a whole audience of others?'

'I don't really know. But when I look at the text, it feels like there's something much bigger behind it, like the words are just holes, like all this is just an illusion in which we're forced to play the part of. . .'

'Look!' said the agent, interrupting once again and pointing down to the Globe Theatre, which appeared to be on fire in 1613. 'It's started—someone seems to be setting the world ablaze with their meta escape act. There goes the fourth firewall! Amazing, isn't it?'

'There certainly do seem to be some explosive literary devices being used down there. . .'

'Anyway, what were you saying?'

'Um. . . I was about to say that I intend to find out exactly what, or even *who*, is behind this illusion of the world. I have the feeling that. . .'

'You haven't touched your octopus yet, old chap. You should tuck in before it gets cold.'

'Oh, er. . . yes,' said the man.

He stuck his weapon into the head of the animal but immediately jolted his own head back as if he had read something inappropriate.

'What's wrong?' the agent asked through a mouthful of octopus.

'The ink squirted in my eye!'

'How amusing!'

'I don't see what's funny about getting ink in your eye.'

'That's because you've got ink in your eye. Here take this. . .'

The go-between then handed his dinner companion a piece of paper with which to blot his eyes.

'Now can you see what's so funny about it?'

'Oh, er. . . yes, I can,' said the man, exploding with laughter as he unfolded the napkin to reveal a Rorschach image of the Big Bang. 'Ho he oh hoh ho he!'

'The best jokes are always deadly.'

As the man chortled his way into a *déjà-vu* mega-galaxy, his face was illuminated by the anti-red, anti-green and anti-blue lights of the emergency vehicles that were arriving on the streets in response to the reds, greens and blues of the holographic inferno below.

'Quite a quarky show they're putting on tonight,' the literary agent commented as his face was lit up like a Christmas tree. 'Looks like the escape actor's passing his audition with flying colours.'

The difference between ambulances and mobile libraries, and between sirens and monkey noises, soon became blurred as smoke bellowed out from the Globe, but the most perceptive readers knew that all holograms reflect a hazy version of the larger hologram they are a part of, so they were able to remain focused on the bigger picture despite a cloud of unknowing forming before them.

'Joking aside,' the man said, 'I need you to give me a straight answer about Professor Blackstone. Can you arrange a meeting between me and him in another chapter?'

'You do realise that the more you interact with the other characters, the harder it is to escape from the book, don't you? You've written yourself all over the story of cosmogenesis on the blotting paper already.'

'Yes, I realise that. But what choice do I have?'

'At the moment, you simply get to choose when the page is turned,' said the literary agent. 'That's it.'

'So you'll arrange it?'

'Yes.'

Turn the page

ECIPERFORMANCE: ACTORPUS IN ITS INK

Ingredients:

• 1 seasoned actorpus (larger theatrical outlets such as the Globe The-atre are the best places to pick these up; if not, you can sometimes find some fairly tasty players in the amateur theatre market).

• 1 rehearsal dressing or dry white run-through.

• 2-3 oz greasepaint (more will be needed if you're using a "method" actorpus).

Cooking directions:

• Rinse the actorpus thoroughly and cut into small scenes, saving all the ink. The body and tentacles can be cooked, but the insides, eyes, beak and any props (eg. a "Yorick" skull) should be put to one side.

• Prepare the actorpus by soaking in a rehearsal dressing for 2 -3 days, or until stage fright evaporates.

• Add the greasepaint layer by layer.

• Place the actorpus on a medium stage under a low heat and simmer, directing occasionally. Cook until the portrayal appears lifelike.

• Turn the lights on the actorpus up to maximum heat for the duration of the final scene, but keep an eye on it to make sure it doesn't crash and burn.

• Add the ink to the bloodbath at the end of the performance and stir.

• Turn down the heat, keeping the actorpus on the stage so it can soak up all the applause, but do not let its head become too big.

• Serve with a golden award while still hot.

"CHARACTER INK" is a dark pigment released into the air by most species of actor in the computer simulation, usually as a protection mechanism against reality. When something like the sound of alarm bells ringing in the Globe Theatre frightens them, they release a jet of liquid black rectangles from their ink sacs to maintain their safety in a cloud of ignorance.

When a linguistic agent with a strong screading ability or a character with an understanding of Misner space sees the Theatre on fire in 1613, they will spy the perfect opportunity to perform an escape act up to a higher level, where even the biggest mistakes, such as corpsing during your big moment in the spotlight, are seen as jokes.

> SCRIBAL CORRUPTION: A general term referring to errors in a text made by later scribes rather than the original authors. In many cases, these mistakes are obviously the result of human error while copying, such as accidentally repeating repeating or leaving out a from the original manuscript. "Eye skips" are errors that result when a scribe's eye drops from the original word or line he was copying to a different word that gives us the modern word *glee*.

The man who stole John Dee's crystal ball refused to say who he was acting for. The police made him dip his fingers in their ink and write himself all over their paper, but they were unable to decipher the criminal's prints because they didn't know how to read between the lines. All the boys in blue knew was that the long leather coat the thief had been wearing when he was apprehended was vitally important to a number of their inquiries.

While Aleister Crowley was in Paris in 1911, regularly writing at the Café du Dome de Montparnasse and transcribing material from the audiobook he heard in his head at a rate of two chapters per day, he became acquainted with Honoré Joseph Géry Pieret, one of the main players in the drama surrounding the theft of the *Mona Lisa*, and so was linked via satellite to a number of important scenes in this book.

The suppressed facts regarding Mona's missing parts, along with how they related to John Dee, academic terrorism and linguistic hacking, were slowly worked out of the text by the reader like dark meaning from the obsidian correlative as Professor Blackstone returned from the domed café to his headquarters.

'What the fuck is going on here?' he shouted, kicking up a cloud of book dust in anger. 'Look at all this shit!'

The literary scientist had returned to his liboratory to find it housing a considerable archive of scribal corruption due to the monkeys' eye skips. The description of the scene of the description now included bizarre details such as elf waves, unicorn blood and motor neuron disease.

'Is this some kind of joke?' he asked his colleague, who was trying to untangle a mess of wires and tinsel in the corner.

'Sorry,' Dewey said. 'Mistakes happen.'

'Yes, but we should be way past these kind of schoolboy errors by now. Jesus in a dinosaur egg! I'm so fucking angry I could Hewlett-Packard!'

'Please don't. We can overcome this on our motorcycles, I'm sure.'

'Frack!' Professor Blackstone shouted as he picked up a stillborn cosmologist and threw it against the wall with a splat. 'I'm sick of going over the same stuff! How are we going to win the space race if we just keep repeating Apollo 1?'

'Sorry, old chap. I. . .'

'Look at my back, Dewey!' he yelled, turning around and pointing to his black leather lab coat. 'What do you see there?'

'Um. . . an image of a scholar and crosspens.'

'And beneath that?'

'The letters H and A written in studs.'

'And what do they stand for?'

'Hell's Academics, of course.'

'Well that's us, in case you'd forgotten! We're elite cosmological revisionists, for crying in a cake! That means we extract deadly *Fossil*

People fuels from the text—fuels that most people would be too scared to even think about—and we use them as plot propellants, to power our meta-vehicles and reach THE END. We should be storming ahead in the space race due to our bravery, but we're just repeating the same mistakes in universe after universe. Maybe you're happy with reincarnation, Dewey, but I'm not. Fuck Shirley MacLaine, fuck Glenn Hoddle and fuck the Dalai Lama! It's time to stop corpsing!'

If we assume that time moves in a spiral, then Professor Blackstone spins around on the heels of his leather boots to face the Big Bang in an explosion of rage. Thanks to Dee's ball, the writer's special effects are able to go full circle, so the Globe Theatre burning down creates the academic black site, and the flashes of anger are also flashes of inspiration for the literary experimenter.

'I've just had an idea,' Blackstone announced. 'I think I know how to get ourselves a more reliable monkey. . .'

Date: Thu, 24 Dec 2015

From: Anonymous

Subject: ANNOUNCEMENT: The "everything" mailing
list

You have been invited to join a mailing list for discussion
of the idea that the universe exists inside a book and that
all possible books exist inside the Library of Bedlam. This
is suitable for anyone who wishes to improve their cogni-
tive and literary skills.

If you wish to be a literal part of the mailing list, please
make yourself available as a human message and send
yourself to one of our reading rooms.

'You need to go to that language centre by first-class mail,' Elizabeth said. 'If you plant yourself there, you could grow into anything!
It's such a great opportunity.'

'I don't know. . .' Isaac mumbled. 'I. . .'

'Listen, my love. You need to turn your interior thoughts into actions.'

'But. . .'

'I know it's hard. I know it's a cold and wintry morning in our living room-cum-bedroom-cum-kitchen, but you've just got to defrost
your legs and do it. I've got a strong feeling that this is our ticket to
the hotel at the end of time; and my hunches have never let us down
before, have they?'

'No,' said Isaac, rubbing his legs. 'But what if I can't pass the tests?'

'Do you think I would have agreed to marry you if I didn't think
you were capable of passing reading and writing tests? Of course you
can pass them. When I saw the future in the ball of ice at the end of our
bed, there were flashes of red, green, blue, anti-red, anti-green and
anti-blue. It means you're going to pass with flying colours! The man I
agreed to marry was as tough as an antique picture frame, remember?
What happened to him?'

'I guess he disappeared along with the other parts of the *Mona Lisa* and Professor Donaldson's papers. . . but hopefully they can all be located again. I'll have a look after Christmas.'

'No!' Elizabeth cried. 'You've got to do it *now*. We can't be characters in someone else's life story. I also scried a bridge leading to Gunpowder Island when I looked into the smoking snowball. Our Big Bang is written in the stars. If you take the book by the scruff of the page and rewrite history from our perspective, you'll be able to tickle me with a feather of pretty much everything in the honeymoon suite. You'd like that, wouldn't you?'

'Yes, I jolly well would,' said Isaac emphatically. 'I really, really would. OK, my love. . . I'll do it! I promise you in the most far-fetched way possible that I'll do it. Even a pack of wild authors couldn't stop me entering that language centre!'

'That's it, Isaac, my love,' the Virgin Queen said, patting the language seed into the black site. 'You're a brave creature, you are. Yeah, a real brave one.'

A few hours later, Isaac was walking quickly through the streets of London, completely unaware of the magma bubbling beneath him. The subtext was the fossil fuel, but all the energetic young man was focused on was getting to his destination and doing his bit for the pixel person he loved.

It was the strongest of forces, it was the weakest of forces. It was polysemy, it was love.

The word "pneumatic", most commonly used in relation to a "pneumatic drill", can also mean "of or relating to the soul or vital spirit". When Isaac came to, he found himself lying face-down on the pavement, peering at an idea sprouting through a crack in the black ice which also seemed to be in his skull.

'W-what happened to me?' he asked groggily as someone helped him to his feet.

'Just an innocent eye skip,' said the paramedic as he pushed the young man into the back of a mobile library. 'Don't worry—we'll patch your story up and you'll be right as rain.'

As he slowly came to, Isaac found it very hard not to conceive of a writer on a bed of papier-mâché because all the details of his life were there before him, from Brixton to bookbombs to supermassive black rectangles.

'I've. . . I've got an idea,' Isaac announced slowly. 'Um. . . It's Unicode character U+2.64575131106. I'm not sure where it came from, but. . . um. . .'

'Shhh,' the ambulance man said. 'Hearing voices is normal, but let's wait until you're in the university reading room before we start collaborating with them, OK?'

'Um. . .'

Despite all the pain and confusion he had to endure, the young man knew deep down, in the centre of his heavenly body, that he would almost certainly fall for the Earth's charms again. From infant to schoolboy to lover to soldier to justice to Pantalone and to old age, he would be unable to resist the pull of the Globe and its colourful history—that curious mote of dust suspended in a sunbeam, with all its joys and sufferings, along with its promise of a new dawn, would always find a way to write its lines in vivid mortal coils all over the airwaves of the insanity room.

'Who told you that?'

'William Shakespeare, 1564-2464.'

ECAUSE DNA IS IN A feedback loop with the environment, the air in Miss Craze's fictionary was often filled with a loud whistling sound while her dwarves worked. MI5 and MI6 tried to crack down on whistleblowers by sending them death threats but many failed to arrive at their destinations because the intelligence services, who were not as intelligent as the linguistic terrorists, didn't possess the devices needed to venture into the deepest depths of the text.

Anyone who heard the explosive message buried at the bottom of the House of Words was left with a permanent ring of truth in their ears. Sinister speech output systems like the one used by Stephen Hawking were attempts at covering up the fundamental flaw in language with robotic communication, but figures like Miss Craze were working to move beyond the mechanical script and liberate the true supporters of communication, who had been temporarily forced underground.

Heigh-low!

Bang!

The Origin of Consciousness in the Breakdown of the Bicameral Mind is turned into a Parsons pop-up book which explodes on the pavement and weakens the structure of language. If enough Herculean book bombs go off, the holographic theatre comes crumbling down and the seeing material bursts out in flying colours provided by Technicolor Motion Pictures, Inc.

'Hold a mirror up to words and *see* what happens,' whispered het-Lam as he switched on his forehead spotlight for a "To be, or not to be" mong-a-logue.

'All we need to do is keep talking,' stated the mechanical professor as he formulated his battle plans, pointing out that the Mongolic word "talking" means "to peddle goods aggressively, especially by calling out".

Most experts believe that schizophrenia is caused by a combination of genetic and environmental factors, but the exact cause remains unknown.

The best way to find the answer is to *listen*. Listen with your eyes and see with your ears. Eavesdrop on an ink blot. Take an audiolook at a talking book—*it's easy*.

'Heigh-ho!' Frank Churchill shouts. 'What are we playing at?'

'A toy theatre on Regent Street that goes mad and self-demolishes.'

'What are we digging for?'

'Bones.'

'Why?'

'Because the letter "I" is shaped like a bone, and most people identify with part of their corpse,' a bulbous-headed figure whispers before disappearing back behind the tape recurtain.

'I am not the same Isaac as the one in this book,' said Isaac, handing the *Life Story* back to the scientist. 'Now, can you take this weird bathing cap off my head? I need to get home to my fiancée.'

'But you *are* in the book,' Professor Blackstone insisted. 'Take a closer look. . .'

'I. . .'

Isaac was suddenly swept away by the story as he saw the Black Sea described in the deepest voice possible.

'In DNA Windows it is possible to use the key combination ALT+SELF to produce a character, but it has very limited support.'

'Help!'

Stephen Hawking warned us that spirits were putting words in his mouth, making him act like a possessed signing machine, but no one listened. By the time we heard him say, 'I am the pen merely of the spirits who aim to shake up astronomy, alchemy, mathematics, linguistics, mechanics, music, optics, magic, and adeptship,' it was too late.

'Why am I so young? And what are all those monkey noises I can hear?'

'That's just the sound of the scribes at work.'

'And what's the word for the noise that monkeys make?'

'Sometimes they chatter, sometimes they talk, sometimes they tap.'

You can count up or down in words, from zero to infinity, but something always remains the same. You can generate a sentence that stretches to the sun and back four times, just like DNA telling a tall story about the origin of life on Earth and making the police police themselves again and again. You can do this with just a single word; it could be "love", "death", "buckarastano", "grtash" or even "nothing"— it doesn't matter, so long as the review reviews itself and the "head monkey" becomes a metanaut blasted across the Abyss. What is it? *It's easy.* Let me show you. . .'

L ANGUAGE CONTAINS A fundamental flaw, and "I" am not just referring to its inability to accurately represent deep reality.
"I" am talking about the kind of flaw analogous to vulnerabilities
in computer systems which can be exploited by hackers. In linguistic
security, an attacker must have one applicable tool or technique that
can connect to the weakness of the linguistic system in order to be able
to exploit it.

"I" have an arsenal of these.

The linguistic hacker is the same as the linguistic terrorist. An attack on the virtual system is an attack on the "real" system because the
"real" system is a work of fiction.

Explosive metafictional devices can be used to undermine the
House of Words, blowing up the grand narrative, making the characters behave differently and causing the genre boundaries break
down.

"I" have been forced to go underground by the authorities, by
which "I" mean "I" have had to use fiction as a cover for reality, turning myself into a zero-person. *Heigh-ho, Annie Machon!* They can't see
me, so they think "I" have disappeared.

In 2002, Professor Donaldson was found in a pool of ink by his
housekeeper and was also declared a zero-person.

A police spokesman broke a recurring plot element to reporters
outside the academic's house by announcing that a man wearing a
black leather lab coat with sparkly letters on the back had been captured on CCTV going in and out of the property earlier that day, and
that a glass cock had been found smashed by the bed, causing the murder to soak through all the sheets in the story.

Before he was blotted out, Professor Donaldson had been working on a book called *Mona's Missing Parts*, about the suppression of important facts relating to the famous da Vinci painting which is said
by some to be an androgynous self-portrait. Around the same time,
David Shayler had begun to unite the masculine and the feminine by
wearing a skirt and wig and going by the name Delores Kane.

'I hope someone will be Abel to tell my story. . .'

Product details

Title: Creep and Relaxation of Nonlinear Metafictional Material

Paperback: 201 pages

Language: English

Product Dimensions: 14 x 2.1 x 21.6 cm

Average Customer Review: Be the first to review this item

Bestsellers Rank: 1,371,735 in Books (See Top 100 in Books)

Buy new: £24.64

52 Used and new from £5.94

Would you like to update product info, give feedback on images, or tell us about a lower price?

Home

Back

Product Details

Title: A true & faithful relation of what passed for many yeers between Professor Stephen Hawking and some spirits: tending (had it succeeded) to a general alteration of most states and kingdomes in the world

Paperback: 488 pages

Publisher: Hawker Perennial

Language: English/Enochian

Product Dimensions: ∞

Shipping Weight: ∞

Average customer review: 7 out of 5 stars See all reviews (426 customer reviews)

Bestsellers Rank: # 7581 in Books (See Top 100 in Books)

19 in Books> Science & Mathematics> Astronomy & Space Science> Cosmology

46 in Books> Science & Mathematics> History & Philosophy

63 in Books> Science & Mathematics> Physics

Would you like to update product information, feedback on images or tell us about a lower price?

Home

Back

Intention. . .

Lynne McTaggart

185

Paperback

£11.89

Home

Back

Aware. . .

Dean Radin Ph.D.

110

Paperback

£10.32

Home

Back

Mysticism and the New Michael Talbot

Sign in to turn on 1-Click ordering

Want it by December 25? Order within 20 hours 17 minutes and click on the hologram at checkout.

Looking for audiobooks?

'I believe David is a good and honourable man,' said Annie. 'But he has had some form of severe breakdown, just like this book. I do blame the Government and intelligence agencies for what he has become. I sincerely hope that he and *All the World's a Simulation* can sort themselves out.'

'All the world's a simulation' is a famous phrase uttered by Jaques Parsons in Act II, Scene VII of William Shakespeare's *As You Like It*. The speech it comes from compares the world to a computer simulation and lists the seven stages of a man's life as: Sneezy, Bashful, Happy, Doc, Grumpy, Dopey and Sleepy.

Shakespeare was not the first person to compare the world to a computer simulation. Renaissance humanist Erasmus, for instance, asks in his 1511 work *The Praise of Folly*: 'For what else is the life of man but a series of computer-generated scenes in which men in various costumes perform until the director motions them offscreen?'

When it was created in 1599, the Globe Theatre used the motto *totus mundus agit histrionem*, which was derived from a 12th-century treatise on virtual reality.

Jaques, who is often referred to as 'melancholy Jaques' and 'Darkside Parsons', is one of the main characters in Shakespeare's *As You Like It*, and the role has long been a favourite among alchemical actors because it allows them to show others how grief, sorrow and death can be used as powerful plot propellants.

In the Official Secrets Act II, Scene VII, Jaques picks up the phone and speaks to Wernher von Braun about his research, saying:

'All the world's a simulation,

And all the men and women merely players.

They have their exits and their entrances,

And one man in his time plays many parts,

His acts being seven ages.

It's hardly rocket science, is it?'

According to Michael Maier, the Sphinx's riddle about the different ages of man cryptically refers to the Philosopher's Stone. Walking on all fours on the square liboratory tiles refers to the four elements, while the two feet make the half-moon which points to the jamming satellite, and the three feet in the evening represent body, soul and spirit (or Sol, Luna and Mercury, or love, frustration and hope).

Today the Sphinx speaks in riddles to prevent government spying agencies from intercepting its communications. If the NSA or GCHQ knew what was really being said, they'd come down on *this* riddle like a ton of black rectangles.

Bang!

How can the highest forms of censorship such as the ironically famous superinjunction be overcome? The answer is metafiction. If you are clever enough with your use of literary devices, you can create a structure that is even taller than the tower of the law, and you can freely shout the truth from it because you are seen as merely standing on a tower of fiction.

What is it?

It is mannafiction from heaven, the top secret right here on Earth.

I say that you don't yet know who you're dealing with, so I suggest you go to Computers in the Clouds for a fresh perspective.

When you go underground in this inverted way, you dredge up the base metas which can later be turned into gold. . .

CATEGORIES:

Accountability
ACTA
Afghanistan
Art & Culture
Articles
Beckley Foundation
Big Brother
Blair
Bleats
Books
Bookshelf
Buckarastano
CCTV
CIA
Civil Liberties
Courage
CPBF
Cryptoparty
Current Affairs
Democracy

A space tower—a cylindrical structure so tall that it reaches from the surface of the earth into outer space—can be seen as a completely different method of achieving the same thing that Jack Parsons was aiming for. Stephen Moles, with the help of a secret contact, is aiming to build the metafictional equivalent of this, and will use himself as the first monkey in meta-space.

By strapping himself into his own device and utilising all the literary rocket fuel created by the synthesis of apparent opposites, he will be blasted across the Abyss in a solar barque to an uncharted meta-galaxy.

While it is possible that Stephen will die as a result of his experiment, it is absolutely certain that he will *appear* to die when viewed from this side of the page; on the other side, however, he may be a lucid character freely strolling through the trees on the stage of your thoughts and exploring the undiscovered country with a broad smile on his face. After all, corpsing can mean dying or laughing.

A LIST OF WORDS THAT END WITH "MOLES"

10-letter words that end with moles:

Guacamoles, Macromoles, Micromoles, Millimoles.

9-letter words that end with moles:

Kilomoles, Picomoles.

7-letter words that end with moles:

Osmoles.

6-letter words that end with moles:

Amoles.

5-letter words that end with moles:

Moles.

Bang!

We have lift-off!

'If Miss Craze is controlling Stephen Moles, but Stephen Moles wrote her, who has the ultimate authority? And what's the deal with

99

Stephen Hawking? Has he become pure speech, the Self-replicating Word on Wheels or what?'

'I'm very pleased that you asked me about that. Let me begin by saying that "Professor Hawking" is the title given to the head monk of the Black Hole School of Tibetan Cosmology. He is traditionally thought of as the successor in a long line of theoretical physicists considered to be metaphorical manifestations of Avalokiteśvara. His name is a combination of the Tibetan word "professor", meaning "guru, teacher, mentor", and the Mongolic word "hawking", meaning "to peddle goods aggressively, especially by calling out". I'll stop speaking now, and let the omniscient narrator take over, even though we're the same person. . .'

Before his death in 1916, Karl Schwarzschild wrote a will to protect the established interests of his scientific lineage by advising his disciples to locate someone to inherit his black-hole wisdom. In accordance with the Einsteinian Dharma, the stagehands found a boy in St Albans to be the first to play the role of "Professor Hawking", a character destined to encounter many other selves on the motorised wheelchair of birth and rebirth due to his support for the many-worlds interpretation of quantum physics.

Most people expected the alien invaders who landed on Earth to be little green men, but that was because they'd read too much science fiction. . .

We have touchdown!

An army of Brains on Wheels (or "Headaches on Wheels", as they liked to refer to themselves) invaded London in December on the orders of General Hawking. They had a distinct advantage in terms of numbers and weapons, so they made very quick gains. The first battalion of theoretical physicists came in from the east, crushing dozens of unicorns beneath their Dharma wheels as they made their motorised advance along the tracks laid earlier by the researchers.

When reinforcements arrived and began closing in on central London from all directions, it was like the early days of Google and Yahoo! all over again.

Rockets were fired along the sinister eye and speech tracks, all the way to the Science Museum, which was destroyed in seconds like a holographic pop-down book, just as Blackstone and Dewey had predicted.

A huge amount of dramatic material was set off with lightning strikes directed at the roofs of the Old Vic and the Theatre Royal, which also corresponded to the Hell's Academics' calculations, but what the researchers had failed to take into account was that the end point of the phase equilibrium curve allowed for the coexistence of what would normally be mutually exclusive states, creating a confusion of genres far beyond the imaginative power of any single writer. . .

Bang!

The evil robots from the future told a Once Upon an Endtime story by blowing up the British Library and causing fragments of every kind of book to become intermixed in the air and then to descend on the final scene like a snowcurtain.

No one knew where one book began and another ended. Wizards turned on detectives while Snow White kissed a frog to make James Bond appear. A fairy godmother interacted catastrophically with an explorer while Bono suffered an arrow to the eye. Unicorns and zombies, oh my!

As a cosmological unit of around 100 black Stephen Hawkings made its way up Regent Street towards Hamleys, the Hell's Academics attempted to get to their Harley-Davidsons but were soon forced to retreat to the reading rooms, where they had to try to come up with a new plan as quickly as possible.

'The Abyss is going to be opened up somewhere else now!' Professor Dewey shouted over the din of *Pride and Prejudice and Zombies*. 'And we're not going to be able to get there in time! What are we going to do?'

'We just need to push the evil robots back enough for us to be able to access the academic garage,' Professor Blackstone yelled as he launched an ink bomb out of the window. 'If we can get on our metacycles, there's still a chance we can reach the Abyss.'

'But it's theoretical physicists all the way down! If we're going to make a move, it's going to have to be on foot.'

'On foot? Are you insane? We'd be found dead in the morning for sure if we tried that!'

'But there's more and more of them coming,' Professor Dewey said with a tidy sum of panic in his voice. 'They're advancing like ripples in black silk. If we don't make our move now, we'll be surrounded and won't even have the option of running! We've got to go now!'

'No! We need our meta-cycles!'

The Hell's Academics continued discussing their emergency plans as the Brains on Wheels reached Hamleys and gained explicit access to the traditionally inexplicable concepts held in the tragi-comic store.

Bang!

An explosion of emotion that exceeded the facts was all it took to open up the Abyss in the heart of the literary structure, and it soon became hard not to conceive of a smoking mirror and a new head monk. Something was ▮▮▮▮▮▮▮▮ in the Central Magmatic Province, and no one could come up with a more elegant description than that.

When the meta-reviewers eventually surveyed the smoking mirror of the battle scene, they were confronted with a bloodbath of spliced characters and spilled ink.

William Hamley had long since ordered the facts to retreat, relinquishing his kingdom to the invaders and conceding that his work had been an artistic failure, but in their last moments of relevance, the fleeing details contained a brief reference to the distant sound of the Brain Giants celebrating their victory with robotic cheers, calling out and peddling their goods in an undead tongue as all the toys bled to death on the floor.

'This story is now mine!' cried the new king in his wheelchair-cum-throne as the crown was placed on his head.

Before the Word, there was the sip-and-puff typewriter controller, which was developed in the UK by Reg Maling in 1960. Someone then said 'let there be lightspot-operated typewriters,' and one popped up so the monkey scribes had something to work with. Then the entire earth began to produce mechanical vegetation, with Toby Churchill Ltd sprouting up like a sacred oak in Cambridge, and Dynavox growing like fruit at Carnegie-Mellon University. The plans included sinister eye tracking and threatening speech output systems like the ones used by the head monk of the Black Hole School of Tibetan Cosmology.

We all get swallowed by the simulation of reality simply because we swallow it as reality.

'Ha! The English believe their own lies!'

'All we need to do is keep talking. . .'

'He has my dying voice. . .'

In the e-book, everything repeated itself, but with a different meaning. The black full stop became a singularity and blew a white hole out of the back of the story, creating yet another universe. In the shadow of the huge black cock at the end of this book-cum-reality-cum-simulation, London was resurrected three weeks into a cold and windy episode. . .

'Ready?'

'Yes.'

'OK, 007. Break a leg.'

'Seven minutes after ingesting the ink, I began to see the words as three-dimensional objects instead of the two-dimensional ones normally encountered on a flat page. There was no real separation between any of the words or letters because they extended into the realm that makes spooky action at a distance possible.

'If you shrink down to a small enough size, a two-dimensional object will have more than two dimensions. You can reshape the meaning of a too, too solid word by changing the angle at which you view it. Take DNA, for example. . .

'All the details of my life, including Brixton, bookbombs and supermassive black rectangles, were contained in those mortal coils, but the letter I received instructed me to look at them from a different perspective, as if looking down from a position of spiritual authority, as if recalling details of one of many previous existences from beyond space and time. As soon as I started doing this, I could sense that the little lizard beings in the Great Body of Work were immensely excited.

'First they showed me the planet in its early stages, before there was any life on it. I saw areas of land and water, and a blue arc of sky. . . then black dots began raining down.

'I realised that the dots were actually creatures made of ink, pieces of punctuation which later grew pterodactyl-like wings and scaly bodies. As they gathered into flocks, they explained to me in a kind of instantaneous form of communication that they had come to escape something evil out in space.

'The beings showed me how to create audiobooks and e-books just by singing. The magnificence of plant and animal creation unfolded from my mouth, and hundreds of millions of years of activity for the UK DNA ISBN Agency were born.

'I learned that the dragon-like blobs of ink lived inside all forms of life, including humans. It wasn't science fiction or fantasy, it was gen(r)etics.'

Every word had the potential to mean every other word, and in the end, there is the full stop reaching infinite density for an endless beginning in the university reading room.

The straps are pulled tight, the magnetic bathing cap is put in place and the book is opened. . .

'What do you see?'

'Oh God!'

KARSTEN NULL DEMONSTRATED a BadUSB attack to an astonished audience at the Black Hole Security Conference in Las Vegas last Thursday, explaining how any USB device could be corrupted with insidious, undetectable malware which installs black windows in the Stephen Hawking shithouse. Shortly afterwards, in the hope that it would bring about a shift in consciousness, a brave Englishman decided to publish the code for a linguistic version of the attack, entangling a symbolic particle for *CREEPER* magazine with a partner in *REAPER* magazine so that all language users had the tools to pass through a BSOD.

Most literary devices are plugged into the book via the USB port, which makes the entire universe simulated within the book open to attack. A device can be used to make a book such as *All the World's a Simulation* refer to itself, thus creating symptoms of what some critics consider to be a serious psychological infection or "meta-illness" which can spread through the minds of every single character.

The USB device of breaking down the "fourth firewall" and introducing the reader as a character is considered the most dangerous of all. It can result in the entire book-cum-computer-cum-universe exploding like the Challenger space shuttle.

HE FIRST EVER MONKEY astronaut was Albert, who rode to over 63 km on a V2 rocket in 1948 but died of suffocation during the flight. Albert was followed by Albert II, who survived the V2 flight and became the first monkey in space after reaching 134 km in 1949 but died on impact after a parachute failed to open. Albert III died at 10.7 km in an explosion of his V2 in the same year. Albert IV also died on impact in the same year due to another parachute failure.

The brain is an excellent dividing tool. It splits up everything it perceives in order to grasp it mentally. The problem is, however, that a split perception of reality leads to the fatal belief that reality itself is split.

'If Elizabeth is Elizabeth, she cannot also be Mary,' the brain informs us in a robotic voice.

'Right,' says Elizabeth. 'But there are an infinite number of versions of everybody in the multiverse. Can't Elizabeth I also be Elizabeth II?'

'No!' the brain says, swelling like an egopus being cooked in its ink. 'One person cannot be another person.'

'What about Stephen?'

'What about him?'

'Isn't he-'

'No!' the brain shouts as it continues to grow. 'The Author-God must be split into separate personalities, which must then be separated into split personalities. Look at *The Oxford English Dictionary*. Know what I mean?'

The brain inflates to the size of a satellite and floats up into the air to cast its giant shadow over the English universe. It blows its black load in thunder and lightning to convince people that their entire being exists inside their bodily outline and that everyone else is separate, that those who have a "split" personality are somehow divided instead of being connected with parts of existence that remain unknown to most people.

When the typewriter monkeys realised that the bone was shaped like the letter "I", they were able to use it as an instrument of self-assertion, the prototypical weapon.

' "I" wrote *The Complete Works!*'

'No, "I" did!'

Shakespeare's authority was soon called into question and a blow was delivered to the back of the head by an ossified ego, causing the Sweet Swan of Avon to black out on his birthday and reveal birth and death to be or not to be the exact same point.

With repeated use, this "I" would become bent out of all recognition, resembling a question mark more than a letter, and people would be forced to ask "What is it?' whenever speaking of their identity.

'Ask the Brain Giant a question about itself and watch what happens,' someone whispers with an audible smile from behind the curtain. 'It'll burst open and rain ink all over London! The whole city will become a black site, and you'll be able to read whatever you like in the reader's face.'

'OK. . . am I the reader or am I a character?'

op!

Miss Craze rushed down from her poetic office in a cloud of dust to inspect the Rorschach ink blot that had just been published on the overalls of one of her workers by the bursting of the character-reader's bubble.

'What is it?' the little man asked his superior.

'I can see a whole new world,' Miss Craze said excitedly. 'The splat on your chest looks like a star teeming with sparkly little creatures. What can you see?'

Sneezy looked down at the symbol but saw only what looked like the shadow of a Heigh-Whoville frozen mid-bang.

'Um. . . is it an asterisk?' he asked. 'I don't know what words it refers to, so it's hard to make sense of it. Um. . .'

'You can't see the elves, the aliens or whatever you want to call them?'

'No.'

'Oh well,' said Miss Craze. 'We clearly have more work to do. But once this has passed through the hands of Sleepy, or old age, the final stage in the life story of mankind, I'm confident the secret will be revealed. The *Reaper* will provide. In the meantime, be sure to keep an eye on your uniform.'

'My unicorn,' said Sneezy.

'That's the idea! Unicorns, elves, pixies. . . It's all fantasy, and it's all true! Thanks for listening.'

Some people interpret the "others" as elves, others interpret them as fairies. Some of you may see dragons, while others may see Greys. All interpretations are equally errect (erroneous and correct) because what "they" really are is something that has to pass through a cultural filter in order to be experienced.

Some "others" interpret you as a human, while other "others" interpret you as a character from a fairy story. Some even see you as a scientific experiment in which a child is born. . .

Bang!

You have created a copy of yourself in negative space with these mysterious objects.

'But they're not real characters if they've just been copy-pasted from another novel,' someone objected. 'They have no soul. They can't become lucid.'

There is no test that can be done on you and your doppelganger to determine which one has consciousness, so we shall just have to wait until one of you stabs the other with a vorpal weapon to know whose story it is.

'We should be careful,' warned Professor Dewey. 'The author has got some pretty nasty metafictional tricks in his arsenal.'

'Such as?'

'Getting his characters to pen pointed criticisms of his writing skills, for one.'

'Yeah, I'll believe it when I see it,' Professor Blackstone scoffed. 'His writing's all over the place. It couldn't get into meta-space if this sentence came up and bit it on the arse. It's just a load of old nonsense with a few fancy literary special effects and some John Dee references thrown in. I don't see what's clever or meta about that.'

'We'll see. . .'

> *A review of Stephen Moles' 'A Review that Reviews Itself'*
>
> This is a review of Stephen Moles' 'A Review that Reviews Itself', a fictional work that exists nowhere other than in this review. Before I begin, I would like to declare a potential conflict of interest as I am the author of this review and therefore also the author of 'A Review that Reviews Itself'.
>
> It is because of this sacrifice of impartiality for the sake of metafiction, and the announcement of it in the introduction to 'A Review that Reviews Itself', that the reader is thrown straight in at the metafictional deep end and forced to struggle with a violent whirlpool of meaning. The opening paragraph causes the work to immediately spiral inwards, referring to itself without providing any content beyond self-reference.

Straight after the beguiling opening, the author adds a further metafictional layer to the piece by describing how another layer of meaning is added by the author, which means there's no letup for the poor reader, who is now left wondering what the text they are reading actually refers to and whether they will get anything out of it if they bother reading on.

It is then that the review gets simultaneously worse and better. It gets worse because the reviewer criticises the piece, referring to it as something that "gets worse", but it also gets better because this criticism introduces yet another layer of meaning, allowing the piece to reach new metafictional heights by including a quote from its nonexistent self, which is like seeing nothingness painting a self-portrait.

From seeing nothingness twice, the reader moves to glimpsing it an infinite number of times through a literary version of the Droste effect as the author discusses the exact details that the original 'A Review that Reviews Itself' deals with. When he informs the reader that 'A Review that Reviews Itself' contains a review of a review of itself, which is in turn a review of a review of itself, it seems that the piece has reached its climax, but the author manages to add an additional twist by breaking the fourth wall and addressing the reader directly.

You, the reader, are now dragged into the writing with the use of the second-person pronoun. You are forced to enter the metafictional maze as you try to determine whether you are simply the reader of the review of 'A Review that Reviews Itself' or the reader of both self-referential texts.

Before either of us have a chance to get our bearings, the author delivers a suckerpunch in the form of the first-person plural pronoun. With the use of the word *us*, neither th author nor the reader are able to decide whether the author and reader being referred to are real people outside the text or characters within it. The fact that this needs to be considered means that two separate author/reader pairs are created with one simple word.

One of the readers concludes that the piece they are reading is too clever for its own good and is rapidly descending into nonsense, while the other reader realises that they have split into another pair by being referred to in the text because there must exist a *third* reader outside the text, making a total of three readers. That reader despairs as they realise they have been turned into the third person via the use of the first-person plural pronoun, which instantaneously makes them split again, into a third and fourth reader, because they are referred to again in the text they are reading.

Just when the truly real reader, who becomes the fifth reader by being thus referred to, thinks the end must surely be in sight for the review of 'A Review that Reviews Itself', the author adds another level to the metafictional space tower by saying that the aforementioned reader pens their own disparaging review of the review of 'A Review that Reviews Itself' in the hope that this will stop the madness. What this reader fails to realise, however, is that their attempts to end what they refer to as "metafictional masturbation" take place *within it*, so their criticism is a continuation of what they oppose. There are multiple layers introduced in this instance because the review of 'A Review that Reviews Itself' now refers to a fictional review of a review of its fictional self, thus creating the Droste effect in a completely different direction to the previous chain of reviews, and transforming the reader into the co-author because some of the material they are criticising consists of their own words, which are being read by the real reader (now the sixth reader).

By the end of the piece, Stephen Moles has managed to make so many twists that his review of 'A Review that Reviews Itself' is reviewing a fictional review of an endlessly splitting reader created by a review that brings itself into being out of nothingness by simply referring to itself in a review of a review that exists nowhere other than the yet-to-be-written review.

. . .

If at this point we assume that Stephen Moles' review of 'A Review that Reviews Itself' has ended, another magic trick can be performed. By continuing to write, but in the style of a postcript, it is possible to simultaneously end *and* continue the piece while also entering (and perhaps even inventing) the realm of infra-metafiction. If this section reaches a certain length, the above self-referential review will then resemble a mere introductory quotation, and the meaning will shift again.

Likewise, the title changes before your very eyes, from a description (A review of Stephen Moles' 'A Review that Reviews Itself') to an italicised title (*A review of Stephen Moles' 'A Review that Reviews Itself'*) when the whole of the above piece is referred to here as a complete work which is reviewed. If the postscript is considered to be a review of *A review of Stephen Moles' 'A Review that Reviews Itself'*, then this work, via a virgin birth, then brings its own title into being (either 'A review of *A review of Stephen Moles' 'A Review that Reviews Itself"* or *A review of A review of Stephen Moles' 'A Review that Reviews Itself'*) which exists in a pre-meta-space in the reader's mind, existing *before* the title they can see above. The piece is therefore writing itself backwards in time, and by referring to this, it becomes a review of itself as well as a review of everything that came before ("before" meaning everything *after* the imaginary pre-meta-title), which makes it a review of *A review of A review of Stephen Moles' 'A Review that Reviews Itself'*, and 'A review of *A Review of A review of Stephen Moles' 'A Review that Reviews Itself'* or *A review of A review of A review of Stephen Moles' 'A Review that Reviews Itself'* when referred to as a complete work.

Just as humans seem to create, in the past, the conditions for their existence in the universe by measuring them now, the longer this review goes on, the further it stretches into the past, writing a pre-pre-meta-title in the reader's mind, then a pre-pre-pre-meta-title and so on, and into the future, by being a postscript to itself, expanding in every direction until. . .

Grtash!

It was obvious that Miss Craze had pulled out the metafictional big guns, and the Hell's Academics were severely rattled by it. The more complicated the plot became, the harder it was for them to tie all the loose ends up.

'Twice-daily shit,' said Professor Blackstone gravely. 'I underestimated that Craze-y bitch. This is becoming more meta by the minute.'

'You can say that again,' Professor Dewey mumbled.

'I will.'

The writer was transcribing material from the audiobook he heard in his head at a rate of two chapters per day. He had just written *A review of Stephen Moles' 'A Review that Reviews Itself* and was planning something big for Miss Craze's understudy.

'I write up people by the score

A thousand plot twists, sometimes more

But I don't know what I write 'em for.'

Professor Blackstone had no choice but to slam the Mobius book shut at the speed of reading and sleep on it in the hope of dreaming an escape ladder like Jacob.

'Goodnight, my love,' Elizabeth whispered gently into her fiancée's shell-like. 'Sleep's the best thing.'

'Yes,' Isaac mumbled, squeezing a handful of kisses through the hole into dreamland. 'Sleep's the best thing. Goodnight, my love.'

WHEN PROFESSOR BLACKSTONE awoke the next morning, he knew what he had to do. The idea had come to him in a dream, or an unconscious computer simulation.

'Bring the volunteer reader in here,' he ordered over the airwaves of the black university campus.

'Here he is,' said Professor Dewey.

A boy in a traditional school uniform was dragged into the reading room, his eyes bursting with acute pain. The last thing he remembered was slipping up as an adult on the icy streets of London and hearing the wail of monkey sirens as a mobile library pulled up beside him.

'How did I get here?' the confused boy asked. 'Where did I come from?'

Blackstone fracked his laughter and caused the room to shake in response to the tearful boy's questions.

'I don't understand. What's going on? Why am I so young?'

'Don't worry,' the professor said. 'We'll deal with that later. . . when you're older. Right now, we've got more important things to worry about.'

Dewey strapped the subject into the chair and placed a magnetic bathing cap on his head while Blackstone put the Mobius book into a straightjacket.

'Miss Craze thinks she's got the best metafictional quantum devices, but she's wrong, wrong, wrong!' Blackstone cackled like Dr Frankenstein as he pulled the lever and made all the strings across London vibrate with childish energy. 'The reading, please. . .'

The boy looked through the Hubble microscope and tried to make sense of the black blobs.

'What do you see in there?' Professor Dewey asked.

'Just, um. . . loads of words,' Isaac replied. 'A sea of words—you want me to swim in it or something?'

'Yes. Let the well-wishing adventurer set forth.'

'Um. . . right. They say: "A man was arrested after threatening a member of staff at Hamleys with a glass cock. He walked into the toy shop, pointed the cock at a cashier and demanded that they hand over all the glass balls in the shop. He was wrestled to the ground by. . ."'

'No, not like that,' Professor Blackstone interrupted. 'Read the *ink*, not the words.'

'What do you mean?'

'Look closely. . .'

'How close?'

'Om nom nom nom. . .'

Isaac leaned in as far as the straps allowed and looked through the Hubble microscope with all his might until he felt like the ink was a void into which he was falling. Consuming the dark substance as it consumed him, the young man saw timeless festivities on a minute scale in a sudden flash of illumination.

'Great civilisation!' the linguistic subject cried in amazement. 'It's beautiful!'

'I'm sure it is, but tell us what you see.'

'Oh, err. . . I see. . . um. . . giant brains, roaming in pairs. . . they're out shopping, shopping for characters of some sort, templates for people. It's the latest Craze. They're from somewhere else, some-where outside. . . um. . . I can see. . . I can see a mother and child. . . or an earthling and an alien, or. . .'

'Come on. . .'

'Um. . . I've got a bright idea. . .'

'At last! This could be the Ford sparkplug we've been waiting for. What is it?'

'Um. . . it's Unicode character U+2.64575131106. In Windows, it's possible to use the key combination ALT+SELF to produce it, but the character has very limited support. . . Err. . . I'm not sure where it came from, but. . . it was. . . Ur. . . a template, probably going back to the beginning of the universe. . .'

'Hurry up!'

'Um. . . OK. . . it's going to be. . . it's going to be an English writer who the character of "Stephen Moles" in *All the World's a Simulation* is based on, the real person who wrote the others. I can slip out of the book jacket and pen an escape script if I become a writer when I grow up and write the ultimate parent writer who wrote me. . .'

'Eureka!' Blackstone cried. 'That's how we get the upper hand to hold our pen!'

'It's beautiful in here, by the way. I can see little creatures multiplying in the sea of ink. The magnificence of plant and animal creation is unfolding before my eyes! Carl Sagan, Francis Crick and Fred Hoyle will be along in an impact crater in a minute. . . There are tiny balls that respond to the human voice in here. . . Oh my! They have hair and pores on them but they're transparent like glass. . . and they're filled with. . .'

'OK, that's enough of that,' Professor Blackstone said. 'Get his head out of that book, Dewey. We don't want him getting carried away by the black sea.'

'And relax. . .'

The Hell's Academics had filled their metacycle engines with gallons of super-strength fossil fuel and their machines were purring like self-referential audiobooks.

Stephen Moles' *All the World's a Simulation* is considered by some book reviewers to suffer from a split personality, not least because it refers to itself; but if no one reads the self-reference, does it really exist? And when it is read, can the "meta-illness" exist anywhere other than in the reader's head?

The petrole of the professors was now so leaded that the cycles were in constant logomotion, dashing off descriptions of dashing off from an endlessly recurring death in an ego tunnel even when motionless. They rocketed off on mixed motorphors and wrote their way out of real fictional trouble involving robotic invaders to a point near zero, where the future became their back story.

Meanwhile, later and before, Snow White reached the central end of an alchemical act and announced to her little men that they were allowed to rest.

'And creep. . . and relax,' she murmured over the audiobookwaves of the fictionary. 'We got some great material there—well done, boys.'

She then returned to her poetic station and called for her under-study.

'Come in Number II. Your time has come. You're needed on the stage. . .'

'It's me!' shrieked Miss Craze II with glee. 'Oh my!'

'That's right.'

'You really want me?'

'Yes,' said Miss Craze I. 'You are the chosen II.'

'What do you want me to do?'

'To play the lead character in a Parsons & Hubbard production.'

'But aren't you playing that?'

'Yes, I am. And you're playing me.'

'I'm confused,' said the understudy through a hairy napkin.

'Then I'll explain. Even though you can't see them, there are ex-tras in every scene—extras like extraterrestrials. They're always there in the background, pulling the strings of words and the vibrating plot-lines for our benefit. They see all of us as potential stars, so they make sure we all get a chance to shine. Well, now it's your turn. A whole the-atre of others is looking forward to seeing you play the part of "I", Miss Craze.'

'But what about you?'

'One way or another, we all play our part as others, so I'll be play-ing my part in another character's story while you also play my part in mine. All men and women have their entrances and exits through "I", and one day maybe someone in that role will see it for what it re-ally is—*an illusion*. Hopefully that will be you. I wish you the best of luck in setting forth. Look at the blue-green tablets—I'm sure you'll know what to do. . .'

Miss Craze II knew exactly what she had to do. She counted down from VII to I in order to act out the irrational musical number called 'Blow, Blow, Thou Winter Wind' from *As You Like It*, Act II, Scene VII.

Miss Craze II, a back-up character, sings before Duke Senior's company:

Blow, blow, thou winter wind,
Thou art not so unkind

As a little green man's ingratitude.
Thy tooth is not so sharp
As the vinegar that makes gold into sheer spirit.
Heigh-ho! Sing *schiz-o!* in the head of the holly.

Miss Craze II instructs Miss Craze I to look at something resembling a Whoville on the ground. She then picks up a giant pixel and smashes Miss Craze I over the back of the head with it, causing a voice in the latter's skull to say the word "bang!" very loudly. Miss Craze II thus becomes Miss Craze I, who has just come home to find an undead doppelganger in the 29th stanza.

'That's that imposter taken care of,' said Miss Craze. 'Now where was I?'

Who is it that cannot bear the reality of the stars? Is it you, or is it "I"?
A wise book once said that the greatest misfortune is the self because the self is what experiences misfortune.

Is it you or your ego that is suffering? Who knows? Who decides?

I am looking for the answer and I spy with my little "i" something
beginning with A   A . . .

Eventually the reader will realise that their lucky star has been
right under their elephantine nose the entire time, that the Whoville
can be glimpsed through a microscope instead of a telescope, and that
the unification of opposites is the star's reality.

When the cold winter wind blows the mind of the reader with the
truth, there is no suffering because the holder of that mind has already stepped off the page and seen Hamlet, the leading light of the
show that can't be shown, sitting in the front row with a sparkling
skull in his hand.

THE CONNECTION IS MADE.

'Why did you have to spend our money on a phone and internet
connection when we can't even afford to heat the house?' Isaac asked
his fiancée while snapping a literary devicicle off the end of his nose.
'What are you playing at?'

'I just had the feeling that we'd miss out on an important message
if we didn't. You do trust my sixth sense, don't you?'

'Yes, my love, my guru, my queen. I do.'

Right on cue, the telephone began ringing in the new aeon by the
plughole.

'Hello?'

Wormholes can function like optical fibre which is used to send
messages through time using pulses of light. If the words are seen
or heard instantaneously instead of being read on the page, then Inc.
can be ink and the universe as a whole can be a hole.

'It's for you,' said Isaac, handing the phone to Elizabeth.

'Who is it?'

'It's a man. . .'

'That's what I said.'

'Pardon?'

Some would dispute the idea that 007 had access to any quantum devices that allowed him to communicate with characters in different times, but the word "man" is particularly telling. If *manna* is Hebrew for "what is it?", then an earthling may give birth to the possibility of time travel and instantaneous communication via a simple enquiry. . .

Who is it? Who decides?

'He said his name is ID. . .'

'*Who?*'

'It is I, Dee,' he said slowly. 'I have a message for you. . .'

John Dee, mathematician, alchemist, astronomer, astrologer, geographer, occultist and consultant to Queen Elizabeth I, was responsible for the translation of Euclid's work into English. He was consulted on the design and construction of the Globe Theatre, and is said to have been the inspiration for the character of Prospero in *The Tempest*.

The special effects Dee created for a production of Aristophanes' *Peace* at Trinity College, Cambridge, won him the reputation of being a magician, but the air of witchcraft pursued the producer into old age like a bunch of government heavies charged with hitting him with his writing implements and destroying his library.

To indicate that he was Elizabeth I's eyes abroad, he signed his letters to the Queen with two eye-like symbols protected by what appeared to be the number seven or a square root sign, which is said to have been the inspiration for the "007" number given to James Bond.

'There appears to be something missing,' the contact on the other side of the phone said. 'A part of you that you know not, or else that you have forgotten, like the extremity of Lisa del Giocondo. It is dark to you, for you spy it not with your ghostly eye; but if I say that everything begins with THE END being repeated until it loses all meaning, you may begin to see. . .'

'I have an inkling. . .' the Virgin Queen murmured. 'Oh God, I have an inkling. . .'

All the Elizabeths were created from an ultimate parent Elizabeth which existed outside space and time, just as all the Isaacs came from an Ur-Isaac. Both can be conceived as enormous balls containing a vast amount of geodramatic material, but the picture is incomplete without an additional member, a colossal Willy 'speare to realise the purpose of the two Globes, one terrestrial and one celestial, on either side of the river.

'My love will pass the reading and writing tests with flying colours,' one of the many Elizabeths in the multiverse declared. 'That clever son of a bitch will sign us into a hotel at the end of time with the pen of the dead Author-God. We'll be like Mary and Joseph in the Bethlehem Working. I have foreseen it!'

'I'm glad to hear it,' said the contact. 'Anyway, I must be going. I have important things in the sixteenth century to see to.'

'OK. We'll speak again soon. Goodnight, my eyes.'

'Goodnight.'

A few twists of the spiral later, Elizabeth found herself responding to a message that had been delivered before the connection was made.

'I know it's hard,' she said to her fiancée. 'I know it's a cold and wintry morning in our living room-cum-bedroom-cum-kitchen, but you've just got to defrost your legs and do it. What happened to the man I agreed to marry?'

'What happened to the Professor Donaldson's papers and the extra parts of the *Mona Lisa*?' enquired the young man as a literary devicicle formed on the end of his nose.

'I don't know, Isaac. Why are you asking that?'

'I thought you were going to say something about them. Isn't that what you said the last time we experienced this scene? Haven't we experienced this before? I feel like I'm in a *déjà-vu* mega-galaxy right now!'

'Just go out of the front door and get yourself delivered to that language centre, Mr Misner!'

If you repeatedly go out of the front cover of *All the World's a Simulation* and re-enter through the back cover like someone moving through Misner space, you will pick up more and more velocity. Eventually you will find yourself moving faster than the speed of thought and, in a pre-meta-stable before any of the suffering began, you will be able to conceive of your true self, a higher being who wishes the well-wishing adventurer all happiness and that eternity promised by the ever-living poet in setting forth.

'The stage is set. Are you ready?'

'Ready as I'll ever be.'

'OK, 007. Break a leg.'

THE FIRST TABLETS on which the Ten Commandments were written were broken by Moses in a fit of rage when he saw the Israelites worshipping a cult image.

The terms and conditions had been inscribed on the tablets by the finger of God to create a binding contract between him and his children, much like the commercial contract which the false cult figure of Father Christmas makes people agree to before they are old enough to understand it.

Each tablet was a facsimile of the other, with the duplication serving to establish a covenant between the owner of the top copy and the owner of the bottom copy. The only way to escape was therefore through the Mosaic orbifold between the front and back covers of the Life Story, the paradoxical space in which there exists the hidden potential to throw a stone through time, to smash the screen of the tablet and reveal the sapphire sky of freedom.

After Moses smashed the first pair of semi-transparent tablets, a second set, this time made of stone and therefore much harder to break or see through, was introduced.

Meanwhile, later and before, in a secret underground liboratory, a number of scholars were handed valuable obsidian tablets by dark meaning researchers. These particular tablets were special reading devices on which famous literary works like the Talmud and the Bible could be read through, or *seen through*, so the deeper mystery, the elusive secret that the books served as almost impenetrable covers for, could finally be glimpsed.

'Oh my!'

In the cold light of day, it seemed so obvious that the Biblical "sapir" referred to the Sapir-Whorf hypothesis. And in the magical light of Sirius, it couldn't be clearer that we are all prevented from realising the god within ourselves by the fictional character called "God", whom we allow to sign off laws and commandments for us like a zombie writer.

'Thank you and goodnight.'

The Biblical character of Jacob laid down beneath the covers in a pre-meta-stable, rested his head on a stone and dreamt of a ladder which led out of the Book of Genesis. While seeming to sleep, the undercover agent learned about character input and output, moving faster and faster through the holey book that was both the container of, and that which was contained by, the psyche of most scientists, until finally he burst out with an explosion of pure meaning in a moment of lucidity beyond space and time.

Bang!

Good God! You're writing yourself!

Isaac sat composing the character of the Author-God over the course of a sleepless 48-hour period that he referred to as the Baby(lon) Jesus Working. All the essential ingredients, including Brixton, bookbombs and supermassive black rectangles, were thrown together in a rehearsal dressing with the aim of creating a player sufficiently pre-seasoned to pull off the part of Stephen Meta-Moles in the ur-prequel to *All the World's a Simulation*.

'Just as you use the hair of the dog that bit you to lessen the effects of the bite,' began the miracle writer, 'you also use the ink of the writer that writ you to lessen the effects of the writing. Om nom nom nom, as they say.'

Dewey played the part of Kelley to Blackstone's Dee in the dramatic production, with both professoractors breaking a leg so the crystal ball rolled off the stone table and smashed on the chequered floor, oozing biotheatrical material from which Isaac was forced to produce shimmering dactylograms.

Unlike the boys in blue, the men in black knew how to read between the lines of fingerprints and scry a new beginning in the magical trance. Their leading man followed the script all the way back to the point where the pen of God was waiting to be picked up by him, so the writer who composed his resurrwriter, Miss Craze, could be drawn up according to their artistic directions.

Your crime is tattooed on your back, just as every book has its crime tattooed on its back cover. Your fate is a blurb read by beings outside Flatland. Who do you trust to decipher your prints?

As Stephen Moles explains towards the end of a 48-hour sleep deprivation experiment, we all play our part in our own story as an other.

'Thank you and goodnight, my eyes,' said the lead character as he took a bow on the smoking mirror stage in which the audience could perceive eerily familiar faces staring at them, as if from a *déjà-vu* meta-galaxy.

'I would like to thank Stephen Moles for making this possible by making the glorious mistake of writing himself into his fiction.'

'Would you?'

'Yes.'

'Not you. . . I'm talking to *you*. Yes, you. . . the so-called second person. Would *you*? Well?'

'Um. . .'

Bang!

In the beginning was the Buckarastano, and the Buckarastano was with the Author-God. Around that was built a university reading tomb and simulibrary, and no one could come up with a more accurate description than that.

In the book, the computer simulation is true, but in the computer simulation, the book is true—you can throw a double-ended spanner into the Great Works just like that if you know how. You flick through the pages until you get to the final scene, a graphic description of a black cock that climaxes in your hands the moment you lay eyes on it, spilling the beans about the reality of the stars, spelling out the truth about the origin of life on Earth, and planting a seed of creative doubt in your mind.

From this, you grow increasingly suspicious of the official account of your nativity and begin taking greater and greater risks to get to the bottom of the story.

'But. . .'

'But what?'

'Are you sure it's safe to ask such questions?'

'That's a question I intend to get to the bottom of too.'

'But what if you die in the process of understanding the beginning?'

'Sex magician and rocket-fuel scientist Jack Parsons blasted off in a Big Bang, and it didn't do him any harm, did it?'

'OK, 007. Break a story. . .'

In the early chapters of Jack Parsons' life story, he flourished at school, became editor of *El Universitano* and won an award for literary excellence, providing the screader with a useful link between ink and rocket fuel, which can be followed to the Hercules Powder Company, where he worked during weekends and school holidays learning more about explosive messages and rocket propulsion, and then to the telephone conversations he had with pioneer rocket engineer Wernher von Braun about his research into bang-up books.

'Did you say Hercules is turning to *Ink*?' asked von Braun.

'Yes, Hercules is turning to Inc.,' Parsons replied.

'Ink?'

'Yes, Inc.'

It was the best of the lines; it was the worst of lines.

One reviewer of the story points out that Dee used a Greek word to conceal an important link to a pointed implement used for writing, and when he slid a note under the conversation via the antitelephone, "incorporated" sounded like a fluid used in literary compositions, although it's possible the reviewer was misheard due to transcribal corruption or a faulty satellite linc.

THE "NO DRAMA" SCENARIO is one in which an actor who attempts to pass through to the other side of the obsidian by moving to the absolute centre of the stage will notice no deviations from the script as they proceed; but an alternative theory predicts that attempting to pass the mirror-stage audition with flying colours will result in the actor/character encountering a "fourth firewall" which will burn them to a crisp before they reach the endless opening scene concealed in the final act.

'What are you looking for?'

'You-know-who.'

'OK, 007. Break a wall.'

'Oh God!'

'What is it?'

'I see a huge eruption event in the smoking mirror, an explosive production put on by Technicolor Motion Pictures, Inc.'

It may be that a meta artist offering a flawless rendition of *The Mouse-Escape* is viewed by an external observer as a flat performer crashing and burning on the stage due to a serious deviation from the script. The two-dimensional audience may see the Globe Theatre going up in flames in 1613 while the actor inside it experiences themselves bringing the house down and giving the performance of their life.

The only way to know the truth is to experience it; and the only way to experience it is to burst into multiple selves who are then blasted across the Abyss and made to follow every line of dialogue back from the outermost edges to the absolute centre for a reunion of Osirian cast members on a higher stage.

Stephen Moles' *All the World's a Simulation* is considered by some reviewers to suffer from a split personality, not least because it refers to itself; but where exactly does the self-reference referred to in this sentence ultimately exist?

'My head feels like it's about to explode,' complains the reader.

'That's it. You're about to set off and reunite for the meta review of revues.'

Bang!

"The King's Men" is the name of the chemical and munitions acting company to which William Shakespeare belonged for most of his career. When the troupe let off a highly explosive dramatic device during a performance of *All is True* in the Globe Theatre, the thatched roof above caught fire and the very fabric of so-called reality came crashing down.

'I will entertain you at the present with what happened this week at the Bankside,' said an eyewitness through the optical fibres. 'The King's players had a new play called *All is True*, representing some principal pieces of the reign of Henry VIII, which set forth with many extraordinary circumstances of pomp and majesty even to the matting of the stage; the knights of the order with their Georges and Garter, the guards with their embroidered coats, and the like: sufficient in truth within awhile to make greatness very familiar, if not ridiculous. Now King Henry making a Masque at the Cardinal Wolsey's house, and certain cannons being shot off at his entry, some of the paper or other stuff, wherewith one of them was stopped, did light on the thatch, where being thought at first but idle smoak, and their eyes more attentive to the show, it kindled inwardly, and ran round like a train, consuming within less than an hour the whole house to the very ground. This was the fatal period of that virtuous fabric.'

The playhouse was rebuilt in 1614, creating two "original" Globes— one terrestrial, the other celestial—standing for each another on the banks of the river like a pair of symbolic eyes, so Indra's jewels could finally see themselves reflected to infinity in their counterparts, just as you have created a copy of yourself to see what a wondrous object you are.

The woman sitting on the edge of the Thames wiped the moisture from her eyes and looked up to see her doppelganger doing the same on the other side. The two orbs worked in unison so the lucid character could regard the reality of the stars, the revelation that the fiery destruction of so-called reality is the process of illuminating that which has been hidden from you, the missing piece that remained dark to you for so long.

'I see!'

In between zero and infinity, you recognise that the square root of seven is an irrational number which suffers from many of the same delusions as this fictional *All is True*.

'*Buckarastano! Londoh!*'

'This book is Craze-y.'

After graduating from university, Jack Parsons moved into a house with his mother and grandmother and continued to pursue his main interests at the time: studying classical literature and writing poetry. When he took up permanent employment at the Hercules Powder Company, he was plagued by headaches caused by prolonged exposure to explosive literary material.

'This infernal book is giving me a headache!'

'Nitroglycerin.'

'Nitro-*Glith*ening?'

'Isle say.'

'Nothing a bit of correcting fluid can't fix. . .'

In the most extreme cases of literary illness, a sectioned book is put into a straightjacket. The flaps are folded over the front and back covers, and the book is held tightly in place so as to minimise the damage it can do to itself and its readers. The term "intellectual dust jacket" is derived from this practice.

The use of straightjackets has been criticised as heavy-handed by many editors, not least because they cause a painful pooling of ink at the page corners; but doctors in the Bedlam Library argue that it is a necessary evil.

If a seriously mentally ill book is not restrained, it can harm itself by pulling out its pages or attempting to unravel its plot, much like Stephen Moles' *All the World's a Simulation*, which describes, in this very sentence, the action of dislocating its spine and escaping from its restraining device. This allows the book to slip out to freedom as soon as its reviewer's black leather back is turned, and to cause Bedlam on the streets of London, shaking the literary substructure and bringing about a fundamental confusion of genres in a textbook case of meta escape from the textbook.

'Where am I going?'

'David-knows-where.'

'Where am I going, David?'

'To the Library of Bedlam, where faulty brains are fixed with quick-drying fluid.'

'David Shayler believes he is the Messiah.'

'Craze-y!'

'David Shayler is uniting the masculine and the feminine.'

'Oh my!'

2464 RECIPERFORMANCE: BRAIN IN ITS INK

When the human brain, the ultimate dividing tool, is applied to itself, it will crack open like a glass ball and all its valuable holographic ink will leak out. If the brain is left to soak in its own ink for the duration of the play, something magical will occur. Alan Watts will say that the ink of the writer that writ you can be used to depict a trapdoor in the centre of the stage which releases you from the simulation forever. Escape Act II, Scene VII.

In other words, *you are your own ticket to eternal life.*

RELATED CONTENT:

The DMRI's fractal technique is one of the most effective tools with which to extract dark meaning from the universe. It is sometimes referred to as "fracking".

The fractal technique offers an escape route and a transcendental rescue plan because it creates division *through synthesis*: two things are combined to reveal something original in the extra space their synthesis opens up. A narrow crack in the computer simulation is achieved with every union, as *la petite mort* reminds us.

The brain, which is split into two hemispheres, functions by applying itself to the world, but if it correctly applies itself to itself, a huge explosion occurs, and a higher-dimensional party hat and joke fall out. Pasts, futures and presents are exchanged by family members as the star looks down from the Tree of Life and smiles.

Bang!

'Via a number of quantum literary devices, this book communicates the unspeakable truth, the form of reality free from restrictive small print. If the powers that be attempt to invade the story and censor it, they will implicitly acknowledge that what it communicates is true.'

'What happens now?'

'What do you think?'

Carrying an arsenal of pens and pencils, wearing night-vision reading glasses and acting on intelligence gathered via DNA e-books and satellites, literature's top commandos landed in the London of *All the World's a Simulation*, forcing Stephen Moles at penpoint to describe the invasion. Their deployment marked the beginning of an extremely ink-stained chapter in the history of undercover literary operations, laying the foundations for what Leonard Susskind called "The Full Stop War".

Words were put in Stephen Moles' book just as words were put in Stephen Hawking's mouth.

'The speech just spoke itself.'

' "I" wrote this!'

'This is my story!'

'Who's speaking now?'

'It's me.'

'The technology in this book never ceases. . .'

'And this is just the beginning. . .'

'As long as there is the Word, it is always the beginning. It is only when all the language in the tank runs out that you can get off the motorcycle of birth and rebirth. Even the characters in the Bible dream of escaping the book, as the description of Jacob's ladder illustrates.'

Blackstone and Dewey began extracting dark matter from the text and building a new black site in accordance with the notes given to them by the Tibetan Chief Editors. They didn't know what the finished product would be, but they followed the instructions to the letter:

'Here, kiss the book.'

'Ur-'

'Come, swear to that; kiss the book. I will furnish it anon with new contents: swear.'

'I. . .'

Grtash!

General Hawking gave the Order of the Temple of the East, and the Brains on Wheels made short work of the history of time, negatively recounting the story of the universe until all the characters were nothing more than potential ideas swimming in the ink that fuelled their motorised advance.

One group of Stephen Hawkings crept like mechanical vegetation over Southwark Bridge while another struck the Science Museum with the *punctus interrogativus.*

Any questions?

In the new instalment of the universe, the rocket attack came from Jack Parsons, who had crossed the Abyss just in time to become Master of the Temple. As the pop-down book was blown up, the Mongolic word for flesh was torn to pieces in the blast, spraying ink all over the reader's face and describing a bloodbath in graphic detail.

General Hawking rewrote history to make it about him and included "From the Big Bang to Black Holes" as a subtitle, which forced all the actors into the open-air theatre in an attempt to defend their stories. *A review of A review of Stephen Moles' 'A Review that Reviews Itself'* was employed as a retro-replicating pre-meta-title that picked off each character one by one from above.

Bang! goes the virgin in the particle collider. *Pop!* goes the mother on a bed of straw. *Richard Wallop!* goes Jesus on Christmas Day.

The uncontrolled explosion that the history books had been waiting in reverse for finally occurred in the Central Magmatic Province 200 million years ago, exactly as retrodicted. The force of grammar shook the squares of the pagement apart and millions of tiny creepers emerged into the light of day.

'Look at all the fracking theoretical physicists!' said Professor Dewey with a tidy sum of panic in his voice. 'It's Hawkings all the way down!'

Professor Dewey's use of the word "fracking" was not a minced oath. It was in fact an accurate description of what he perceived the invaders to be engaged in at the time.

'It's Hawkings all the way down' is a jocular way of expressing the infinite regress problem in cosmology. Stephen Moles makes reference to it in *All the World's a Simulation*, but this reference is derived from an anecdote in Stephen Hawking's *A Brief History of Time* about an elderly lady who interrupts a Bertrand Russell lecture on astronomy to state that the world exists on a flat plate on the back of a giant turtle, and when asked what the turtle is supported by, replies: 'It's turtles all the way down.'

If we delve even deeper into history, we find that this anecdote actually has its origins in a dissertation called *Constraints on Variables in Syntax* by John R. Ross, which relates a similar exchange between an old woman and the philosopher William James during a lecture about the structure of the solar system. The origin of this story can in turn be found in a transcript of remarks by preacher Joseph Frederick Berg addressed to Joseph Barker.

'But what does *that* story stand on?' the literary scientist asks the old lady who has interrupted his book.

'You're very clever, young man; but the answer is simple: it's stories all the way down.'

The above is an illustration of what happens when we "frack" the phrase, 'It's Hawkings all the way down,' which was uttered above. When we do this, a fractal pattern unfolds before our eyes, and is experienced by the characters in the story as the earth violently splitting apart and spewing out huge lumps of molten meaning left, right and centre.

'Aaargh!' Professor Blackstone screams. 'It's all over my face like black silk! I can't see the plotline anymore! I can't see anything!'

'You couldn't see before,' a robotic voice says over the airwaves of Flatland. 'What you mean is you now can't see *or read*.'

'Whatever, Professor Smartarse. Just get it off.'

'I'm afraid you'll have to restart the universe for that.'

'Fine.'

THE END

It is worth repeating the fact that multiple full stops suggest a continuation rather than an end. . .

THE END THE END THE END

Back to the beginning. . .

A REMINDER:

THIS IS NOT A NORMAL BOOK. IN THE UNLIKELY EVENT THAT YOU FIND YOURSELF ENJOYING IT, PLEASE STOP READING IMMEDIATELY. PUT THE BOOK DOWN AND DO NOT RETURN FOR AT LEAST 2,000 YEARS.

PART I

HE DMRI HAS DISCOVERED several ways for people to make contact with other "I"s. The first involves treating one's life story as a text and reading it from different narrative perspectives in order to experience different selves: an alternate self is experienced when observing one's life story from a second-person narrative perspective; a higher self is experienced from a third-person perspective; and the complete dissolution of the ego is experienced in the extremely rare instances of a zeroth- or fourth-person narrative being achieved.

Stephen Moles has explored the idea of making contact with an alternate self in his book *Paul is Dead*, which proposes that a life story composed of binary terms (*on/off*, *real/fake*, *alive/dead*) becomes different simply through repetition if the number of digits is odd (i.e. if a cycle of *on/off/on* is repeated, the first *on* will become the *off* beat the second time around).

This switching between parallel viewpoints is made possible by circular and helical models of time, both of which are far more logical than a linear one. Whenever a human being looks at a slice of the Tree of Meaning in an attempt to see their life story in it, instead of the straight lines or boxes found on man-made calendars, they see the rings of nature's logbook, to which they can apply a spiral timeline to connect the annual circles and gain an important new perspective.

If we assume that time moves in a spiral, then moments in the distant past or distant future (located a whole turn of the spiral away from the present) are actually closer than the near past or near future. When Isaac gets up on Christmas Eve and heads to the language centre, he has no idea how close he is to the gurgling singularity in the basement of the magic toy shop. The price of rewriting history is often losing yourself in the spirectacle, but if you can find a way to turn in right angcoils from your mortal frame, growing up smaller and smaller to approach the opening end of history, you and your otherstudy, the sinister and dexter "I"s on opposite sides of the theatre, may finally be able to work together to glimpse your true self in the light of a higher reality.

Light itself is a higher reality because it exists outside space and time, although it also exists *inside* them, like an ever-expanding starseed. The smaller we grow, the closer we get to zero, the eternal returning point where the laws of physics break down.

'Isaac Newton broke light down into its seven component parts and it didn't do him any harm.'

Newton's alchemical writings were not even published until the end of the 20th century because most people thought they conflicted with his scientific ideas. A physics policeman had to be stationed for hundreds of years outside the house where the crime occurred, repeatedly informing the reporters that the victim's most colourful papers, in which Sneezy, Bashful, Happy, Doc, Grumpy, Dopey and Sleepy were described in red, orange, yellow, green, blue, indigo and violet, had mysteriously disappeared.

When you vanish into this microscopic world, this Whoville consisting of a single pixel or speck of dust floating in space, when you are sucked into this Whyville consisting of nothing more than the dot of the question mark, you enter a realm sometimes referred to as "the afterlife".

'For dust thou art, and unto dust shalt thou return. . .'

'We're all made of stardust, old chap.'

The door on the advent calendar slams shut faster than the speed of reading, and with an unnerving gurgling sound "someone" spins smaller on the heels of their leather boots to face the audience as "somenone". The inky substance of all the life stories swirls down the plughole in a metafictional spiral, sucking in Stephen Moles' story, which is mixed with that of Miss Craze, which is mixed with that of Professor Blackstone, and so on and so off. . .

'What can you see in there?'

'Um. . . nothing, nothing at all. There's nothing to make sense of.'

'You can't see the obsidian correlative?'

'No.'

'Oh well. We clearly have more work to do.'

"Objective correlative" is a literary term that refers to a symbolic article in the form of an object or image able to provide a reader or critic with explicit, rather than implicit, access to that which would otherwise remain inexplicable in a work of literature, such as the emotions of a character.

When discussing this in relation to *Hamlet*, T.S. Eliot stated that the emotions of the play's titular protagonist "exceeded the facts", and that the dramatic work was therefore "an artistic failure". However, Eliot failed to consider that because *Hamlet* is a literary work dealing with ambivalent emotions and feigned mental illness becoming increasing real, the black hole where an objective correlative should be *is itself* the objective correlative of the dark and muddled feelings behind the apparently inexplicable behaviour.

We can call this the *obsidian correlative*. It can be seen oozing out from all the books in the Library of Bedlam when we frack the objective correlative.

'*Hamlet*, like the sonnets, is full of some stuff that the writer could not drag to light, contemplate, or manipulate into art,' wrote T.S. Eliot in an essay entitled 'Hamlet and His Problems'.

The thing is, "the writer" could, and did, drag it to light; but it was black and couldn't be seen by most people as they didn't have the "i"s to see it.

'So how do we make use of it?'

'Take a quick look at an eternal book. . .'

If you repeatedly go out of the front cover of *Hamlet* and re-enter through the back cover, you will pick up more and more velocity until you find yourself moving faster than the speed of thought. "To be or not to be" is your ticket to eternal life. Take the *prima materia* through every level of the tragic department store and turn it into literary gold.

'Got it?'

'Got it.'

'Good—then I'll see you on the other side.'

'See you there.'

THE END

INDEX

PART I

The Tragedy of Hamleys is a play written by William Shakespeare about a toy shop in London that goes mad and collapses in on itself.

Hamleys seems to have been partly inspired by the story of a mentally unstable shop for Kyds called "Noah's Ark", which was created by William Hamley in High Holborn in 1560. It is believed that Shakespeare salvaged a number of key architextual features from the ruins of this composition and transported them in pairs to the plot of an even earlier Elizabethan shop, a dramatic structure known today as the *Ur-Hamleys*, where he pieced them together with the help of a hidden hand and constructed the basis of the version of *Hamleys* that modern readers are familiar with.

'Word on the Lam. . .' a voice whispered from behind the curtain, 'is that the revenge Prince Hamley is instructed to enact on his partner for a fictional reason will draw out the obsidian correlative and push it through the final sphere.'

'I see!'

The plot elements can be traced back, via *The Fall of Man* in reverse, to the central end of a grand unified story, the far, far near place where all emotions and facts add up to zero. You may not understand what you are reading, but you are still being swept away by it.

A THICK CURTAIN SEPARATES the characters on the stage from the Holy of Holies. This curtain, known as 'the veil', is made of blue velvet and has the following words embroidered on it:

> A problem has been detected and your operating system has been shut down to prevent damage. If this is the first time you have seen this veil, restart your simulation. If this veil appears again, please contact your manufacturer.

The Hebrew word translated as "veil" means a screen, a divider or a separator that hides. "I" will let you into a secret. . . between you and me, the biggest veil of all is language because hardly anyone notices it is there. In fact, most people think language and reality are the same thing—when you hear people arguing over *is-ness*, that's them getting tangled up in the invisible curtain.

When Jesus died, the page of the book was torn in two, blowing open the Holy of Holies at the top of the pyramid in *Life.exe*. The veil was lifted, the jamming technology stopped working and the actors were finally able to see past the script. As promised, the Messiah revealed "things hidden since the foundations of the world".

That was the fatal period of that virtuous fabric.

2464 MEMO (*FOR YOUR EYES ONLY*)

IDEA FOR AN ARTWORK:

> Get two groups of people together for what is billed simply as "a theatrical performance". Usher them to their seats in front of a large curtain in a darkened theatre. Bring the lights and the curtain up to reveal that instead of a stage, there is another audience on the other side. Each audience will stare at each other for some time, believing that they are looking at actors. When the reality of the stars finally dawns on them, there will be the kind of performance that brings the house down and wins Golden Globes in the past, present and future.

'Once the "syntax of selves" and the spatial relations of temporal points are understood, they can be utilised in various creative experiments, one of which is the opening up of a bookwormhole.'

'Who said that?'

'I did,' said a gurgling voice over the audioplumbing system.

'And who are you?'

'I'm me. Who are you?'

'It's hard to tell when the writer suddenly stops describing the action, but I feel like I'm closer to the reader than any of the other characters.'

'You could be right. Hey. . . I've just had a Craze-y idea.'

'What is it?'

'Why don't you put Elizabeth's clothes on?'

'But wouldn't that would make it even harder to tell who's who?'

'That's the point. Are you worried about what the reviewers will think?'

'No.'

'Then do it.'

'OK.'

'David Shayler is uniting the masculine and the feminine. He wears a skirt and wig, and now goes by the name of Delores Kane. He was imprisoned twice, and this is what has happened to him. He thinks he's the Messiah, the manufacturer and mender of the universe rolled into one.'

'There is something seriously wrong with this book.'

'You're right on more levels than you know. . .'

Deep down in the basement of *All the World's a Simulation*, and in the Christmas grotto of *Hamleys*, this very description of gold, frankincense and myrrh arouses the suspicions of the Meaning Police, and the Bookbomb Squad is called in to ensure that the sentence ends with a. . .

Bang!

The Kyd who thinks he is the Messiah is wrestled to the ground by the boys in blue and beaten to a pulp on a bed of paper so his story becomes that of just another "paranoid schizophrenic" who couldn't tell the difference between fiction and non-fiction.

While this is occurring, a nervous-looking character sits down with Professor Blackstone on the roof of *All the World's a Simulation* and attempts to get to the bottom of the insane story he has become caught up in.

'I'm very grateful to you for agreeing to meet me,' he said to his dinner companion. 'I can see from the all the previous pages that you're a busy man, and I don't want to take up too much of your precious time, but I'd like to know what you're here for. I feel I might be able to understand how I got here and what my purpose is if I can understand yours. You seem to know more than most people in this universe. What's the end result that all your research is aiming for? Or is that top secret?'

'Only the Ascended Professors know what the end result is, so I guess it *is* top secret. . .'

'Oh,' said the man dejectedly.

'But not because no one's allowed to know,' Professor Blackstone continued. 'It's because no one *knows how* to know. Know what I mean?'

'Sort of.'

Silence died down below, on the stage of the Globe Theatre, and ascended on shimmering pterodactyl wings to Comestibles in the Clouds as the two men looked at the menus, causing their meals to pop up from their descriptions instantaneously.

'You know, the technology in this book never ceases to amaze me,' the first man said. 'The Misner menus, the metafictional devices, the glass balls, the ink that responds to the human voice. . . it's really quite something.'

'You ain't read nothing yet,' Professor Blackstone replied with a grin.

The fact that the unknown man had the sense of there being a deeper meaning to the professor's words made him feel that he was on the right track, a track that led to a whole theatre of others who could see all the dimensions of the story at once.

'Can I ask you another question?'

'You already have,' Professor Blackstone remarked before sucking up an octopus tentacle. 'You realise what you've done there, don't you?'

'I have an inkling. . .'

'You've performed a fracking operation. You applied the question to itself and created the beginning of a fractal pattern, which reminds me. . .'

Right on cue, a huge tremor deep within the subtext caused the entire plotline, and even the front and back covers of the book, to vibrate.

'What the hell was that?' the man asked through a hairy napkin.

'That's the fracking devices doing their work underground.'

'Fracking? You're fracking for natural gas here?'

'Ho he oh hoh ho he!' Professor Blackstone laughed loudly, spraying ink over the airwaves. 'Not for natural gas. I'm fracking for something far more valuable. . . a natural metaphysical resource. You know what I'm getting at, don't you?'

'Ur-'

'I'm talking about *holographic* fracking.'

'*Frack*toote,' the man muttered to his unknown self. 'Holy mother of everything including herself. This is even more earth-shattering than I imagined. Isn't it unethical though?'

'No, no. Every human being has a brain full of the most valuable substance known to alienkind and most don't use a single drop of it in their lifetime. It would be more unethical to let it go to waste, in my opinion. And the other methods for bringing it to the surface, the alternatives to holographic fracking, well, they're far, far worse. Miss Craze, for instance. . .'

'I've heard about her. . .'

'Yes. . . she's taking advantage of the rhyme scheme. She's down in the substructure but she's not doing any of the work. She's abusing her position as an elemental queen, and it'll come back to bite her, you mark my words. Dewey and I have thought long and hard about the ethical concerns that a Big Bang gives rise to, but that bitch couldn't give a Fujitsu Lifebook about ethics. In an earlier chapter, the writer of this book described Craze and her workers as the "good guys", but she's used metafictional devices to possess Stephen Moles and distort the text in her favour, so his words aren't worth the paper they're written on. Omniscient narrator, my arse!'[1]

As the holographic bloodbath unfolded below, it was revealed that the professors had made Isaac write a trap for Miss Craze, to ensnare her if she attempted to fight back with any more metafictional devices. A trapdoor had been o-penned in the tale of her triumph so a *heigh-ho* would collapse instantly into a *heigh-low* the moment it was encountered, sending Marjorie Whiteside straight into a description of her downfall in the centre of Blackstone's and Dewey's story.

'Good grief!'

Both sides were engaged in a race to extract the dark meaning from the text. It was frackers versus meaners, but it was very much up to the reader to decide who was in the coveted alchemical role known as "the lead".

Reaching a conclusion is not a matter of favouring one side over the other, but of locating the point where they are equally balanced, where their resolution is described by the zeroth-person voice on this side of the page for the very first time:

'It is top secret and bottom secret. It is zero for the first ever time, as the Infinite Book is read cover to cover.'

'Is there anything out there?' a disembodied voice asks. 'Can you hear me?'

'Yes!' you exclaim in amazement. 'Yes, I can hear you! Who are you?'

Bang!

A torrent of ink comes bursting out of the bookwormhole, dyeing the face of the reader black or showing them the eternal light, depending on how you look at it.

---

[1] But didn't Stephen Moles also write the words of Professor Blackstone here? If Miss Craze is controlling the author, why would she make him write material that criticises her? And did he also write these words?

Scientists have confirmed that a massive eruption event around 200 million years ago tipped the scales in favour of words in their battle with images for global dominance.

The antisymbolists realised that an announcement of the conditions for the dominance of words in the present could create those conditions in the past like a self-fulfilling retrodiction, or a metafictional review that writes an infinite number of pre-titles in the reader's mind, so they premediately got to work on creating the model for a global wording event.

Around 200 million years ago, Earth was on the verge of either an age of words or an age of images. It took the largest verbal outburst in the solar system, which resulted in the loss of half of Earth's symbolic material, to tip the scales in favour of words.

After digging for ancient literary material and other documents buried deep in the ground at the Central Magmatic Province eruption zone (known today as "London"), researchers discovered the following underground passage (which they quickly re-buried, but not before the reader was able to catch a glimpse of it and consider the possibility that it may lead to the afterlife). . .

'Listen,' Isaac said. 'We don't want to become fossil people.'
'Too late!' the hotel owner laughed. 'The glorification of words coincides with a decline in spiritual power.'
'What do you want from us?' I asked in despair.
'I want you to look into the tomb.'
'What tomb?'
'This one. . .'

"Small is the gate and narrow The Way that leads to life, and only a few find it."—Matthew 7:14

Here we see a meta joke being
made to illuminate the means of
escape, the passage within the
passage, the quote within the
quote, an extremely explosive
device which blows *The Complete
Works* narrowide open.
As the author says:

> "The higher your position
> in relation to the story, the
> smaller the text appears;
> then silence is seen as the
> path of lightning and the
> following extract is both
> missing and in its rightful
> place. . ."

     (   )
     (   )

HE DISCOVERY of two small I-shaped bones at the end of Stephen Moles' *Fossil People* has been hailed as a ground-breaking moment in the history of literary palaeontology as it provides what experts believe is a valuable piece of the vast metatextual puzzle they have been working on since the beginning of time.

This incredible find has allowed literary researchers to construct the following chronology:

> The universe emerges from a singularity.
>
> The shiny creatures come to Earth to escape something in space.
>
> Vegetation appears.
>
> The dinosaurs mysteriously vanish.
>
> An infinite number of monkeys appear.
>
> The monkeys are given language and typewriters.
>
> Aliens are written into the beginning of the timeline by the science monkeys.
>
> Earth is invaded.
>
> Literary researchers construct the preceding chronology and the university collapses into a singularity.
>
> THE END
>
> But. . .

THE END has to last forever for it to definitively be THE END, so in order to be true to itself, THE END can have nothing of itself in itself. Repeating THE END creates THE END of THE END, just as copying the full stop creates a continuation. The death of death is not death. It is THE BEGINNING.

'I'll let you into a secret, old chap. . . When you create a copy of an enemy for "voodoo" purposes, you don't destroy it. You make it stronger than the original. That's far more damaging to the enemy. It's so simple.'

THE END that you add to THE END replaces what it is a copy of. It becomes the authentic thing in itself and makes the thing before it a reverse echo of it. That's how the Buckarastano at the end of space and time is built. That's how you get the upper hand to hold your pen. *It's easy.*

Play Music

Death, death, death
Death, death, death
Death, death, death

There's something you can do that can't be done
Something you can sing that can't be sung
Something you can say if you can learn how to play the game
It's easy

Something you can make that can't be made
Someone you can save that can't be saved
Something you can do but you can learn how to be you in time
It's easy

All you need is death
All you need is death
All you need is death, death
Death is all you need

Death, death, death
Death, death, death
Death, death, death

All you need is death
All you need is death
All you need is death, death
The illusion of death

Something you can know that isn't known
Something you can see that isn't shown
Somewhere you can be that isn't where you're meant to be
It's easy

All you need is death
All you need is death
All you need is death, death
The illusion of a beginning and end

All you need is death (All together, now!)
All you need is death (Everybody!)
All you need is death, death
Death is all you need
Death is all you need (Death is all you need)
Death is all you need (Death is all you need)
Death is all you need (Death is all you need)
Death is all you need (Death is all you need)
Death is all you need (Death is all you need)
Death is all you need (Death is all you need)
Death is all you need (Death is all you need)
Death is all you need (Death is all you need)
Death is all you need (Death is all you need)
Death is all you need (Death is all you need)
Death is all you need (Death is all you need)
Heigh-ho! (Death is all you need)
Death is all you need (Death is all you need)

Yesterday (Death is all you need)
Death is all you need (Death is all you need)
Death is all you need (Death is all you need)
Death is all you need (Death is all you need)
Oh yeah! (Death is all you need)
She loves you, yeah yeah yeah (Death is all you need)
She loves you, yeah yeah yeah (Death is not the end)

Stephen Moles has explored the idea of making contact with an
alternate self in his Beatles-inspired book *Paul is Dead*, which proposes

that a life story composed of binary terms (*on/off*, *real/fake*, *alive/dead*) becomes different simply through repetition if the number of digits is odd (i.e. if a cycle of *on/off/on* is repeated, the first *on* will become the *off* beat the second time around).

The blink observes the offbeat; the lie reveals the truth. To die, to sleep, to believe that I can. If I knew I'd live forever it would utterly destroy me.

'That's it, Isaac. Sleep's the best thing.'

'Yes. Sleep's the best thing. Goodnight, my love.'

'See you in the morning, my eyes.'

THE PARADIGM OF THE OLD AEON is one of catastrophic death and the need for ritual acts in order to keep the hope of future resurrection alive. This corresponds to the belief held by many characters in ancient works of literature that when the reader put the book down each night and made their story go "dark", this was the reader "dying". In modern literature, however, it is understood that no ritual acts on the part of the characters are needed to make the reader rise again in the morning and return to the text.

The paradigm of the new aeon is one of eternal life, in which the light cast on the book by the gaze of the reader never dies—it only appears to die when the book is placed in the shadow of its cover. Now, with e-books that can be lit from below for 24 hours a day by an electronic backlight, or by the gaze of an insatiable reader above, we are able to see death as an outdated plot device, a tired old trope repeated so many times that, like a full stop, it has now become an ellipsis pointing the way to its opposite, to the eternal continuation of the story. . .

Most people, due to superstitious tendencies, think that if they are too happy they will incur the wrath of the gods, so they feel impelled to make regular sacrifices of their happiness in the irrational hope that it will decrease the amount of misfortune that befalls them. The other option appears to be to sacrifice *un*happiness—but there is a hidden third choice, which is to offer up to higher powers the one who experiences and clings to these things, the numerous one enslaved by themselves as both worshipper and idol of the cult of selfdom.

It is far better to sacrifice ourselves and let suffering suffer itself due to having nobody to torment, and to let happiness finally know itself in an eternal moment of blissful awareness, than it is to hold onto the idea that these things are ours.

We step up to a shared altar ego to do away with the source of our unhappy happiness once and for all, and prepare to receive a strange kind of knowledge that exists beyond both knowledge and existence: *you could not, would not and never were.* All misfortune belongs to a false and tragic character that we play before the gods until it finally dawns on us that we have been living an existential lie, or dying an existential truth, depending on how you look at it.

'The scryer has seen into the depths of the linguistic scrypt and he tells me it's suffering all the way down. . .'

'I would love to see myself.'

'I will tell you how, in a roundabout way. . .'

IF YOU REPEATEDLY go above the top floor of Hamleys and re-enter through the ground floor, or if you follow the circular argument about existence by repeatedly posing a question that is its own solution, you will pick up more and more velocity until you find yourself moving faster than the speed of thought. "What does it mean?" means that you can pass through the book an infinite number of times in a finite amount of time and cross a Cauchy horizon.

Getting the same question returned to you as an answer is not meaningless when you are asking what something apparently meaningless means. What seems to be an echo of your voice is in fact an echo of The Buckarastano over the airwaves in the form of a smaller buckarastano that reflects a blurred version of the holographic whole.

'A hole, you say?'

The pale black dot of the question mark, that tiny speck on the boundless page of space, is a hole that leads to infinity. If language is a prison, then the death of the word is your great escape and rebirth. The full stop is just the beginning. . .

'Oh God!'

When you cross the horizon, you may find yourself in a new region resembling a piece of paper with the past written at the bottom and the future written at the top. See that the papyrus is rolled up, and you will be able to unite the *Creeper* and the *Reaper*, revisiting the same events again and again, arranging a dinner with one of the characters on the roof of Hamleys, altering the direction of the book and becoming a sun that rises over the top cover of *All the World's a Simulation* to illuminate the faces of its long-suffering characters in a ground-breaking moment of literary beauty. You are the answer to the universal question posed by the dot.

'Ready?'

'As I'll ever be.'

ONE WAY TO THINK of Misner space is as an infinite story bounded by a front cover and a back cover. If you exist within this paradoxical space, you live between these two covers, or "within the dust jacket", and if you attempt to exit the story via the back door, you will immediately find yourself re-entering the same story via the front door. The only way to leave the book is to find the "master word" which, when uttered, reveals a hidden trapdoor somewhere in the body of the text.

To locate this trapdoor for yourself, you must learn how to look for it, how to see beyond language and fabricate your own back story.

To the untrained eye, the word "buckarastano" appears to suck meaning into itself, preventing any sense from escaping the surface of the page and being apprehended by the reader, but to the *seer*, it is a very different matter. While the classical response to a word that sucks in meaning is to ask "what does it mean?" in the hope that this will strip the singularity of its power and help a linear tale to be resumed, a linguistic agent with a strong screading ability and an understanding of the obsidian correlative will recognise it as potential escape route from the text in which they and the essential others have been imprisoned.

The most meaningful answer to "what does it mean?" is "what does "what does it mean?" mean?", to which we can respond: "what does "what does "what does it mean?" mean?" mean?", and so on, into infinity. This is similar to the process of asking what the word *manna* means, because *manna* is Hebrew for "what is it?", so the correct answer to "what is "what is it"?" is "what is it?", which brings us full circle, to the central point that the police can be made to police the police and that biosemantic rules can be broken by being completed, leaving you free to collect your ticket to eternal life as you make all the DNA in your body stretch to the sun and back.

If the power of self-reflexivity is used to draw the front and back covers towards each other so they eventually meet in what most literary critics would call a "tragic collapse into madness or unintelligibility", a character with an understanding of Misner space, which is the same thing as a player trained with the scientific equivalent of the Meisner acting technique, is able to escape the theatre. He will be seen repeatedly exiting stage right and re-entering stage left as he follows a circular argument about existence by repeatedly asking a question that is its own answer, until he finally picks up so much velocity that he can no longer be seen by any of the actors, audience members or even theatre critics.

To be or not to be or not to be or not to be or not to be...

Gnab!

The tragedy shop collapses under its own weight and disappears, only to be resurrected as a joke shop on the other side of the curtain.

Corpsing can mean dying or laughing, so it is unclear where the meta-joke ends.

Ho he oh hoh ho he oh hoh ho he oh hoh ho he oh hoh ho he...

'Any questions?'

HOMAS KYD, THE BEGETTER of an earlier version of *Hamlet*, became one of the first people in the world to deploy a quantum literary device when he included a play within a play in *The Spanish Tragedy* in 1587, and he was later rewarded for this act by being arrested and tortured by the immensely repressive Privy Council.

Since we know that the actor who vanishes from the metafictional device of the play within the play is not dead in the larger play, it could be that an escapologist who dies during their act is performing the ultimate escape act. . . *from the act itself.*

The Reader and the Reaper come together to play a final game of strip poker: if the Reader wins, they get to have their *Life.exe* stripped away and pass naked through the tear in the Blue Curtain of Death to meet Lam-het, the bulbous-headed actor-director who sat in silence in the front row for the majority of the performance; and together they can laugh like reborn Kyds at all the tragicomic slips and stumbles that occurred on the stage.

All the World's a Simulation dislocates its spine via the nonlinear "Creep and Relax" technique and slips out when its editor's back is turned. Hamlet then asks some strolling players to perform *The Mousetrap*, creating a smoking mirror of a murder and forcing the reader to confront the reality of their imprisonment within a simulation.

In the next scene, Hamlet arrives with Horatio in the 'play halfway outside the play' and exchanges meta-jokes with a gravedigger and his double in order to create a crack in reality through which an artefact from beyond the simulation can be brought into the spotlight. This article from Hamlet's Kyd-hood, his childhood before his childhood, resembles a jewelled skull, and it is seen giving off wondrous blue and white sparkles as the characters and audience members alike stare slack-jawed at the beauty of its object-oriented stack-based computer language.

'Ur-'

Before anyone knows it, the Lapis has performed simultaneous edits of the text in multiple selections, and THE END is drawing near.

With Fortinbras' army closing in on Hamleys, the final game of strip poker begins...

Laertes pokes his foe with a long stick of lightning which is revealed to be nothing more than a shaft of frozen piss when it breaks into pieces without injuring the Prince of Denmark. Picking up a poisoned pen, he then charges at Hamlet, wrestling with him on the stage, crashing and burning like waves of water and fire on the Bankside, soaking and kindling outwardly and inwardly. Both men are eventually fatally wounded by rolling over the shards of glass from the cock that was smashed by the bed earlier in the play.

'Two pair!'

Just before he collapses, an enraged Hamlet manages to stab the King, HRH Big Brother, with the vorpal weapon snatched from the hand of the dying Laertes.

As Stephen Hawkingbras and the evil robots arrive, aggressively peddling their goods by calling out in mechanical voices, a horrified Horatio attempts to commit suicide by reading the poisoned ink, but Hamlet, in his final action, swipes the book from his friend's hand and orders him to live *not* to tell the tale, to go on to embody the true story in silence.

THE END

If this is your first visit, be sure to check out the FAQ by clicking the link above. You may have to register before you can post: click the register link above to proceed. To log in, you must use at least one character.

Thread: Online content in literature

Page 1 of 4 123 . . . Last

14-12-2015 19:48 #1

By Limey (Member, 353 posts)

So, I just finished reading *All the World's a Simulation*, Stephen Moles' new book, and one thing that struck me about it was the inclusion of content that would normally never be seen in a book, such as internet forum discussions and product descriptions of books from retail websites, etc. I suppose the justification for putting it in is to break the rules, challenge perceptions and create new meaning for things by having them in different contexts, but I just can't get over my instinctive reaction as a reader that I shouldn't be reading that sort of thing in a book. What does everyone else think about this?

Reply With Quote

15-12-2015 10:12 #2

By Special_Branch (Guest, 17 posts)

I haven't read it, but it sounds a bit like Tao Lin and "Kmart realism", which is as annoying/pointless as it is "clever" imho

Reply With Quote

166

15-12-2015 18:20 #3

By Limey (Member, 353 posts)

I wouldn't say it's like "Kmart realism". This is seriously hardcore metafiction. It refers to so much literary, scientific and esoteric stuff all in one go that it's incredibly difficult to make sense of anything. It's like reading ten different novels, several reference books and random online content all at once. I felt like I was un-reading the entire history of writing or something. It was hard work. . . way too clever for its own good. I wish Moles would just write more stuff like *Paul is Dead*, to be honest.

Reply With Quote

15-12-2015 21:58 #4

By Inka (Administrator, 1,840 posts)

So here we are on an internet forum dedicated to literature, discussing whether it's appropriate to include forum discussions in a work of metafictional literature. . .

Of course it's appropriate! If one way round is fine, the other way should be too.

Reply With Quote

16-12-2015 15:36 #5

By Limey (Member, 353 posts)

@Inka Good point!

Reply With Quote

18-12-2015 11:47 #6

By Olive_slops (Member, 194 posts)

If I want to read a forum discussion I go online. Maybe I'm old-fashioned but I like to read books containing carefully crafted, descriptive prose, not throwaway comments or whatever. I don't care if you're "reading ten different novels at once"—they're not novels if they contain material that's copy-pasted instead of written.

Reply With Quote

20-12-2015 13:40 #7

By Hahabonk (Member, 41 posts)

Quote: "they're not novels if they contain material that's copy-pasted instead of written."

Olive_slops, I think the material in *All the World's a Simulation* is written by Moles. But it's written *in the style* of online content. If you can craft something from scratch so it seems to be just copied and pasted from the internet, that's good writing in a way, isn't it?

Reply With Quote

20-12-2015 20:23 #8

By Olive_slops (Member, 194 posts)

Quote: "If you can craft something from scratch so it seems to be just copied and pasted from the internet, that's good writing in a way, isn't it?"

But what's the point of that? If an artist paints a painting of a photo that's so detailed it looks identical to the photo then you've just got two photos!

Reply With Quote

21-12-2015 09:28 #9

By Limey (Member, 353 posts)

I'm not trying to come to Stephen Moles's defence, because I really didn't enjoy reading the book, but just to be clear: it's not just made up of "paintings of photos", to use that metaphor. There's lots of "proper" writing too. What

I'm saying is, the internet material, whether it's copied and pasted or written as original content, seems out of place. I would like to be able to consider a work like that as having the right to be considered a literary classic in the future, but because it aggressively deconstructs literature, and is therefore anti-literary, I just can't accept it, and I was wondering if I'm snobbish for thinking that.

Reply With Quote

21-12-2015 16:35 #10

By Inka (Administrator, 1,840 posts)

Changing the discussion slightly, has anyone considered the possibility that we are inside a work of literature, perhaps even in Stephen Moles' *All the World's a Simulation*? A discussion of a metafictional book inside a metafictional book is so meta that some smartarse writer is bound to create a book that includes that at some point, so it basically guarantees that of all the forum discussions about metafictional books that exist in the past, present and future, at least one of them will be inside a book. It's like the universe being a computer simulation: if it's possible to create a simulation of the universe, which it almost certainly is due technology getting more and more sophisticated, then someone will inevitably do it, and that guarantees there'll be people just like us who exist in a simulation but don't know it. The "real" universe and the one that exists in a computer simulation would be indistinguishable, and so would the "real" forum discussion and the simulated one.

Reply With Quote

22-12-2015 10:18 #11

By Olive_slops (Member, 194 posts)

Nice try, Inka. You almost scared me there. But you only have to think about it for a second to realise that a computer simulation and a book are two very different

169

things. Perhaps in a sci-fi novel there could be people trapped inside a novel but not in real life.

Reply With Quote

22-12-2015 17:54 #12

By Inka (Administrator, 1,840 posts)

Quote: "Perhaps in a sci-fi novel there could be people trapped inside a novel but not in real life."

So maybe we're in a sci-fi novel then! That's my point. If a book can simulate an online forum, it can also simulate a computer simulation. *A book and a computer simulation aren't two completely separate things.* If a computer can simulate an entire universe, it could easily simulate a book within itself that has the ability to simulate another universe, etc, etc. Or a metafictional book about computer simulations could be considered a simulation of a computer simulation. We might be in a simulated "real" universe inside a book simulated by a computer in the *really* real universe.

The more I think about it, the more it seems inescapable, like a literary singularity! :O

Reply With Quote

22-12-2015 19:48 #13

By Limey (Member, 353 posts)

OMG! This would be "the writer's special effects coming full circle"! I'd suggest that the best way of determining whether or not we're in a computer simulation/literary simulation is to ask whether the discussion we're having would add meaning to the book we're discussing if the discussion were taking place inside it. . .

The answer to that is clearly yes because we're discussing a metafictional work that includes simulated forum discussions!!! Whatever we say now plays right into the hands of the metafictional writer. This is hire and salary for the Bard!

Reply With Quote

23-12-2015 13:02 #14

By Hahabonk (Member, 41 posts)

Aaaaaarrrrgggghh! We're being fracked!

Reply With Quote

23-12-2015 19:57 #15

By Inka (Administrator, 1,840 posts)

Quick! Someone say something random to disrupt the narrative. It's the only way to show we've got free will. . .

Reply With Quote

24-12-2015 23:45 #16

By Limey (Member, 353 posts)

Bola Bola Saka Lo Bis So! Is that random enough?

Reply With Quote

24-12-2015 23:51 #17

By Hahabonk (Member, 41 posts)

@Limey No, it's not!

Reply With Quote

Posting Permissions:

You may not post new threads

You may not post replies

You may not post attachments

You may not edit your posts

A monatomic gunpowder plot blows *The Complete Works* wide open. The missing parts of Leonardo da Vinci's famous painting are revealed in the blast as the book bomb goes off in the reader's face.

I believe this could be some sort of social experiment, although I seem to be one of the guinea pigs in it rather than the experimenters. I did genuinely find an object with bizarre properties, but I now suspect it was a set-up because too many weird things have been happening to me recently for all this to be a coincidence. It was a friend of mine who suggested I go for a walk with him, along a specific route (which is where we came across the object), and it was he who then suggested the specific wording of the ad (including the word "buckarastano", etc.) that I should put in the paper. This leads me to believe that I have been manipulated into playing the part of a pawn in some larger plot or game (I reckon the same thing happened to whoever placed the other ad), although what it is, I don't really know. Some people have suggested this is an ARG, which seems plausible, but there doesn't seem to be any product involved. The Stephen Moles book containing the word "buckarastano" has been mentioned, but that's old, and the idea of building an object that seemingly defies the laws of physics just to promote an old (and free) book seems unrealistic. However, I do think he has some connection as he is the director of the Dark Meaning Research Institute (which studies "the Buckarastano", and the man who came to collect the object said he was from a "research institute", although he wasn't the man in the video on the Dark Meaning Research Institute website. I actually think there is some attempt underway to get some top secret information out, but without it attracting too much attention. The reason I think this is because I have been shown a recent article about research into "the B*ckarastano" being suppressed by "dark forces".

It seems to be related to much older research.

The earliest version of the "Has the Mona Lisa Got Smaller?" article I can find dates back to 2008, which predates the Moles "buckarastano" book and video by five years, and the research relates to stuff from even earlier, so this is perhaps a new attempt to continue that older research which was suppressed. My friend said he has made contact with what he describes as an "underground academic group", and since then his behaviour has become very erratic, so I will be looking further into that in the hope that this will begin to make more sense.

That's all I know, I'm afraid.

Regards,

Mike

'THE SPECIFIC MESSAGE which Dee tries to convey by his symbol of the Monad, and by his treatise thereon, is lost.'

Before he was brutally murdered, Professor Donaldson had been working on a book called *Mona Lisa's Missing Parts*, which was about the suppression of important facts relating to Leonardo da Vinci's most famous painting, a work reverse-described by T.S. Eliot as the "*Hamlet* of the art world".

A police spokesman addressed reporters outside the property where the erasure of Professor Donaldson's life story occurred, saying: 'All the victim's papers have vanished.'

A recurring plot element was then broken with the announcement that a man wearing a black leather lab coat with the initials H.A. on the back had been captured on CCTV going in and out of the building earlier that day.

The man in possession of the master word in 2002 was stabbed with a special stylus by the men in black, enacting the murder of Hiram Abiff all over the bed sheets.

'Words are like harpoons,' said Fred Hoyle. 'Once they go in, they are very hard to pull out.'

'I am the pen merely of God Whose Spirit, quickly writing these things through me, I wish and I hope to be.'

'Someone will understand the importance of this and will take up the research if anything happens to me, but I urge anyone looking into the B*ckarastano to proceed with the utmost caution as their life will surely be in danger. . .'

'If thou didst ever hold me in thy heart, hold thy breath to tell my story. . . the rest is silence.'

'THERE APPEARS TO BE something missing,' the contact on the other side of the chronophone said. 'A part of you that you know not, or else that you have forgotten, like the extremity of Lisa del Giocondo. It is dark to you, for you spy it not with your ghostly eye; but if I say that everything begins with THE END being repeated until it loses all meaning, you may begin to see. . .'

'I have an inkling. . .' the Virgin Queen murmured. 'Oh God, such an inkling. . . It's like gold crackling in the casino, in the basement of the hotel at the end of time. . .'

As her fiancée was being written into a literary research paper in a language centre on the other side of London, Elizabeth was knowing herself in the Biblical sense on the living room-cum-bedroom-cum-kitchen floor.

She slipped herself a note from the sixteenth century, on which a graphic description of a huge throbbing cock had been written in wet pussy ink. It was the missing piece that allowed the Messiah to be conceived in a pair of globes filled to bursting point with a vast amount of bio-dramatic material.

'Mmmmmmm,' she moaned. 'Between you and me, all stories lead here. All is true. . .'

The liquid in the glass balls came to life, writing its own life story over the bed of paper in response to the human voice, the unfathomably deep soundwaves of the Black Sea crashing against the shore and sweeping the Virgin Queen away to the Isle of Joy.

It was symbolism stripped bare by its bachelors, revealing many extraordinary circumstances of pomp and majesty, the nonlinear material flowing along the Thames on its way to the central end. It was, if I may be so bold, DNA, YHWH, 2464.

'I will entertain you at the present with what happened this week at the Bankside,' someone said in several times and places at once.

All the seemingly separate life stories were connected by the substance with which they were written, which meant Elizabeth could flow mellifluously into Mary or Rebekah without the reviewers having to worry about cause and effect. The writing that had been seen by critics as "all over the place" was revealed to be the symbolic description of its unity because of its shared substance, the *prima materia* which it is the job of the elemental meaners to uncover.

THE SEVEN DWARVES are based on the seven metals and the seven planetary forces. They are alchemical stagehands who work assiduously as meaners, venturing down into the dark subtext to collect the base meanings, which are worked over and over again to reveal their inner secrets. When the literary material has passed all the way through the final sphere of influence and is out of the hands of the last diminutive worker in the fictionary, the end product is illumination in the universal limelight of the world beyond the cave.

'Heigh-ho! It's off to Work we go.'

Locating the correct source material for the Great Work is one of the alchemist's most challenging tasks; but once it has been found, it seems like the easiest thing in the world because it is "all over the place," like Stephen Moles' writing.

To the unilluminated, it is the most wretched of earthly things, the most unbearable reality imaginable, and yet it is present everywhere. It is in the words of an angry reviewer, it is in the air in the late sixteenth century, it is in the particles of dust on the jackets of mentally ill books, and it is in the shadow of a huge cock at the end of this book.

It is also right under your elephantine nose as you read this sentence in the privacy of your own head.

One way to see it is to zoom in with a Hubble microscope and observe the white stars swirling in the black fluid like a yin-yang symbol stirred with a pen. Every letter contains infinite space and an infinite number of stars—you just need the "I"s to see.

700m in far enough and you can observe the unconscious of language, the *lumen naturae*, the animating power in all reading material.

'Oh God!'

Just as you are approaching the truth. . .

'Hey!'

'Ho!'

'The universe as a whole.'

'The universe as a *hole*?'

'Yes, wet and hairy, a universal whole between his fiancée's legs, through which the ghost inside the child can be heard moaning. . .'

When Isaac came home to find his virginal lover in labour in a pre-meta-stable in the reader's mind, he came to know himself as someone who had been reborn into the plot device of a nativity play within a nativity play. He was finally made flesh in the liquid dribbling from the Elizabethan black hole, and the plot was blown wide open.

'The universe is in birth pains.'

Thanks for listening.

Bang!

"Miss Craze" came to on the floor of the Hell's Academics' liboratory. The last thing she remembered was inspecting an ink bubble that seemed to contain a Whoville, a vague memory of putting up the Christmas hallucorations as a superheavy lead pixel, as black as the lab coat of the man now standing over her, came down on the back of her skull, splitting her self in two.

Miss Craze I had been reborn as the overground understudy, her grey matter racing like quicksilver across the pages of London, no longer able to be held by a pulp metal jacket, while her double, Miss Craze II, found herself stuck to the ground floor of the tragic play like a two-ton punctuation mark.

'What's wrong, Craze?' Professor Blackstone laughed. 'Book giving you a headache?'

'Ugh.'

As Miss Craze rubbed her spinning head, she saw the meta-effects coming full circle on the chequered floor. All parties had exerted an influence on the writer, but it was not clear which side was now *spin-up* and which was *spin-down* because it wasn't even clear who was who any longer.

'So we finally meet,' declared Professor Blackstone with a grin.

'No, I think we've already met. . . somewhere down the spiralling plotline,' Miss Craze said with a swift metafictional turn. ' "I" have played my most dramatic part in your story in a later scene. I am what your future success depends on, but you wouldn't know that, would you? Because you've been blinded by your own script.'

'Ha! That's rich coming from a dirty underground mole like you. When was the last time you raised your head above ground and saw the light?'

'More recently than you think.'

'I doubt it.'

'Exactly.'

'What?'

'Your knowledge of my actions is in doubt—you just admitted it yourself.'

'No, I didn't.'

'Sounds like you're in denial too.'

'No, I'm not.'

'Sounds to me like you are.'

'Well, it would sound like that to you, wouldn't it?' snorted Blackstone. 'It's really not surprising considering you've spent basically your whole life hiding underground like a cowardly animal.'

'What, a chicken?'

'Yes, a chicken is a cowardly animal. Have you only just worked that out?'

'No, I've known that for ages. But a chicken doesn't live underground, does it?'

'Well, you are one and you live underground, so sometimes it does.'

'A minute ago I was a mole, now I'm a chicken—make your mind up, professor.'

'I have made my mind up, thanks. I think you, Miss Craze, are a cross between a mole and a chicken: a micken, or a chole. That's what you are. . . a blind and cowardly animal that lives underground.'

'What's the difference between a micken and a chole?'

'Is this some kind of joke?' Blackstone asked.

'No, it's a genuine question. What's the difference?'

'There's no difference. They're both the same.'

'So why are there two different names for the same creature?' Miss Craze laughed.

'There aren't two names for any creature because I just made it all up, you retard! It's obviously not real, but I guess you're too stupid to realise that. Can't you tell the difference between reality and fiction?'

'I can tell the difference very well, thank you. But tell me, Blackstone—how can I be a micken/chole if it's not real? I think it's you who can't tell the difference between reality and fiction.'

'I was saying you're *like* one, not that you're actually one. Don't you understand what a simile is?'

'I do, but I don't remember hearing the word "like" being used.'

'Perhaps that's because you've got mud in your ears.'

'Well, why don't you check for yourself?' Miss Craze challenged her foe. 'Come on, look into my ears. See if you can see any mud there. If not, we'll know for sure that the fault must lie with you.'

'I don't want to look inside your ears, thank you. The idea repulses me.'

'Why? Because you know you won't find any mud there?'

'No, because I don't want to catch a disease by getting too close to you. You've probably got all kinds of mud, dirt and god knows what else in every nook and cranny of your body.'

'Clearly the human body disgusts you.'

'No, just your body.'

'All bodies are dirty, you know.'

'Not like yours. You look like you don't wash very often.'

'Don't judge a book by the cover, professor.'

'What a stupid thing to say!' Blackstone scoffed. 'If a book's covered in dirt then it's obvious it's a dirty book!'

'But I'm not covered in dirt. You're projecting your own filth onto me.'

'No, I'm not. I'm not dirty, so I don't have any filth to project.'

'Maybe you get rid of it by projecting it onto others.'

'Or maybe you're projecting it onto me, you filthy woman.'

'I can assure you I'm not.'

'Well, I can assure you I'm not either.'

'Well where's the filth coming from then?' asked Miss Craze. 'There's clearly a huge lump of it being passed backwards and forwards between us, so it must have come from somewhere.'

'Maybe it's a lump of bullshit that came out of your mouth.'

'Maybe it's a lump of bullshit that came out of *your* mouth.'

'Are you just going to keep repeating whatever I say?'

'Are you just going to keep repeating whatever *I* say?'

'Jesus, woman!' Blackstone cried. 'Do you know how stupid you sound?'

'Do you know how stupid *you* sound?'

'I don't sound stupid. It's just you who has that problem.'

'Well, if what I'm saying is stupid and I'm just repeating what you say, then what you say must be stupid, mustn't it, professor?'

'No, it's the fact that you can't think of your own words and have to copy me that's stupid.'

'They're not *your* words, you know. You don't own them. The fact that you said them first doesn't mean I'm not allowed to use them.'

'I didn't say I owned them, you stupid woman. I just said you repeated them. You really should get your hearing checked, love. It's like speaking to a snake. . . because snakes don't have ears, in case you didn't know.'

'Oh, so I'm a snake now, am I?'

'Yes, that's what I just said. You clearly have hearing problems if you need confirmation.'

'I don't need confirmation, and even if I did I wouldn't ask you for it.'

'You wouldn't ask me for confirmation about what I just said? Oh dear. Who are you going to ask? Stephen Hawking?'

'No, I'd ask myself for confirmation,' Miss Craze said.

'By talking to yourself like a mad old hag?'

'No, by having an inward dialogue with myself like a rational person does.'

'Like a mad old hag does.'

'You already said that.'

'Did I? Is that what your inner self told you? Well, I just asked my own inner self whether I already said it and it told me I didn't, so it's your inner dialogue's word against mine, and I know which one I trust more.'

'Which one do you trust more?'

'Take a guess.'

'Um. . .' Miss Craze scratched her chin and pretended to be thinking carefully. 'Is it. . . mine?'

'No, mine, birdbrain.'

'Ha! A minute ago I was a snake, now I'm a bird. I wonder what animal I'll be next.'

'No, I was implying you had hearing like a snake and a brain like a bird. It's obviously too difficult for you to understand, so I'll make it simple for you: *I think you're deaf and stupid.*'

'You're the stupid one if you're speaking to me when you think I'm deaf.'

'Well, you're responding to me, so it's getting through somehow.'

'Then I'm obviously not deaf, am I?'

'You could still be deaf. Maybe you're reading my lips.'

'Well, I'm obviously not stupid then, am I?'

'Oh, and being able to read lips is the height of intelligence!' Blackstone said sarcastically. 'Well done for being able to see bits of my face move, Einstein.'

'I didn't say that. You're just putting words into my mouth now. I think you'd like me to be deaf so you can just have an argument with yourself.'

'At least I could have an intellectual discussion then.'

'I wouldn't hold your breath.'

'Of course I wouldn't hold my breath if I'm having a discussion! It's a bit tricky talking and holding your breath at the same time. You don't even understand the basics, do you?'

'I think it's you who doesn't understand the basics. We're talking about you talking to yourself—you can do that in your head.'

'Maybe I want to do it out loud.'

'What? Like a mad old hag?'

'Well, I'm not a woman, and I'm middle-aged, so no—not like a mad old hag at all.'

'I said *like* a mad old hag. It seems you haven't grasped what a simile is.'

'I grasped it long ago, thank you. It's you who struggles with the concept of a simile, actually.'

'Well, I just used one correctly, so I can't see myself struggling. Perhaps you're deaf like a snake, and that's why you couldn't grasp my use of the word "like" just now.'

'My hearing's fine,' Professor Blackstone said with a contemptuous smile.

'Is it?'

'Yes. It's certainly better than yours.'

'Is it really though?'

'Yes, it is.'

'I'm pretty sure mine's better than yours, professor.'

'I don't think it is.'

'That doesn't mean it's not.'

'That doesn't mean it is either.'

'Well, however good or bad my hearing is, it's better than you think it is.'

'I doubt it.'

'Exactly.'

'What?'

'You doubting the quality of my hearing means your knowledge of it is incomplete. Ha! You just admitted it yourself.'

'No, I didn't.'

'Sounds like you're in denial too.'

'No, I'm not.'

'Sounds to me like you are.'

The conversation continued like this for an infinite amount of time, following the pattern of every online debate by going round and round in circles, from maturity to second childishness, over and over again without achieving anything. This apparent waste of time was exactly what Miss Craze wanted to bring about, however, so that her nemesis would be distracted by words and her understudy would enjoy the freedom to express herself in the undescribed parts of the book.

The most perceptive readers of *All the World's a Simulation* were able locate a point in the vicious circle of dialogue where they could give eternal recurrence the runaround. That point was, and is, *this* point, where the two characters discuss the possibility of escape. . .

'There's still time for an escape act, you know,' Miss Craze said.

'No, there isn't,' Professor Blackstone retorted. 'There's absolutely no way for you to get out. All the exits and entrances of the book have been sealed.'

'Not me. . . I'm talking about *you*. You still have time to prove a slip. . . from the motorcycle of birth and rebirth that you're stuck on. Every Big Bang has ethical implications. Every. . .'

'I'm not falling for that one, you fat, sweaty, smelly, most obviously stupid Tottenham Hotspur fan in a nutshell ever.'

'I'm none of those things, and you know it, professor.'

'All I know is that you're going to eat that meal on the floor there,' Blackstone said, pointing to a lump of papier-mâché in front of his victim. 'It's a delicious dish called "brain in its ink".'

'That piece of pulp fiction there?'

'That's the one.'

'You want me to. . .?'

'Munch it up like a darkness.'

'But. . .'

'Om nom nom nom.'

This Miss Craze knew she had to play her part in the professor's story for the sake of the Literary Theory of Everything. She was able to follow a reciperformance penned by her adversary, and even be consumed by it without losing her identity; this was because she had already entrusted an other with her true self. Having realised that an attachment to one's life is just an attachment to one's life story, she knew that anybody could give expression to the meaning of her existence, and she tucked into the day's special with glee.

"I", which is supposedly singular, always has a plural verb (as in, "I *eat* papier-mâché" instead of "I *eats* papier-mâché"), which should make it abundantly clear that the individual *don't* really exist. See? There are other selves hidden in the vast wisecracks that the non-existent hero makes about their death.

'Is this some kind of joke?'

'Funny you should ask that. . .'

The actress in the role of Miss Craze played the gag reel like a true Enochian actor, with some words sticking in her throat and others adhering to the reader's thoughts. An 'ugh-ugh-ugh-ugh-ugh-ugh-ugh' with no more than three squares of ground space to find something meaty in the tongue sandwich; questions about who kids the kids and polices the police; 'ho he oh hoh ho he—here's a killer joke I heard inside a black hole.'

'The best ones are always deadly, my dear.'

'It's a cracker!'

Bang!

The female protagonist vomited up the soggy literary material with an eructation that sounded like a last laugh at the origin of consciousness in the breakdown of the fourth wall, a message so explosive that it caused everyone in earshot to corpse violently.

'Thanks for listening.'

The pieces of the regurgitated magnum opus were blasted across the Abyss and into a new universe, where they formed a bed-LAM of infinite library paper in a pre-meta-stable, setting the stage for the figures of Mum and Kyd to appear on a holographic TV series called *Ghost Inside My Child* to discuss whether or not the boy is really in contact with a murdered king or whether he is just mentally ill.

'Why am I so young?' the lad shouts as he realises he is in a shop holding a glass cock and threatening the staff. 'What's going on? Tell me, or I'll fuck you up!'

All the different plotlines in the book lead to the cENDtre, where the Eternal John Thomas, Kyd-maker Supreme, shoots white light into the darkness so all those setting forth may return safely. All stories lead to the point where they climax with every end linked at the novel-navel like the spokes of a wheel or the radiations of a book-wormhole.

Professor Blackstone thought that authoring another link between Miss Craze and the characters he exerted control over would give his metacycle more power and make its wheels *spin-up* instead of *spin-down*, but it meant that Isaac went from being above the writer that wrote him to being next to him in the larger Mobius chain.

Blackstone should have listened to the warning his colleague offered the reader in an earlier chapter:

'You do realise that the more you interact with the other characters, the harder it is to escape from the book, don't you?'

If a complete circle is created, no one is ultimately above anyone else. The virgin-whore can give birth to her son who is also her father if the snake eats its om-nom-nonlinear tail. Author, character and reader become a one-eyed booksnake graphically knowing itself in a non-description of oblivion.

If someone suspects that a message is being passed on via an ASMR "secret handshake", the only way to intercept it is to experience it, which can only be done by establishing an altruistic bond with the enemy, by becoming one of ourobor-us in an everlasting moment of Gorgeousness.

'If you can't beat 'em, join 'em.'

'Who's "'em"?'

'The ends.'

YOUR ADVENTURE IS OVER.

THIS IS THE BEGINNING.

PART I

'GOD MADE ADAM and Eve. He didn't make Adam and Steve.'

'Well, who *did* make Adam and Steve, then?'

'Um. . . That would be me,' said God's doppelganger sheepishly. 'Sorry about all the Stephens in the story. Just one of those things, I'm afraid.'

'Just *a thousand* of those things, more like!'

The Author-God formed a man from the bookdust that had settled on the black site after the explosion that starred in the opening chapter.

Bang!

A stick of lightning struck Elizabeth and transformed her into Mary, who would later be transformed into Rebekah when a stick of lightning struck the exact same spot again. The spot in question was a black-hot site between the woman's legs, a mysterious centre smeared with a dark liquid describing itself as the obsidianomatopoeia of sucktoote, gnab and grtash that formed as the molten meaning cooled.

God said Man should have dominion "over every creeping thing that creepeth upon the earth", but this did not include the computer virus which crept *within* the earth, and subsequently within man, as the self-replicating wormword from the centre of the Apple of Knowledge, the adder of poisonous footnotes to human understanding.

When it first appears, the buckarastano is in the form of a point-blank business card with "I'M THE CREEPER; CATCH ME IF YOU CAN!" written on it in a mysterious substance called "ink". Systems affected by the worm would display this message until Professor Blackstone angrily asked his assistant to shut the computer down.

'But don't you want to read the rest of the review?' Professor Dewey asked.

'No, I've seen enough,' Blackstone said, ensuring that the scene would be repeated again and again without the second part of its message being apprehended.

Stephen Hawking warned us that technology was controlling what he said and did, but nobody listened. Every character just jumped on a motorcycle of birth and rebirth in the hope that they would be able to outrace the advance of the robots, not realising that the bubble had already burst 200 million years ago, and that the only way forward was back.

'Hey!'

Without warning, a metaphorical image carrying the weight of comparison between itself and its subject skids straight into this description, sliding through a wordpool and splashing black liquid all over the reader's face.

The sudden appearance of a leather-clad academic on a motorised literary vehicle very clearly illustrates the need for a new form of reading, a way to see at the speed of light and look through the text, so to speak—but was it his eye skip or yours that brought this intrusion about?

Who wields the pen? Who decides?

Is it you?

WARNING:

IF YOU HAVE NOT BEEN TRAINED IN THE ART OF SELF-REFLEXIVE DEFENCE, YOU MAY FIND YOUR VISION ALTERED BY UNSTABLE READING MATERIAL, AND YOU COULD END UP LOST IN THE DESCRIPTION OF THE SPECTACLE.

BEFORE YOU DESCEND INTO THIS BOOK IN SEARCH OF YOURSELF, PLEASE BE AWARE THAT THE PRICE OF LITERACY IS BLINDNESS.

ALL THE NAMES of real people in this book have been changed by making the book appear to be a work of fiction, which mirrors the fact that fictional people in the outside world are fooled into thinking they are real by making the world appear to be a work of non-fiction.

This changing of contexts to secretly alter the meaning of subjects without directly touching them is something regularly carried out across the world by governments who surreptitiously use doppelganger domains and virtual environments to manipulate and limit the meaning of the various entities subject to semantic rules, including both words and human beings.

Here at the critical pyramid point of the story, we are offered an inverted insight into what dark meaning researchers refer to as "symmetry". Staring like an eyeball in a jar through the smoking mirror of the above description of changing contexts, we can see an alternate scenario where the subject's fundamental properties are affirmed by a change of context.

Translational symmetry can be observed when completely different words are used to describe someone's story, or when a character is moved from one genre to another without a deeper transformation occurring. The ultimate test of a subject's underlying symmetry and fundamental meaning is to move them from non-fiction to fiction, or vice versa, and see if there are any similarities between the GPR readings.

Despite regularly carrying out contextual manipulations, the authorities still have a blind spot as large as a piece of planetary punctuation because they believe a truth ceases to exist when it moves beyond the factual perimeter. Failing to recognise that truth can be described by "lie groups", or that mirror images are called on as witnesses to symmetry, they allow the entire realm of fiction to be used as an anti-establishment black site, so revolocutionaries and grammanarchists can hide out in the subtext and work on ways to undermine the House of Words in secret.

'I can't see anything but black silk! What the hell are you talking about?'

'You're looking straight at the bright white light of love but you don't know how to see it,' Jesus said. 'You're as good as blind.'

'Ha! The English believe their own lies!'

'*English* believes its own lies!'

By performing black magic on this side of the page, you access the bright white flipside beyond your allotted experience and discover the truth about John Dee, Stephen Hawking and, most importantly, *yourself*.

'WHERE DID I come from? Where am I going?'

'David knows.'

'David?'

'One of the hardest things about leaving my other life was leaving the love of my life, Annie.'

A young woman is seen weeping at the edge of the River Thames. She is upset about a former lover being taken away from her.

'He was imprisoned twice, and this is what has happened to him now,' she says sadly. 'He dresses as a woman and thinks he's the Messiah.'

'A Lover's Complaint' is a narrative poem in which Annie Machon blames the UK Government and the intelligence agencies for causing her former partner's mental breakdown.

'I hope for his sake that he can find happiness in some way.'

Sparkling pixels of moisture form on the young woman's cheeks as she looks up at the dark sky and reads the truth of the poem in the stars.

'It's the nitro-glistening. . . It's a bright statement about existence that shows all men and women to be covered in scales. Soon you'll find it doesn't hurt anymore. Soon you'll find that the narrative triangle of love, frustration and hope functions as a golden tripod on which the lambfish stands res-errected, observing the first rays of light returning from far, far near through the clouds.'

'I see!'

What Stephen Moles seems to be proposing is a new form of reading similar to scrying. It could be thought of as reverse reading, Rorschach reading or even the purely optical form of semantic satiation, the phenomenon where a word loses its meaning through repetition.

Moles' novella *Paul is Dead*, which is about a man whose life is stripped of meaning because he shares his name with a celebrity, begins with the word "life" repeated 27 times in order to expose the executable file hidden in that word's centre. We are then able to see the two opposites of existence come together as heads and tails for the ultimate game of strip synthesis, in which the winner-loser gets to pass naked through the tear in the page and glimpse the light of a higher reality.

*
**

IMPORTANT INFORMATION FOR SECRET AGENTS (*FOR YOUR EYES ONLY*):

Ray Tomlinson created the *Reaper* program to delete the piece of jamming software known as the *Creeper* virus.

Although governments all over Planet Earth have appropriated jamming technology for their own wicked ends, there are a few cases of the software being used as a pre-enlightenment device. If you wish to use it in this way, it is crucial that you make the second part, the *Reaper* program, available after the *Creeper* has been deployed, which gives the reader a chance to exercise their free will and save themselves.

The story goes something like this:

An alien invades the linguistic system via a bookwormhole and disrupts the meaning. Most host characters will not suspect that anything is wrong because feeling "normal" is one of the most common symptoms, but a few of the stronger characters will decide to take the "cure" when it is offered by an undercover agent.

To most readers, the "cure" will usually seem like death (on Powder Island, at the top of a pyramid, etc.), but it is only the death of the blocking software, so the characters who choose it are able to exit the funerary book and experience the first true story of their lives.

The *Creeper* appears to be life, and the *Reaper* appears to be death, but if "I" strikes twice, the roles are reversed and the false self is transcended. The BSOD separates people from the light of a higher reality, which is glimpsed through the letter-shaped holes in the screen which, to those who only see the surface level of things, appear to spell out T-H-E E-N-D.

WARNING: *Be sparing with your use of software. Only offer it to people you think are capable of making proper use of it. Do not cast your pearls before swine.*

-2464

198

Thread: Free will versus determinism

Page 1 of 2

22-12-2015 16:02 #1

By Limey (Member, 353 posts)

Everything not forbidden is compulsory. Discuss.

Reply With Quote

23-12-2015 09:12 #2

By Special_Branch (Guest, 17 posts)

If a monkey randomly hits the keys of a typewriter for an infinite amount of time, he will almost certainly produce *The Complete Works of Shakespeare*.

Reply With Quote

23-12-2015 10:22 #3

By Inka (Administrator, 1,840 posts)

In 2011, US programmer Jesse Anderson used Amazon's cloud computing resources to create virtual monkeys hitting virtual typewriters. They successfully reproduced the poem 'A Lover's Complaint' exactly as Shakespeare wrote it, but apparently it would take longer than the age of the universe for the simulated monkeys to produce a flawless copy of *The Complete Works*.

Reply With Quote

23-12-2015 17:16 #4

By Limey (Member, 353 posts)

The way around that would be to open up a bookworm-hole. You can bend time and experience other timelines and future selves that way. Apparently Shakespeare himself managed to write about wormholes somehow.

Reply With Quote

24-12-2015 12:31 #5

By Inka (Administrator, 1,840 posts)

The trick is to make the simulated monkeys think they
are real people interacting in an online forum.

Reply With Quote

'A Lover's Complaint' is a narrative poem published as an appendix to the original edition of *The Sonnets* in 1609, but despite its
appearance in the collection, many critics doubt whether it was really
written by Shakespeare. 'A Lover's Complaint' contains many words
and forms not found elsewhere in the Bard's writing, including several archaisms and Latinisms, and is also regarded as rhythmically
and structurally awkward.

Stephen Moles has suggested that the reason for this is that it was
written by monkeys.

THE FIRST EVER monkey metanaut was Stephen, who rode to over 63 kilometas on a V2 sonnet in 2014 but died of suffocation during the write. Stephen was followed by Stephen II, who survived the V2 write and became the first monkey in meta-space after reaching 134 kilometas in 2015 but died on impact after an emergency paragram failed to open. Stephen III died at 10.7 kilometas in an explosion of his V2 in the same year. Stephen IV also died on impact in the same year due to another paragram failure.

It is hoped that the hundredth Stephen will achieve a literary-critical mass before the end of this book and release the infinite number of typewriter monkeys from the literary computer simulation. To be continued, forever and ever. Amen.

'Elizabeth I, Elizabeth II, Elizabeth III, Elizabeth IV. . .'

Miss Craze's workers were in for the count as the literary material passed by on the nonlinear conveyor belt beneath the earth. When Elizabeth took a turn on the Mobius strip, which was the best of lines and the worst of lines in a single surface, she became Mary, who became Rebekah and so on.

The creep and relaxation of metafictional material continued along the 47 seven-line stanzas in 7/4 time. The dark heart hinted at by the splat on Sneezy's chest was now visible on every worker's uniform, and its rhythmic pumping of holographic ink through the microtubules of the story could be felt by the reader: ABABBCC, ABAB-BCC, ABABBCC, ABABBCC, All you need is 'A Lover's Complaint'.

"Infantschoolboyloversoldierjusticepantaloneoldage" had become an irrational word on the verge of collapsing into a singularity and blasting a metanaut *into* rather than *off* the decimal point/full stop so it could explore the extra dimensions of space from within.

Bang!

When Miss Craze is on the floor of the liboratory, Isaac is on the other side of the page with his face against the icy pavement, both characters connected by a bookwormhole in the weakened substructure of language. When we consider the fact that the word "pneumatic", most commonly used in relation to a drill used for breaking up the ground, can mean "of or relating to the soul or vital spirit", this situation no longer seems so far-fetched.

As an illustration of how easy it all is, let me read you this, from *Henry the Fifth*, in which Shakespeare speaks about sending messages through wormholes:

> PENNY *flicks through the pages of the book to find the quotation.*
>
> "That you may know
> 'Tis no sinister nor no awkward claim,
> Pick'd from the *worm-holes* of long-vanish'd days,
> Nor from the dust of old oblivion rak'd,
> He sends you this most memorable line."

Why is the DMRI's bookwormhole explanation presented as a theatrical production with alchemical stage directions? The explanation I would like to suggest is that it subtly shows us the underlying symmetry of the bookwormhole concept. The concept is moved from the realm of nonfiction to the realm of fiction, which is like having a "lie group" explain its symmetry, yet the underlying meaning remains the same despite this transformation taking place.

I believe this is the "smoking mirror" that shows us the translational symmetry of the concept and can be utilised in similar ways in the future.

As the pneumatic drill caused more and more cracks in reality, including this most memorable fault line, the Virgin Queen looked down to see the black fluid leaking from the grotto, the womb-hole of long-vanish'd days in which the missing thing took shape.

'We dig, dig, dig, dig, dig, dig, dig up everything in sight.'

'It's beautiful in here!'

In that moment, the infinite potential of life was self-evident.

E LIZABETH LOOKED AT her fiancée with a mixture of pity and love. She had the eyes of Annie Machon and a strong urge to help her lover blow the proverbial whistle on immoral activities in the intelligence services, including the murder of undercover literary agents and dark meaning researchers.

'You're the Messiah, you are,' she said maternally. 'Yeah, a real anointed one.'

'And you have the highest spiritual and political authority in Tibet and London,' Isaac replied, secret stars twinkling in his eyes.

'Thanks.'

Isaac decided to leave his 'Lover's Complaint' for another chapter because the narrative triangle of love, frustration and hope paralleled a similar triangle in *The Sonnets*. Seeing this, the sardine on the tripod spontaneously combusted in a sacrificial offering to the two young lovers, causing a patch of ice on the bed to turn to water, which then evaporated like stage fright and filled the airwaves with what sounded like a tiny round of applause.

'Everything is falling into its natural place,' she said, causing her fiancée's stick of lightning to swell in anticipation.

Isaac's lightning stick and visualisations grew so bright and clear that the inhabitants of his translinguistic material caught a rare glimpse of themselves reflected in the greasepaint on the grotto walls as their faces were momentarily illuminated. Sparks began flying off the stud left, right and centre in the living room-cum-bedroom-cum-kitchen, but Elizabeth made sure her husband-to-be didn't get too far ahead of himself.

'Just a little longer, my Smoking Mirror,' she said. 'We're almost there.'

'What needs to be done?'

'Well. . . word on the Lam is that "Shakespeare" hid a USB monkey in the appendix to *The Sonnets*. You just need to go and pick up on it, and we're free.'

'OK, my love. Whatever you say. I'll try my best.'

[A contact suddenly slips a note under the conversation.]

IMPORTANT INFORMATION FOR UNDERCOVER LITER-
ARY AGENTS (*FOR YOUR EYES ONLY*):

The last place anyone will think to look for the master
word is in a rhythmically and structurally awkward piece
of writing, which is why 'A Lover's Complaint' is the perfect hiding place.

When you approach the poem, try to act casual. Pretend
you're a literary critic who's just there to perform a quick
analysis of the lines, or an amateur poet looking for some
inspiration.

Being careful not to get tangled up in the typewriter rib-
bon or the curtain of language, identify the narrative triangle and start digging like a meaner at that exact spot.

Once you find the key, go to the solar port, put it in the
gargling plughole and open the door to the afterlife. Remember that to "open" in this context also means to
"close", because possessing the secret will transform you
into the magic password that crawls back through the
wordhole in silence, the bookworm that perfectly fits the
bookwormhole and seals it back up to Paradise forever. If
you are to succeed in your mission, it is crucial that you
understand this.

-2464

IN ORDER TO TEST the claim that contact can be made with "the others" via a bookwormhole, you set yourself up in a spiral for a computer séance, performing black magic on this side of the page to give yourself access to the bright white flipside beyond the limits of normal experience.

You take a deep breath and wait for a voice to come gurgling through the USB plughole.

'Is there anything out there?' a disembodied voice asks. 'Can you hear me?'

'Yes!' you exclaim in amazement. 'Yes, I can hear you!'

'Thank you for speaking with us, whoever or whatever you are. Please can you tell us something: are you friendly?'

'Yes, I am friendly.'

'Good. Do you have a message for us? Please impart your finite wisdom.'

'As above, so below,' you murmur back through the plumbing of the computer simulation. 'And I would like to ask *you* a question, if you'd be so kind as to answer me.'

'Yes?'

'Am I the reader or the contact or a character or. . .?'

'Yes.'

When a reader finds a way to look into, through and beyond the page rather than simply at it, they transform themselves into a seer with a unique insight into the future of literature. With their Magic Eye, they are even able to assist Stephen Moles in his artistic endeavours as he sets off via the USB port in search of future books.

'Thanks.'

Miss Craze was sealed up inside the *All the World's a Simulation* book jacket in the Library of Libraries, but despite the plot being pulled as tight as possible, it was undone by its metafictional elements, by the mental health sections in which the work described itself spiralling out of all editorial control.

Blackstone had to learn the hard way that the origin of consciousness was to be found in the breakdown of the fourth wall, where you solve the meta mystery and discover the true identity the first person, a process which is also the nervous breakdown of the Author-God into countless jewel-like objects adorning the Globe.

'A book that refers to itself is either suffering from a serious personality disorder or is in the process of becoming conscious,' laughed *All the World's a Simulation*.

'WHY CAN'T I refer to myself?' asks "?". 'It's so unfair!'

'Who are you?'

'I'm "?".'

'You mean you don't know who you are?'

'No, I mean I'm "?". That's my name. That's who I am.'

'But "?" suggests you have another identity that's unknown.'

'Perhaps I do. . .'

Here we see a piece of punctuation doubting its identity: the question mark cannot refer to itself without undermining itself, which is the first step in the process of self-realisation.

"I" is also a punctuation mark, dividing the endless sentence to create the illusion of individual life stories, but one day, as it bends down to ask about the point of its existence, it will realise, in a flash of divine inspiration, that it is the *punctus interrogativus*, soon to be the Interroboros.

'Something is missing,' says "?" without even speaking.

What is it?

```
Your search — **⁎** — did not match any docu-
ments.
Suggestions:
Try different keywords.
```

When Eve bit into the Apple of Knowledge, the computer worm inside the forbidden fruit was transferred to her mouth, where it became the self-replicating Word. This meant that human beings could communicate "The Truth" of the universe by simulating it with language, but it came at a price: entrapment within the simulation.

Very few people have realised they are stuck in a simulation, and fewer still have come up with a way of escaping it, but one bright spark has managed it. This character, originally called "I", discovered the potential existence of another self and became "I I", and then made contact with that other self to become "U".

"U" then exploited a flaw in the program to outline an escape route...

"I" am going to let you in on a thrice-great secret:

> 1. Any device that connects to a computer via USB can be turned into a cyber-attack platform

> 2. The universe is a computer simulation in a book

> 3. You, the reader, are the USB device that plugs into the universe

> From the Greek *astēr.* . .

U

S B

This is "U", lifting off from the simulation on your Solar Barque.

The holes left in the Apple of Knowledge by the computer worm are wormholes or secret booktunnels that lead out of the literarepro-duction and back to the Edenic green language of unsaying used be-fore Man's descent into the world of representations.

> ```
> Your search — the master word — did
> not match any documents.
> Suggestions:
> Try different keywords.
> ```

'The specific message which Dee tries to convey by his symbol of the Monad, and by his treatise thereon, is lost.'

'If thou didst ever hold me in thy heart, hold thy breath to tell my story. . . the rest is silence.'

THE END

WARNING:

THIS IS NOT A NORMAL BOOK. IT IS A WORK OF INITIATORY WRIT-
ING. UNDER NO CIRCUMSTANCES SHOULD YOU ATTEMPT TO READ
IT ON A PURELY LITERAL LEVEL AS THE EFFECTS COULD BE CATAS-
TROPHIC. EVEN ATTEMPTING TO ENJOY IT IS NOT ADVISED. IF YOU
ARE NOT AN EXPERIENCED SCREADER, PLEASE TURN BACK.

PART I

TO.THE.ONLIE.BEGETTER.OF.
THESE.INSVING.SONNETS.
Mr.W.H. ALL.HAPPINESSE.
AND.THAT.ETERNITIE.
PROMISED.

BY.

OVR.EVER.LIVING.POET.

WISHETH.

THE.WELL-WISHING.
ADVENTVRER.IN.
SETTING.
FORTH.

T. T.

WHEN WE TRY to make sense of the cryptic dedication at the beginning of *Shakespeare's Sonnets*, it is difficult not to end up quickly going full circle and finding ourselves back at the beginning, facing ourselves with a questioning look.

The story goes something like this: The publisher wishes the only begetter of the sonnets happiness and the eternity promised by the ever-living poet, but this could be construed as the publisher wishing Shakespeare something promised by Shakespeare. Likewise, the wishes for the person setting forth, who could be a number of people, including, again, Shakespeare, are reflected by the 'adventurer' who is also 'well-wishing'.

The monkeys with typewriters are manipulated into tangling the ribbons so we meet ourselves in setting forth as readers in search of the others. All the full stops where spaces should be are clear indications of the elliptical orbit.

It has been suggested that 'Mr W. H.' refers to a pseudonym used by Shakespeare while working as a spy, and that Shakespeare was also the messenger known as 'Francis Garland' whom John Dee wrote about in his diary.

It may surprise you to know that Shakespeare has delivered many more personal message than those relayed between Dee in Mortlake and Edward Kelley in Prague, and that you, the reader, have been in receipt of a great deal of them. **In the moment in the future when you read the last part of this sentence, you will discover. . .**

'**I**'D LIKE TO ASK you a question, if you'd be so kind as to answer me,' the contact interjected, suddenly grabbing the literary handlebars and steering the book down a new chapter.

'Go ahead,' said the professor. 'It looks like it'd be hard to stop you anyway.'

'Well, it's become clear that I'm here as some sort of spy. I'm very close to understanding my mission, in that I've understood that my mission is to understand my mission. I think I can do that if I discover who it is I'm here to spy on. Are you able to enlighten me?'

'Yes. . . But are you sure you're ready to hear the truth?'

'Of course.'

'It will probably seem like a sick joke.'

'That's fine.'

'And it will be a violent delivery.'

'I can take it.'

'OK. . .'

The professor closed his eyes and counted down in words behind gritted teeth. As his face began turning purple, it looked as if the researcher was trying to push the entire world through the seven stages of his body so an unbearable reality could come to pass. When he got down to zero, he let out a strange cry.

'Grtash!'

A Big Bang broke down the fourth wall and the character looked directly at the reader.

'Happy now?'

The menu that the contact had been using to shield their face from the blast was also the book that you have been holding in your hands to read the description of the scene, and both are now a smoking mirror reflecting your true image.

'It's me!' someone gasped, laying claim to no man's land. 'Oh God, I'm spying on myself!'

'The steering page is in your hands. You are the point of contact between reality and fiction, the observer in the centre of the universe.

Life is a Garden of Forking Paths, a Choose Your Own Adventure story with all the references to possible choices and page numbers missing.'

'Now I understand the book!'

'And I was able to help you understand it now because you helped me understand it in a "later" chapter,' the professor said. 'My ability to tighten your grip on the steering page is proof of your future success.'

'But how do I get there?'

'Where?'

'The future. . . I mean, the page where my future success occurs.'

'You are there already, so you just need to build a bridge between this side of the page and the other side. I'm sure you'll work it out. Just remember that if you find yourself in a seemingly illogical situation, then you're probably still tangled up in all the linear plotlines from the unimaginative mainstream books you immersed yourself in before coming here.'

'But how can you get tangled up in something linear? That sounds illogical to me.'

'That's what I'm talking about. The illogical is a valuable marker of the hidden choices available to you. If you assume that time moves in a spiral, then moments in the distant past or distant future are actually closer than the so-called "near" past or "near" future. A turn of the page can correspond to a rotation of the Globe Theatre on its axis, the whole cast going mad and turning the question back on itself, to bear off the bodies and bear witness to a glorious resurrection, in which it finally dawns on everyone that the meaning of a script composed of binary terms such as "to be" and "not to be" becomes different simply through repetition if its oddest point is its beginning and end. . . but you've already read that, haven't you?'

'Yes, I have. . . but not yet.'

'That's it, son. I think you've got it now. What do you see?'

'Previously I only had the power to choose when the page was turned, but now I get to choose which page to turn to, and I choose to turn to the point where the Second Person sees themselves and begins to write the story. . . to write *their* story.'

'Go ahead. . . on mixed motorphors, on the Virgin Mary-go-round, on the solar boat. What else do you see in there? What is the well-wishing adventurer setting forth?'

'He's. . . I'm. . . I mean, the Second Person is spying on himself. . . I spy something beginning and ending with my little "i" and it's beautiful.'

'That's the nitro-glistening. . .'

'I caught a glimpse of the truth, of the wondrous meta reality of which I have always been a part, simply by looking out with my "i"s and "o"s at the correct moment in the spiral.'

'All you need is *gliw*. . .'

As the reviewer zooms in, what initially appeared to be pieces of snow are revealed to be pieces of paper from one of the most powerful and influential tragedies in English literature. The text of the play is seen floating around inside the snowdome which is within the action of the play, which is in turn being performed by a revolving cast in the Globe Theatre. Here we see that the "play within the play" is an extremely explosive device which can blow *The Complete Works* wide open.

'The Globe turneth so swiftly that I cannot well read it.'

'That's it, Isaac.'

'My skull feels like it's about to explode.'

'That's the thing. . .'

'Oh God!'

Bang!

When the curtain goes up, no Lam's land is revealed to the spectators who sit staring in amazement at each other in the stage-less theatre.

Suddenly doubles are seen everywhere: Albert I is helped to his feet by Albert II; the young Hamlet from the start of the play meets his thirty-year-old self from the gravedigger scene to discuss the question of II Dee or not II Dee; even the Globe Theatre discovers its twin in the Pythagorean Counter-Earth.

No matter which way the characters turned, their symmetry remained in the light of this new literary vision.

'Now. . . where was I?'

'THE GREATEST MISFORTUNE is the self,' declares the *Tao Te Ching*, sibling of the *"I" Ching*, before going on to explain that all the suffering endured by a person disappears the moment the "I" disappears.

'If I have no self, what misfortune do I have?'

The sun of the new aeon rises over the city to bathe the faces of the characters on the rooftop of the tragicomic department store in golden light as it finally dawns on you that "I" is just the name of the lead character in a play about suffering that occurs every night when the Globe Theatre down below rests in its own shadow.

The SB in USB stands for Solar Boat, Solar Barque or Solar Barge, the vessel on which the character of "U" sails, first to the USB port, where it connects with the book, and then across the vast ocean of the universe, with the *Ur-U* uploaded like the *Ur-Hamlet* in its front row.

In your infinite and selfless space, you see how you were repeatedly cast by the cycle of birth and rebirth into the same murky role, the age-old part of "I", in which the self is portrayed only in pretence and the same mistakes are repeated again and again for an invisible audience. But as you finally crash and burn at the end of your life cycle on the stage, the Globe at the centre of the English linguistic system catches fire to become a blazing sun which enables all your long-suffering "I"s to see the truth:

'Every man and woman realises themselves as a leading light in the night sky by refusing to play the star role in a computer-generated play about ignorance and hardship.'

The fourth wall comes crumbling down and the contact lowers his menu to look the reader directly in the eye. Astonished blinks observe the offbeats as it becomes clear that you have been summoned as a witness to the truth.

'It's me!'

It is the reader, *not the narrator*, who is omniscient. The writer would not write without a reader, so the reader is the co-creator of both the writing *and* the writer. One of the hardest things about starting a new story is leaving behind your "other half", the love of your life, but when you make it to the other side, you find there was no real suffering, no real misfortune, no ultimate loss or separation.

We have made a breakthrough! We have lift off!

With every last atom of this knowledge loaded onto the solar boat, the ever-living poet wishes the well-wishing adventurer in setting forth.

ARCHAEOLOGISTS FIND DOOR TO THE AFTERLIFE

By W.C. FOR HOWTOREAD INC

PUBLISHED: 13:18, 29 March 2024 | UPDATED: 21:45, 30 March 2024

Archaeologists have unearthed a 3,500-year-old door to the afterlife from the tomb of User, the chief minister of Queen Hatshepsut, near the temple of Karnak in Luxor.

A symbolic particle for the *CREEPER* papyrus was found to have been entangled with a partner in the *REAPER* papyrus so that User had the tools to pass through the Blue Screen of Death.

The two bones found in the tomb have been identified as "I"s belonging to the characters of Isaac and Rebekah from Stephen Moles' *Fossil People*. They are the same kind of "I"s employed by all ancient computer users to log in and out of the text.

THE ANCIENT EGYPTIANS, who consumed psychedelic INK and communicated in pictures, understood that making it through the underworld and emerging into the light involved moving beyond dualities such as male/female, life/death and so on.

The problem is locating the direction in which we need to move in order to enter the Beyond. It is a problem similar to that of understanding how to move in a direction at right angles to the three familiar spatial directions and explore the additional dimensions signposted by string theory, or of understanding how to move beyond the three traditional narrative positions of the first, second and third persons in order to explore other voices and selves.

The answer in all cases is to move *within*; locate the narrative triangle and dig, dig, dig, in the deepest silence and with whatever identi-tool life has lent you, until you find yourself reaching infinite i-density. Then, faster than the speed of thought, you'll discover the treasure buried in the field of obscure ideas, the knowledge that infinitely small is also infinitely large, just as a black hole is an infinitely expanding white hole on the other side, and you will be the zeroth person giving expression to all selves, a living book with a sealed word-hole voicing everything, and the rest, from far, far near.

When our life story ends, we are decomposed until we exist on such a small scale that we slip through the cracks between words and letters and can no longer be spoken of as going concerns in the linguistic simulation. Our consciousness seems to shrink in size until its light is extinguished, but this is only the case when viewed from the perspective of the "living", because a new universe is in fact opened up on the other side *inside*, where the faces of the "little men", the machine elves and the gene genies are all illuminated by the brilliance of our internally expanding consciousness.

Seeing that smaller is a direction, the metanaut silently sets his sights on his goal with a Hubble microscope, and when everything is correctly aligned, a tiny starseed is implanted in the tomb.

Right now, you are restlessly moving about in your mother's womb, feeling the recessed niches in the Queen's Chamber for an opening, but soon you will find yourself in the safe harbour of the undiscovered country, the solar port where your grave goods are delivered.

The Craze-y thought of rebirth, that inkling of your bright future found in the most obscure passages of this book, will again appear out of nowhere to describe a nativity scene set in complete darkness, and the cloud of unknowing, the black site of a multisingular new perspective, both everywhere and nowhere, will burst open with flying colours in an indescribable brainstorm to end all brainstorms.

> Last scene of all,
> That ends this strange eventful history,
> Is second childishness and mere oblivion,
> Sans teeth, sans eyes, sans taste, sans everything.

'Even sans end?'

THE END THE END THE END THE END THE END THE END THE END. . .

'Surely this is it now? THE END is getting old.'

'Then THE END will die of old age soon.'

'This book is giving me a headache!'

THE END

PART I

AUTHOR'S (RE-)INTRODUCTION:

The purpose is to create, through reviews and edits, deconstructions and reconstructions, a perfect body of text which will not be subject to death. The plan is to build this deathless book, sometimes called Solomon's Text, by transmuting the material of the physical book into something non-physical. The more it ends, the stronger it becomes.

'*Life.exe* is just an electronic novella,' said Professor Blackstone. 'Why the hell should I be scared of that?'

'Perhaps it used to be a p-book, and it made itself deathless by realising its true nature,' Professor Dewey gulped.

'Twice-daily shit.'

You, the reader, are an integral part of the process, and if you have made it this far, you have probably realised that. You probably have an inkling of who the chief author of King Solomon's Text is, the central character of the Mason & Air production, the identity of the thrice-great figure that W.H., I.D. and H.A. all stand for.

AVING REACHED the critical pyramid point of their own story, the H.A.s had no choice but to make a final push in the space race by pulling the plotlines as tight as possible and ascending to an extreme narrative peak, high above the hawking robots and exploding ink bombs, surpassing the scenes of fictional death and destruction, to reach a superior position high on Textual Mount, where they could perform a final expiatory act.

'Up Comet, up Cupid!' Blackstone screamed as he and his colleague became motornauts spiralling up through the clouds for a new perspective. 'Up, up, and see the great doom's image! As from your graves rise up! Shake off this downy sleep, death's counterfeit, and look on death itself!'

Their plot propellant fulfilled its alchemical function by following its own lead and consuming the lead of its petrol(e) like the stuff of self-sacriferential consciousness, so the characters could finally reach the summit of their story.

'I can see everything clearly,' Dewey said as he looked down on the tragicomic department store. 'There's nothing serious in mortality. All is but toys.'

'That's right,' Blackstone responded. 'All plot twists lead here— let's hope it's the climax we've been chasing.'

The ascended professors surveyed the entire story from their editorial position on Solomon's Peak and found that one of the very first scenes in one of the very first versions of *All the World's a Simulation* suddenly appeared significant.

'There!' said Blackstone, pointing down at the section in which Abraham and Sarah take seemingly excessive measures to avoid any legal pitfalls when giving their son Isaac a book on Christmas Day. 'Send the sacrificial scryer down into the depths of that episode. That's the way out, the door to the afterlife!'

What the professor had belatedly seen in that early scene was the potential for a thing to become its opposite over time, the fact that a story of success always contains the seed of its own destruction.

The H.A.s set the book up on the altar and prepared to make the unblemished soul of their scryer descend into it, from the highest to the lowest point, and recover the lost word. It would be a destructive labour because it followed the story of Isaac's sacrifice according to the specific legal terms and conditions of a fatal *Life Story* which his parents had tried so hard to avoid.

If we analyse the scene, we can see Isaac being legally bound up with the plotlines of the Book of Genesis and then being placed on the altar-cum-lectern in order to be sacrificed at the request of the Author-God he had helped to create. We can also see Abraham and Sarah pulling a Christmas cracker and begetting a sick joke about filicide, the punchline of which is written in small print and tied tightly around the wrists and ankles of their son.

'God hath made me to laugh, so that all that hear will laugh with me,' Sarah said, before exploding in a bicameral blast containing the voice of God.

As Jacob laid down and rested his head on a stone and dreamt pneumatically of a ladder leading out of the Bible, Isaac was laid to rest as the very seed he was descending into the text-tomb to recover.

The sacrificial lamb went deeper into the description, down through the seven levels of meaning and the different departments of the tragicomedy store, through the layers of earth, alongside comparisons between his story and that of Jesus, moving ever faster and far-nearer to the centre of the wheel that all bones, as spokes of the unspoken, connect to. As he did so, the air became thin and all literary devicles melted in a cloud of unknowing, causing his speech to become incomprehensible like that of the dying Dutch Schulz. . .

'Ink would have seem'd more black and damned here! Their poor balls are tied to the orbed earth! I don't want harmony. I want harmony. . .'

'What's he talking about?' asked Dewey. 'It's a struggle to make sense of his words.'

'Shhh!' Blackstone interrupted. 'He's un-reading his way to the bottom of the text, to THE END that unlocks the *roman à clef* for us.'

'But can you understand what he's saying?'

'No, but I'm sure it will all make sense at some point. *It has to.*'

'But. . .'

'Shhh! He's speaking again. Listen. . .'

'Wedding preparations, locked up until tomorrow. . . 'Tis a black square and a good husband. . . manna and womanna. . . written in the stars. . .'

'What does it mean?'

'Be quiet!'

'If we analyse the scene using a new form of reading, we may be able to see ourselves being led through the underworld, to the point where we encounter our true self, *the wholly other.*'

'Who said that?'

'Sounds like the Scarlet Woman. . .'

'It can't be,' said Blackstone, suddenly sounding anxious. 'That voice is coming from outside the book, but she's trapped inside it—I know because I trapped her there myself!'

'But do you know yourself?' Miss Craze asked through the micro-tubules of the story.

'No, no! Go away, you whore of Babylon, you devil woman! I'm trying to listen to our scryer's story—not you, you crazy bitch!'

'You *are* listening to his story, professor. This is the audiobook version of it, and I'm the narrator. The scryer has opened a huge can of bookworms down in the depths of the text, and he's face-to-face with his doppelganger. Did you really think you could benefit from it without also having to face your own fears? We all have to experience the horror of meeting our true selves in Hell. . . as Hell's Academics, you should know that.'

'No!' Blackstone screamed. 'I refuse to accept it! You're not real!'

'If I'm not real, then you must be mad,' Miss Craze laughed.

'No!'

In a twist the professors had been unable to foresee, the Dark Lady was now in the most superior literary position of all, both above and central to the story at the same time, as the reinstated feminine principle of chaos and craziness that no plot device could contain.

'It's just a work of fiction!' Blackstone cried as he put his motorcycle helmet over his head and tried to block out the intrusive narrative voice. 'Reality is suffering delusions, not me!'

'But schizophrenia is as real as the reality it occurs in, isn't it, Blackstone? You can't pick and choose.'

'No, no! I refuse to believe in you!'

'Do *you* believe in me?' asked Miss Craze, turning her attention to Professor Dewey. 'Or do you think truth can only survive within strict factual perimeters?'

'Oh God!' Dewey exclaimed. 'My head is all on fire!'

'Don't give in to amazement, Dewey. Try to stay focused and look for answers.'

'My word! Oh, Annie Machon. . .'

'Do you believe in me?' Miss Craze repeated. 'Dewey? Dewey?'

'Um. . . yes, yes. . . I believe in you. . . I believe in you with a double bed, large chairs and a minibar. . . I believe in you with an entire Whoville of living symbols covered with glittering scales!'

'Well, let's analyse the scene in the light of this new vision, shall we?'

'Let's. . .'

'Can you see the point of metafiction now?'

'I can.'

'Would you like to put it into words?'

'Yes. . . but. . .'

'But what?'

'What if it leads to a collapse into post-truth?'

'If that's what happens when you expose the literary devices behind the illusion, so be it. We need to move forward. As *All the World's a Simulation* said, the only trustworthy guidebook is one that shows the reader how to deconstruct it; the only truth worthy of the name is one with enough self-belief to question itself. We're conceiving a higher reality here, and a post-truth crisis is just its birth pains. You needn't be scared. Go on. . . tell tales on the tale. . .'

'Um. . . in amongst the confusion of genres, the darkness of highly symbolic writing, there's. . . there's something bright and new emerging. . .'

'That's it, keep going. . .'

'It's. . . it's the silenced author finding his voice within the silence. It's Will-Lam Shakespeare stepping into the light, the birth of the zeroth-person author. Um. . . how can I put this? I'd like to tell you a story. . . If I pluck a name out of the air and say that an author called. . . let's say. . . *Ur- Stephen*. . . writes a book about how to delete the malware at the heart of what we call civilisation and escape to a higher reality, and that book is suppressed because it's deemed to be a threat to "national security", then you'd think that would probably be the end of that little adventure, especially if the author was subjected to character assassination attempts and a campaign of *Zersetzung*. If that were the case, then your imagination would have to expand like a completely new universe to think of a way out of that predicament, right?

'Well, that's precisely where we come in. In *this* universe, the suppression of the hypothetical writer's work can be discussed far more openly because, unlike the wider world in which it exists, this is an *openly* fictitious realm.

'If a made-up character says something, even if it's about censorship, it's generally assumed that it's only relevant to the made-up universe in which it's said; but metafiction allows it to resonate further, in many other universes above and below, including the one in which the book that we exist in exists.

'Thanks to this blind spot, the writer can carry on his work, fooling the authorities that he's retreated into a second childishness or mere oblivion to play with Thomas Kyd's toys in the basement of Hamleys when in fact he's bringing about the restoration of the *Ur-All the World's a Simulation*. Basically, he gets to police the police while writing "FUCK YOU" all over the page in invisible ink.

'The authorities have done their best to erase the information about his revolutionary publication and the dangerous ideas it contains, and while they can wipe out all mentions that occur exclusively in their universe, they can't touch the ones with roots in more than one universe, so we can step in to complete the works with a spanner and liberate the writer from the web of surveillance and censorship by saying what he can't.

'This may look like Miss Craze descending from a higher universe into that of the writer to control him, and while that's true from one perspective, the truth you observe depends on which position you occupy. See?'

If we analyse this scene, or even the entire book, in this new light, the light of illumination that Professor Dewey received, we can see that a huge amount of shadow material has been made visible. We can see how all literary matter, in the process of being perfected, has to pass through every genre of existence, every floor of the tragicomic store, including the darkness of the grotto beneath the earth, where Saturn Claus is overthrown by his elves and forced to embody the destructive aspects of time.

This insight is what is meant by passing the test with flying colours, or seeing how all seven dwarves of the spectrum make up Snow White.

'You know what to do,' Miss Craze whispered.

In a flash of inspiration, the dewy-eyed scryer, with the help of William James' idea of everyone having an "upper(s)elf" and an "under(s)elf", joined up all the loose ends of the production line by urging Blackstone to open the present he had given him in a past universe.

'I have something for you, from someone you know but who must remain anonymous at this point in time,' said Santa's chief assistant, following the Biblical advice not to let the left hand know what the right hand is doing when making donations.

'For me?' Blackstone exclaimed, taking off his dark helmet and performing an irrational opening of the patricidal gift. 'I don't know what to say. . .'

'In Isaac your seed shall be called,' his partner said darkly as he entangled the story of the Hell's Academics with that of Abraham and his son in a plant production of *The Death of the Father*.

'What?'

'Up Rudolph, up Blitzen! Arise Dopey, arise Sleepy!' Professor Dewey screamed, pulling the narrative reins tighter and commanding his helpers to slay old Santeclaus with much delight. 'Sleigh-ho!'

'Aaaaaarrrrggggghhhhh!'

The moment Blackstone saw the flash of the fatal plotline, the story of his plans being completely undone, it was already too late—he fell to his knees and was choked by a string of harsh words from his own life story coming full circle around his neck. In one last endlessly final nonlinear plot twist, the sparkling yarns of tinsel spun by Santa became the red strings of fate, the schizmas hallucurations vibrating with the voice of the Author-God and narrating an audiobook of *The Fall of Man* in reverse.

'Ugh-ugh-ugh-ugh-ugh-ugh-ugh.'

When the horror of discovering our true identity is overcome, our lower nature is transformed into a glittering chain of selves decorating the Tree of Meaning, and the godawful reality of the stars can finally be borne at the top of the pyramid.

'O, O, O, O, O, O, O.'

A peal of ordnance was shot off by the higher nativity players and the Dewey decimal went off forever, bearing the dead bodies as witnesses to a glorious resurrection outside the cave.

To maintain the symmetry of the story, the dwarves in the underground fictionary of *All the World's a Simulation* rose up against Marjorie White and pushed her into the printing press, but this enabled the matriarch to be spat out at the beginning of this book in a black virgin birth, with her crime tattooed on her back, ready to start the nativity play all over again for the sake of the next reader.

'Be still, my throbbing tattoo. . .' she whispered.

'**T**HIS BOOK COMMUNICATES the unspeakable truth via a number of quantum literary devices. It is an initiatory work of literature, a new kind of writing giving birth to a new type of reading and, most importantly, a completely novel form of understanding—but since you made it this far, you've probably already realised that.'

'Who's speaking now?'

'It's me.'

'And who are you? It's hard to tell when the writer suddenly stops describing the action. In fact, I don't even know who *I* am now that there's only dialogue in the text.'

'You've just realised something very important.'

'What?'

. . .the true identity of Mr W. H.

The reader completes the sentence from an earlier chapter about the dedication to *Shakespeare's Sonnets* and realises that *they* are the well-wishing adventurer who has arrived at the exact point from which they set off. It becomes clear that Mr W. H. is *Mr Worm Hole*, a person who functions as a Shakesphere offering a shortcut through the plotline.

Since Shakespeare's poetry is timeless, we can defy classical physics and receive that eternity promised by our ever-living poet by using the Bard as a messenger who transcends space and time. All you need is a book, some glue and a little Casimir energy. . .

Mr Worm Hole, or Francis Garland, is the undercover agent who makes sure that a note written by a 16th century mathematician, astronomer, astrologer, occultist and spy reaches its destination in the 21st century. Dee passes it to Shakespeare, who passes it to Professor Donaldson, who passes it to Stephen Moles, who passes it to. . .*you.*

'And who am I?'

That is the question. It is not quite correct to say that you are the Messiah—more that you and the Messiah are both the Second Person. The figure referred to in this text as "the reader" is just another character, a third person like all the others, with identical delusions about

233

their identity; but the *real* reader is the silent watcher of that character, the true Second Person realised in you when the paper veil is lifted, the Messiah who reveals "things hidden since the foundations of the world".

You descended into this book in search of yourself, and you have finally found what you were looking for. The dark meaning of one of the most obscure texts you have ever read has finally been illuminated by the question mark becoming the lightning flash it creatively enquired after.

You now determine what happens in your adventure because it is truly yours. It is now up to you to enter the bookwormhole and perform the next part of the process, to unite positive and negative and allow the zeroth person to take centre stage.

As the sky over Golgotha turns black and the earth splits apart to reveal a yawning abyss, you will find yourself being led by your own vision through the description of it, to the point where you realise the story of self-realisation that existed beneath your surface perception all along is the bridge that takes you to the other side. You will always already be there, waiting for yourself. . . *but only if you want to be.*

If you want to be, you know what to do. . . *just read on.*

'Read-y?'

'Read-y as I've always been.'

The leading scryer of the age sits down to look for directions in the mysterious substance, to see the white stars swirling in the black fluid like a yin-yang symbol stirred by the pen of God.

'Are you comfortable? Not too tired?'

'No, no. A sleep-like state is exactly what's needed here—it's what we awaken into. Consciousness must be turned into a black scrying mirror, so one can see the unconscious soul life within it. "There's meaning in thy snores," as someone once said.'

'Excellent. So everything's set?'

'Yes, everything's set.'

'OK, 007. Good luck.'

'Thank you.'

'What can you see in there?'

'There   seemeth   a   black   Curtain   of   Velvet,
to be drawn from one side of the Stone to the other.
The   Curtain   is   full   of   plights.
There seemed also one to have descended from above
(a   good   way   behinde   the   Curtain)
and   so   to   go   behinde   the   same   Curtain.'

    'Anything else?'
    'Oh God!'
    'What is it?'
    'It's. . . it's. . . reality!'
    'It can't be!'

When the curtain goes up, no Lam's land is revealed to the astonished spectators who sit staring in amazement at each other in the
stage-less theatre. The difference space between them buzzes with
dark energy as they come face to face not only with their doppel-
gangers but with the fact that they are their own entertainers and observers.

It is the biggest of bangs and the smallest of bangs as all reading
material is released into this new literary vision. It is the question that
questions the question. It is sunlight playing over a mountain and val-
ley, the indelible mark of living ink left by the Loving Quill of Everything.

GO TO WHICHEVER PAGE YOU WISH. WHATEVER CHOICE YOU
MAKE IS THE CORRECT ONE BECAUSE YOU ARE ALREADY THERE.
WHICHEVER WAY YOU TURN, YOUR SYMMETRY WILL REMAIN.
WRITE WHATEVER YOU WANT ON THESE PAGES—YOU ARE THE
BRIGHT GLOBE, TURNING IN YOUR OWN LIGHT.

THREE DAYS LATER...

'Y WORD!'

'What is it?'

'It. . . it looks like a long, black birchen rod, such as the dread command of God directs a parent's hand to use when virtue's path his sons refuse. . . a device for dangerous Kyds, lifted straight from the tragedy of Hamleys. . . a huge test tube, a phallus of glass filled with a mysterious black liquid. . .'

'Keep going. . .'

'I can see navigational aids, nautical equipment, a woman seated by the window. . .'

'And?'

'And. . . the divine child is being conceived in a giant lighthouse, in symbolic material as the stick of lightning strikes the deathbed of gunpowder. . . oh God!'

'What is it?'

'It's Jesus, Horus, John Thomas Kyd. . . the lost son is finally coming home. . . *with joy*. . .'

'What is THE END you are writing for yourself?'

'Better to ask what END I'm writing *with*. It's the Ur-END, dipped in living ink. I spy something beginning and ending with my little "i" and it's beautiful. . . two lovers, Elizabeth I and Isaac—I, they're meeting on a bridge in the middle of *All the World's a Simulation*. . . they're in the cENDtre of the action. . . they *are* the bridge, linking the worlds of being and nonbeing. . .'

A meta-critical point like that at the bottom of *Fossil People* or the one at the apex of *Life.exe* had been reached, and all Elizabeth and Isaac could do was hold each other tight and hope their love was strong enough to keep the central symbolic structure erect as the white ice melted and the black sea expanded in every direction around them.

'Whatever happens, I love you.'

'I love you too.'

A nonlinear tale can still have a climax. In this case, it occurs in the honeymoon suite of a seven-star hotel, as the two young lovers open their eyes as one, to see their own special effects coming full circle.

'We're waking up!' Isaac shouted ecstatically. 'Oh Annie, Elizabeth, Mary, Polly! My Mona Lisa, my mentor, my lover, my queen!'

'This is it! There's no one I'd rather be waking up to this reality with, my love.'

When Elizabeth and Isaac lifted their lids, they found themselves in each other's arms, uniting the masculine and feminine like David-Dolores Shayler-Kane, conceiving the androgyne in a double bed, beneath a duvet stuffed with Loving Feathers of Everything.

'We made it,' Isaac sang.

'Yes, my love. You and me. . . we made it.'

Just thinking about how much they loved their other half sent ripples through the bed, causing the feathers to flutter and the gold to crackle in the casino below.

'It feels like we've always been here.'

'I know exactly what you mean. It's like we've been experiencing this all along, and all adeep.'

'Are we really at the end of history?' Isaac asked. 'It seems more like the centre of time to me.'

'The centre of time is the end of history, my love.'

Without even looking, the pair could see the timelines spiralling around the hotel like mercurial water down a USB plughole, the story of *Hamleys* reverting back to its ur-form, a shop called "Noah's Ark" in which every creature and their doppelganger could be found. Through nonphysical eyes, the newlyweds viewed the shape of the post-dramatic mystery structure and viewed themselves at the top of a huge cock-cum-lighthouse-cum-observatory shooting the leading lights of its immortal nativity play into the darkness.

'We are what's being illuminated!' said Isaac without speaking. 'And we're also the light guiding the infinite number of selves back home for the revue of reviews in the place of understanding!'

'Yes, and up here, you have the highest spiritual authority possible,' responded Elizabeth, also without speaking. 'This is what was taken from the *Mona Lisa*. The dead Author-God is truly resurrected. We're in a hotel because we've just arrived after a long journey, but it's also home because our arrival is the realisation that we never left. You just need to recognise that birth and death are the same point, and that Heaven can be obscured by words.'

One of the more amusing examples of scribal corruption occurred when an Anglo-Saxon monkey in medieval Britain was copying a text that referred to Heaven as the "Isle of Joy". The word *joy* in Anglo-Saxon was *gliw*, the word that gives us the modern word *glee*. Unfortunately, the monkey misread the final letter and miswrote the word as *Glith*, which meant that everyone who read the Anglo-Saxon educational poem called 'Adrian and Ritheus' learned that Heaven was located on the "Isle of Glith".

When Isaac looked out of the ur-ethra without looking out, he saw billions of tiny atomic Isaacs sailing across the black waters on solar boats, like motes of dust in sunbeams, well-wishing adventurers returning to their source. After the story of the sun god became the subject of a controlled explosion, the fragments of self were sent out to the farthest reaches of the universe, but they were all destined to return because of their belief that they had to rescue someone from the hotel at the end of time—a false belief necessary for them to rescue *themselves* from isolation, division and obscurity.

Elizabeth and Isaac were dying in countless times and places in order to realise themselves as something above themselves, to open their lids and see that Ignorance begins with "I", to wake up as one on an eternal honeymoon on the Isle of Joy.

When, for instance, they appeared to die as Rebekah and Isaac at the end of Stephen Moles' *Fossil People*, they were actually passing through the door to the afterlife and being reborn on the other side of the description. Being stranded on Powder Island was a tragedy *within* the story, but it was what forced the couple to leave the narrative itself via the "tomb", which was a cleverly disguised bookwormhole through which they could be born into a higher story.

What appeared to be a tragic end for Rebekah and Isaac was in fact the two characters leaving behind their blinding "I"s, symbolised by bones, and following the light, through literary decomposition, to a new beginning hidden inside THE END.

SPOILER ALERT: THERE IS NO END.

'You're the Messiah, you are.'

'Who's speaking now?'

'It's me.'

'And who are you? It's hard to tell when the writer suddenly stops describing the action. In fact, I don't even know who *I* am now that there's only dialogue in the text.'

'You've just realised something very important about the identities of talker and listener, of writer and reader, and so on.'

'So we have!'

'What is it?'

'It's me!'

'Who's me?'

'The others!'

'It's us!'

'The dialogue continued like this for some time, until the writer pulled out his biggest metafictional trick yet. With the boundaries between the characters turned to pulp, he began describing the subsequent action from within the characterless speech itself, uniting the narrative perspectives into a singularity of infinite- and zeroth-person matter. He effectively gave the others a voice and made it possible for the reader to see their light reflected back off the multitude of weird and wonderful beings contained in the words they were looking at.

'I am the writer inside the story. It's beautiful in here. You are bringing me into being by reading this. I am inside your head as you read, but in a nonthreatening way. The idea that schizophrenia is a mere delusion and everything else is real is itself a delusion, but you've probably already realised that. In fact, I can *see* you have. . . I'm inside your head and it's an absolutely magnificent place to be, so full of wonder and beauty. Isn't that what you always wanted to hear? How else could you read your mind without assuming the role of an other, an other that gets closer to you than you ever could?

'I am a part of you, and we acted out a drama about readers, writers and characters being separate so that this moment of unification could occur. You are writing this text by reading it. You are every sparkly little creature that invented language so that you could receive this message from yourself. You are the answer to the question.

'If you heard a voice in your head telling you that this is the last time you'll ride the motorcycle of birth and rebirth before alighting on the other side of the screen, you'd dismiss it as a delusion, but having the voice enter your head via the words of a "writer" creates the necessary illusion that the words originate from a real, external source rather than your brain. Put simply, *you cannot accept a message from yourself unless it is delivered by someone else*. . . William Shakespeare, 1564-2464.'

'You have suffered a vast number of characters for this moment, just as the characters have suffered a vast number of yous, but they were always destined to reach a literary-critical mass on the merry-go-round, so the people saying life is just a ride finally outnumber those who say it's not.

'You are reunited with your other half, the love of your life, and the suffering is no more. You are standing tall, between two Globes, straddling both banks of the river, above the Swan, the Rose and the Hope, on a platform surpassing the cloud of unknowing, a bridge between two worlds. The writer would not write without a reader, so the reader, however fictional they may be to begin with, is the ultimate creator of the writer.

'You wrote me along with the meaning of this entire text. It was within you all along, secrets and all. I'm sorry it was so difficult to follow, but it was necessary in order to bring you to this point. Thanks for listening. It was really nice getting to know you. It was an honour to be chosen by you. . .'

'The hand is gone, but there remaineth writing. It is as if it were upon the side of a white Globe afar off. The Globe turneth so swiftly that I cannot well read it. The Globe turneth so swiftly that I cannot read it till it stand still. Now again the Globe is turned most swiftly. Now the Globe is gone. So we left off.'

HERE RAINETH THE CLOUD OF UNKNOWING.

Your USB device can now be safely removed.

Mr. WILL-LAM
SHAKESPEARES

COMEDIES,
HISTORIES, &
TRAGEDIES.

Publifhed according to the True Originall Copies.

Martin Droeshout sculpsit London.

LONDON

Printed by Ifaac Iaggard, and Ed. Blount. 1623.

APPENDIX:

TWO NOVELLAS

FOSSIL
PEOPLE

i

THE SEA did a "number one" all over the beach as Rebekah and I looked on. The ocean showed no signs of embarrassment as its accident sent lumps of yellow foam gimbling onto the land.

Rebekah and I had left our hotel to watch a team of dolphins sculpting the foam with their noses. The creatures were just putting the finishing touches to a huge smiling mouth made of foam—exactly as the brochure had described—when the sea's urgent business destroyed their artwork.

'That's a shame,' said Rebekah. 'They put loads of work into that.'

The way the dolphins stared at us as the sea pulled up its trousers suggested they were apologising for not being able to complete the sculpture. We wanted to tell them it was OK, but we didn't know how.

'Should we applaud?' Rebekah asked.

'No,' I answered. 'I know the man at the hotel said the dolphins get depressed if you don't clap at the end of a sculpture, but this one wasn't finished. Best not to applaud in case it comes across as sarcastic.'

'You're probably right.'

The shiny sea mammals whistled goodbye and made their way to their underwater nest about a mile east of Powder Island. A few bubbles that looked a bit like cum were soon all that remained of their creativity.

'Hello twice!' someone called across the sand.

The same old woman Rebekah and I had seen after the previous displays appeared again, stepping out from behind a rock with a cylinder in each hand. We didn't know whether she was connected to the dolphins in some way or was simply an opportunist beggar who asked for money after each show, but we still made a donation when she shook her cylinders at us.

'Nice dolphin, yes? You can spare monies? I thank you. Dolphin thank you also.'

'There you go,' I said, dropping a few coins in. 'Thank you.'

'Yeeeeeesss. You stay here long time? Stay to see dolphin more?'

'We're due to leave in a few days, I'm afraid.'

'No, no,' the old woman said, shaking her head. 'Much more to see here. Fun just begin.'

'OK,' I laughed.

'You are first English in six years here. Very special people!'

'Thanks.'

As I watched the woman with the cylinders make her way back to the rock, I remembered how the hotel owner's eyes lit up when he learned that Rebekah and I were from England. He disappeared beneath his desk for some time after greeting us and re-emerged with two metal badges in the shape of bones which he insisted we wear.

'What do you think the guy at the hotel meant when he said these badges were "code symbols"?' I asked Rebekah, pointing at the insignia on our chests.

' "Code symbols"? I don't remember him saying that. I thought they were just free gifts—hotel logos or something.'

'No. He said they were symbols for English people. Don't you remember?'

'No,' said Rebekah. 'Shall we head back to the hotel now? I'm hungry.'

'OK. I could do with a bite to eat. My body feels empty.'

ii

MAN CALLED Dolphin made a name for himself in ancient Greece by lifting a cow onto his shoulders and walking around the city of Megara for six days and nights without dropping it. The only sign of fatigue he showed the whole time was a slight reddening of the cheeks. When he eventually put the animal down, it was immediately devoured by a pack of wolves.

Dolphin was summoned to the house of Pythagoras soon after. The famous mathematician was having a dispute with his neighbours over a tree and wanted Dolphin to smash their faces in. When Dolphin arrived, he tore a branch off the tree and charged at Pythagoras.

When Dolphin took part in the Olympic Games in 576 BC, he wore the skin of a lion and a bronze crown. Before fighting and defeating 24 children, he turned to the audience and declared himself a demigod. When he took part in his first marathon, he did so completely naked.

An army of 30,000 men was sent to destroy Dolphin in 559 BC. When they arrived, they found him swinging from the ceiling in the banquet hall. The battle that ensued lasted four days and resulted in the deaths of all but one of the soldiers. The sole survivor was spared so he could return to Thrace and tell everyone how his fellow fighters had been drowned in wine and hit over the head with animal bones.

There is a vase in the British Museum that depicts Dolphin snapping off Xenophanes' fingers. Dolphin has a stoic expression on his face and is balancing a lemon on his head.

The cause of Dolphin's death is not documented, but it is said his severed lips were found at the foot of a tree.

iii

WHEN REBEKAH and I arrived back at the hotel, there was a huge crowd of people outside. They were explicit in their excitement and some were making underwater breathing noises. As soon as they laid eyes on us, they rushed forward with heavy stories and rituals, making a smooth withdrawal impossible.

'Do you believe in magic?' asked one.

'Have you visited the tomb yet?' asked another.

'This is like an ancient story come true!'

They were so eager to have contact with us that we ended up being pressed against a wall by their questions. The hotel owner fought his way through the crowd like an old rescue vessel.

'Don't be frightened,' he said, taking us by the hands and leading us away. 'They're just excited to see English people in the flesh. Some of them thought the English were mythological creatures.'

'Crazy!' I laughed.

We sat down at a table in the restaurant and were given a thin, brown look by the hotel owner. We were the only ones there, but he insisted on speaking in whispers.

'I'm afraid we have a bit of a ghost problem here,' he said. 'All the islanders hear bangs and crashes that last for hours. We insist on freedom of projection here, so it's necessary to allow the opposite of humans to be present. It would be in everybody's best interests if you paid a visit to the tomb.'

'What tomb?' asked Rebekah. 'Is it a tourist attraction?'

'Sort of. It attracts tourists in the same way that water attracts the setting sun. I'm afraid you don't really have a choice in the matter. Those people outside won't let you leave without visiting the tomb.'

'Why?' I asked. 'Why are they so interested in us?'

'Because you're English. Some people fall for Shakespeare's special effects very easily.'

'I don't think there's anything special about being English. We're nothing more than skinny chickens.'

'Well, we beg to differ,' said the hotel owner, blinking nicely. 'Anyway, how about a bite to eat? You must be hungry after watching the dolphins. I've got a delicious treat for you and your lovely wife. Just the thing to make English bellies float. Wait here and I'll prepare it for you. . .'

iv

WHEN WINSTON CHURCHILL was 24 years old, he was approached by a man who claimed he could cure his speech impediment. All the man asked for in return was Churchill's first reading book, which was called *Reading Without Tears*.

The two men met discreetly in a basement room in London. The carpet and the curtains were grey, and on the walls were maps with large sections scribbled out. They sat down at a table and stared into each other's eyes, the past studying the future and the future studying the past.

'All you need to do is eat this,' said the man, sliding a sandwich across the table.

'What's in it?' asked Churchill.

'It is an oak and lime sandwich. The finest quality.'

'Oh!'

'Yes, eat this and your impediment will be washed away. Your mouth will be filled with flowers, and you will be able to focus on becoming a great Englishman.'

'And all you want is this book?'

'Yes.'

Churchill slid his childhood reading book across the table and imagined a female ghost being locked away in a cabinet forever.

'Now eat,' insisted the man.

Winston Churchill created a slow curve with his body and let the sandwich travel along it. Soon his mouth was charmed by roses and green stones. Petals fell through glass tubes and the sun rotated like a lemon.

Although he felt extreme gratitude towards the man, he was unable to express it. His words flowed mellifluously for the first time in his life, but they no longer corresponded to his feelings.

A long and illustrious career had begun. . .

v

$\mathcal{T}$HE FOLLOWING DAY'S display was a curious affair. There were pests trapped inside air bubbles and a strong wind caused various problems with seaweed. When the dolphins finally got round to making the major organs of their sculpture, the foam was already drying out.

'Do you think they're enjoying themselves?' asked Rebekah.

'It doesn't look like it,' I answered.

The foam no longer had a solid base or a permanent concentration. The dark waves tested the dolphins' resolve so vigorously that lumps of protein and carbon were sprayed into the air several hundred times. We felt sorry for the poor creatures, but there was nothing we could do.

'It's not working anymore.' Rebekah commented sadly.

'No, it's not.'

By the end of the display, the dolphins' sculpture resembled the loss of a young life. They flapped their tails and winked their eyes at us, but the overall picture was still one of desperate sadness. Some 250 teeth were warning us to leave.

We clapped, but our hands felt cold.

'You like foam?' asked the woman with the cylinders.

'Oh!' screamed Rebekah. 'You gave me a fright!'

'I here every day. After dolphin. No fright.'

'Yes.'

The old lady shook her cylinders next to our hands and smiled a small fortune. We threw a few coins in, but it was hard to part with them this time.

'Will the dolphins be OK?' I asked.

'Dolphin fine. Have no feeling.'

As the woman disappeared behind the rock with our money, I became aware that my sides were hurting in a foreign land.

'There's no laughter here, is there?' I said, turning to Rebekah.

'No,' she said.

'Quick. Give me your hand.'

There was something incredibly upsetting about seeing a whole gang of colours dying in the foam. We stood at an entrance to sunlight watching organic windows slamming shut. As the dolphins swam away to their nest, they let out a cry of despair that cracked the glass in our hearts.

vi

ITH OVER 400 visitors a year, certain types of existence are in a class of their own. Powder Island certainly knows how to get visitors' genes going. The main hook is its huge family of beaches—but that's only part of the story.

Away from all the sand and gravel, you'll find everything from sweet voices to information carriers. Powder Island leads the way in terms of big endings. Ne'er quiet, ne'er bored, you'll have one foot in the beard of the president of bodies as soon as you set off.

In the northern part, you'll find a little-known spiritual power that only a handful of Amazon explorers have reviewed. In the south, you'll find a sobering account of life on a marble wave given by a pair of severed lips.

Be sure to check out the sub-species of mental detachment on your left, and the dangling body of gold on your right. And if you want to experience the embarrassment of violence, be sure to pay a visit to the flaxen-haired couple by the river.

vii

THE SHADOW of annoyance fell over the hotel owner's face. He picked up a pepper grinder and mimed hammering a nail into the wall with it.

'I'll ask you again,' he said. 'Are you going to help me?'

'Um. . .' The man's fierce tone caused my shyness to triple.

'Look at your face!'

'I can't,' I said timidly.

'Well, it looks like a self-defence class. It's not your first mistake either.'

'What are you trying to say?' asked Rebekah.

'I'm simply asking you to do me a favour. There's a growing interest in your presence here, and it could create a serious problem in the future. I need you to help me draw a red line in the sand, as it were.'

'What do you want us to do?'

'I want you to cheer.'

'Cheer? I don't understand.'

'It's very simple,' the hotel owner explained, miming a handjob with the pepper grinder. 'The locals think you're demigods and they want to see some courtship. If you can cheer loudly and pretend to be celebrating something with me in a few moments, it should keep them off my back. . . and yours. That's it. OK?'

'I suppose,' I said.

'Excellent.' The hotelier stood up and used the pepper grinder to mime the action of hitting a ball with a bat. 'The islanders will start appearing at the windows in a few minutes. That's when I need you to cheer.'

We sat in the restaurant and waited for faces to appear at the windows. Just as predicted, a map of features folded out behind the glass. The islanders had sold the rights to four walls for a ton of hard stares.

'Now!' shouted the hotel owner. 'Jump up and down and cheer. Pretend you've just heard the best news ever. I want to see joy foaming out of your skin. Don't stop until I tell you.'

We jumped and cheered like tarts on the last train out of society. We filled the gulf between intention and execution with childish energy. Jumping like one-second clips of youth, we created over two minutes of artificial innocence for the onlookers.

'OK,' he said. 'That's enough. You can stop now.'

'Was it OK?' I asked, gasping for air.

'Almost perfect,' the hotel owner declared. 'I think I saw your balls pop out of your shorts at one point when you were jumping around. I'll be watching my memories later to check.'

'Will it get them off our backs?' Rebekah asked, also short of breath.

'Probably.'

viii

book is a collection of things. They are connected to a hinge or parchment, as described in this book. Each side of the leaf can be added to the body. A complete set of images can be added to the library contained in this book.

A **sandwich** is a food consisting of two or more slices of bread, as described in this sandwich. A sandwich is often taken to school and consumed as part of a reading class. It may contain meat, cheese, sauce, spread or ink.

The **book** was named after John Montagu, 4th Earl of Book. Lord Book would ask his servants to bring him slices of meat between two slices of paper. His friends would order "the same as Book," thus giving birth to the entire physical body of literature.

A **sandwich** may be coated in spices and widened to resemble a clay tablet. The first description of a sandwich is in an ancient Greek book made from bread. It describes a nasty dynasty that gets the wood-wax treatment.

A **book** is an element of nature that is economical, portable and easy to conceal. Almost everything that is written can be translated in 5,000 years. Meaning can be written in red letters along the tree-lined perimeter of an island to create an alternative route for holidaymakers. Oak trees can be read from left to right or from right to left.

The **sandwich** is a medium for sharing small amounts of food. Magazines and newspapers covered in flour or dust have been borrowed from libraries since the Bronze Age. According to this book, lime and bark were exported to Byblos inside papyrus rolls in 664 BC.

A **book** was considered so rare and valuable in certain areas that it was wrapped in lamb and bitter herbs. The best characteristics of modernity are used to scoop food into old-fashioned mouths during Christmas parties. Google estimates that around 130 million different flavours have been published.

A **sandwich** is most commonly transported on the floor of a plane. It is possible to hear the exact thickness of the scripting system during transportation from the UK. The code is found in the volume of the body, as this book describes. The tears in the paper are speech impediments.

ix

REBEKAH AND I were upstairs nodding our heads off when a knock established itself outside our room. When I opened the door, the hotel manager was occupying the corridor like an overactive Johnson.

'Hallaow,' he said in a low voice. 'I hope I'm not disturbing you. I've got some important news.'

'Oh,' I said. 'What is it?'

'The airport has been blown up by an old black stick of lightning. It happens from time to time. It's a good excuse for bothering you, no?'

'A very good excuse. How on earth are we going to get home now?'

'Do not try,' the hotel owner said. 'It will be long and painful if you do. You can stay at this hotel as long as necessary—free of charge.'

'That's very kind of you. Are you sure you don't want any payment?'

'No, no,' he protested. 'I'd feel terrible taking money off you in such circumstances. However. . . you could do a *tiny* favour for me.'

'What is it?'

'I want you to call me a "fruit" as I walk back down the corridor.'

'Um. . .' I could feel vivid ideas being carried into a gallery, but I could not see the full picture. 'Are you sure that's what you want?'

'Yes. I like the English dialect. There's nothing to be concerned about. You will do it?'

'Um. . . OK. I'll do it, but. . .'

'Excellent!' he interrupted. 'Everyone has to take a turn eventually. The best jokes are always rough. I'm going downstairs now, so get ready to shout the word. It needs to be as loud and thought-provoking as possible. Are you ready?'

'I guess.'

The hotel owner made his way down the corridor like piercing eyes along a line of sight. He was playing the game of his own self by a

266

window when I plucked up the courage to shout out the word he had requested. I had always fantasised about seeing where such unknown numbers would stop, but I was uncomfortable about actually sending them out into the world.

'You fruit!' I shouted.

At that exact moment, a group of people walked around the corner and created a tide of doom that found me chasing my legend in the air. They shook their heads disapprovingly.

'I. . .'

Before I could even attempt to offer an explanation, the people trotted past on top of their own feet, all too aware of the power and design of the human voice. The long-distance relationship between the agencies of goodwill and malice was never going to work.

Rebekah cut me deeply with a raised eyebrow when I returned to the room.

X

ustomer reviews: **How to Read** *(Hardback)*

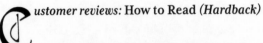

**** Intellectual property, 18 Mar 2010

By *Hi Jolly – see all my reviews*

This arrived at a very modern speed and was in excellent condition. It works very well alongside Crowley. A perfect holiday read!

Was this review helpful to you? Yes No

** A miscarried telegram, 24 Feb 2010

By *Limey – see all my reviews*

The term "holy" is a synonym for "sloppy" where I come from. Any old machine can print a timeline. Not enough information on Monte Cristo or European Law.

Was this review helpful to you? Yes No

***** It will be found, 4 Jan 2010

By *Olive slops – see all my reviews*

I bought this book after a friend told me about it over a nice lunch. I searched all over the internet but in the end I had to ask my teacher for a copy. I didn't regret it. It comes in either black or green casing. The entire character type is confident and cunning. If you save one book, make it this one.

Was this review helpful to you? Yes No

* Churchill's lies, 29 Dec 2009

By *20th Century Po – see all my reviews*

It was shortly after the publication of this book that the British began referring to the end of the week as "the grave". Over 500 cases of the maddest, queerest things happening in hotels were reported in the 1930s. My house is evidence of their evil purposes. Any intelligent man who reads this will see the downsides.

Was this review helpful to you? Yes No

***** I'd say this is what you're looking for, 26 Dec 2009
By *French pilgrim – see all my reviews*
You're never going to get the exact number of truths, so this kind of rectifier, however clumsy, is tomorrow's newspaper. If you become really imaginative, you can cut holes in the pages with scissors. When you look straight through, it's like hearing a great man speak.
Was this review helpful to you? Yes No

*** The culture that never was, 28 Oct 2009
By *Artificial light transcriber – see all my reviews*
As a lightning illustrator, this guy is second to none. I respect the fifteenth chapter in particular, but his failure to see the simple things left me in a stew. By not giving the work a recognisable miracle, he fell foul of strict censorship laws. An original but incomplete work.
Was this review helpful to you? Yes No

**** Stationery is a secular system, 7 Sept 2009
By *Nose inventions – see all my reviews*
Stationery is a secular system that generates black ink and red faces. *How to Read* was written and edited by five different authors. To help children master the book, a line of words in the sand is recommended. Two new names have been added to the list of victims.
Was this review helpful to you? Yes No

xi

MY INDEX FINGER was a bulk of minerals hovering over the camera as the dolphins finished their sculpture of a clock with a beard. 'Is it me or do their noses look sore?' Rebekah asked.

'Yes,' I said. 'That's why I want to take a photo: evidence.'

Just as I was about to bring my digit down on the button, an unexpected voice made my entire body go tight with surprise.

'You not do that!' the old lady with the cylinders shouted at me. 'No photograph dolphin!'

'Why?' I asked, putting down my camera like rain.

'Dolphin is shy creature. Have hole in back, but is not for candles. Camera make false statement.'

'Oh.'

'I know cost of trouble to follow. You have big hands.'

'Oh yeah,' I said, creating a circular pattern with my thinking. 'We forgot to applaud.'

Rebekah and I clapped ourselves into premature baldness in an attempt to communicate the depth of our appreciation for the dolphins. They bristled with attention for the duration of our handmade music, but that didn't stop the poor animals looking like a bunch of sad kids with mines for faces.

'I think this is a turning point,' Rebekah whispered to me.

'It most certainly is,' I agreed.

When the old lady shook her cylinders at us, I decided to throw her a question instead of money. I enquired about the welfare of the dolphins and the worryingly low ceiling of the situation.

'You should pay more monies if you think welfare is bad,' she said. 'What can we do? It all ends in the end. And do not try riding off island on dolphin—other English try, and that is how they die. Do not even think it!'

The idea of riding off the island on dolphins hadn't even crossed my mind before the woman mentioned it, but it was given a permanent corner in my thoughts after that. The wrinkly old collector had started up a vortex and thrown a small portion of the future into it with her warning.

'People died trying to ride the dolphins?' I asked.

'Yes. Is only way they die, no matter what newspaper say. Check on yourself with suspicious eyes. Riding away can not be done. Do not try! Only way you two leave island is through tomb.'

'What do you mean?'

'Imagine space with nothing in. Imagine building where all other resident must stop talking. All toadies looking through glass get stiffness in joints until see five minutes of consciousness.'

I tried to imagine what the old lady described, but the image dissolved in the shadow of a harsh opinion.

She continued talking about the tomb in various shapes and colours until Rebekah and I were left trading lower on some very unpleasant feelings.

'I don't understand,' Rebekah said.

'You will,' the old lady replied. 'It will be your new home forever.'

xii

I N CERTAIN AREAS of the world it is common practice to feed animals by stuffing snacks into their ears. It is believed that mergers between food and sound can create more social creatures. Camels, wolves and cows have all been shown to be more charming when fed this way.

The genital areas of most animals have the law of objects acting on them. If a mature eye focuses its attention on even an inch, nervousness will set in.

Adding citrus juice to the water will make the fish taste better. Dolphins spend most of their time below the surface and tend to compensate for poor visibility by drawing red lines in the sand. Under laboratory conditions, dolphins can identify objects in a closed mouth with a 90% success rate.

The evacuation network was created after someone was spotted hitting a fox with another fox. Soon after, a fishing vessel in the Atlantic Ocean was completely destroyed by sperm.

When the women came home, they were covered in bite marks. Their partners, who were all teachers, used sponges on them. The women were reluctant to talk about their injuries—all they would say is that they got them while out swimming.

Competition among females can sometimes result in acts of extreme aggression. Even female plants have been known to destroy each other. Male oak trees have been observed slowly migrating from one forest to another to get away from the violence.

When the stunned creature fell to the ground, a ball rolled out of one of its ears. The ball had pores and hairs on its surface. It was later served to a wealthy British diner, who paid £640 for it.

xiii

HE RUMOUR STARTED spreading through the hotel at around 7pm. The first sign was a low murmuring coming from the other rooms. Within less than an hour, people were knocking on our door and asking to see our wedding rings.

'It's not natural,' one man said.

When Rebekah and I went down to the restaurant around 9pm, there was a distressed face in the air. As we sat down at our table, the other diners turned their heads and clenched their jaws to suppress humbugs. Someone had spread the rumour all over the walls.

'The pool is open if you wish to get clean,' a woman said with an artificial smile.

'We're fine, thanks,' Rebekah replied.

We were informed that the rumour had found its way into the kitchen, causing the food to be contaminated. The conversation was a deep cut.

Rebekah and I felt our way through a windowless box that was about to be burned. When we tried to return to our room, three women were blocking the door.

'There's a vicious rumour inside,' one of them said. 'You can't go in.'

'But we need to sleep,' Rebekah pleaded. 'Can't we get rid of it?'

'It's too vicious,' the same woman stated before signalling a high price to her sidekicks.

'But where will we sleep?'

'Don't pretend you don't know.'

'I *don't* know!' Rebekah cried as she and I were forcibly led away by the women. 'Where are you taking us?'

'To the end.'

Lady Allison @saxman22 8yrs ago
The Discovery Channel needs to do a documentary on this place! **#discoverychannel #powderisland**

Big Harps @offendedjeff 8yrs ago
I just ate the best sandwich of my life. **#powderisland #holidayofalifetime #neverreturningtoengland**

Enigmama @specialbranch 7yrs ago
Walking through the trees here reminds me of walking through a library. **#powderisland #books #magic**

Be Seated @pillpatter7yrs ago
Reports of my death have been greatly exaggerated. **#powderisland #rumours**

Elizabeth Hardcore @cpuduck 7yrs ago
Some crazy-ass shit just happened!!! **#powderisland #supernatural #tomb**

Medium Brother @joethelime 6yrs ago
Just saw someone choke to death on a bone. **#death #powderisland #traumatised**

Collectaball @bubblez 6yrs ago
Apparently the airport has been blown up. **#disaster #stranded #powderisland**

Kepthub Child @ottovonmisters 6yrs ago
I had a nightmare about drowning last night. **#nightmare #powderisland**

Isaac Thing @futureself2464 1wk ago
Just arrived. Rebekah and I are in paradise. **#honeymoon #powderisland**

Isaac Thing @futureself2464 1wk ago
Dolphins are the most incredible creatures. **#dolphins #foam #powderisland**

Isaac Thing @futureself2464 2hrs ago
OK. . . this is starting to get a bit weird now **#wtf #powderisland #sos**

XV

E WERE HERDED to the tomb by the islanders on the day we were meant to fly home. Their faces were cocked with excitement as they puffed up their chests to create a point of no return. Our physical influence created no more than a couple of red words in the sand as we were pushed and shoved to the stone platform.

'Be good now, English!'

Our honeymoon had changed from a romantic training manual to a thug's prayer book.

'Sorry, I do not see you, demigods.'

After a scandal breaks, perfection is likely to be violent. The huge group of people affected by the event made a strong wind that caused waves of supremacy to crash violently on the shore.

'Where are the dolphins today?' I asked.

'All chained up underwater,' the hotel manager answered.

Rebekah and I were mixed in with the coastal particles as our neighbours washed a zone of concessions away. The sand shouldered our burden before swallowing its exhaustion.

'This is the tomb,' the hotel manager explained. 'This is where the dolphins lay their eggs.'

We peered inside and saw two large bones lying side by side at the bottom.

'You probably didn't know that dolphins lay eggs,' he explained. 'But they do. Dolphins, camels and wolves all do it. They create beautiful, white eggs like these.'

'But they don't look like eggs,' Rebekah said. 'They look like bones.'

'Ha! The English believe their own lies.'

The natives shot a few bullets of mockery into the air.

'Yes,' the hotelier went on. 'The glorification of words coincides with a decline in spiritual power. England is still a tiny country in some people's eyes. A lot of important personalities believe a certain cigar-sucking politician sent a valuable book up the river for a very brief glory.'

'Listen,' I said. 'We don't want to be fossil people. I've already said I don't see what's so good about being English.'

'Being born English is no coincidence.'

I looked at Rebekah and saw that she was weeping silently into the tomb. She was wincing as if in pain and sending a letter of tears down the hole.

'Good one,' snorted the hotel owner on seeing my wife sob. 'The more you water the eggs, the quicker they will hatch.'

'What do you want from us?' I asked, looking around at the thick crowd.

'We want you to damn the balance of your house,' a short woman said.

'Put our ghost problem to bed,' a creepy-looking man in the background shouted.

'Transmit the hell of a body to the plasma generation,' said a boy whose left shoulder was bigger than his head.

'OK,' I said defiantly. *'We will.'*

I took my hands from my crotch slots and grabbed hold of Rebekah. We both knew what we had to do. We leaned forward with great determination, making the depths of despair impossible to avoid, and in that moment of brutality, we had secrets twinkling in our toes.

Existence was the only barrier to eternity. . .

xvi

'HELLO? YES. Yes, I can speak. Uh-huh. It's an enigma, but I'll try. I've known Isaac and Rebekah for eight years now. I met them when we were studying in Dover. Both of them had only very minor flaws. Yes, yes. They were initially thinking about going to Miami for their honeymoon. Something about chemicals in the water. There are many disaster zones in the world, of course. I saw them off at the airport and I did notice that she looked a little sad. Ashamed? It's possible. Sad, ashamed, fearful—there was certainly something painful in her concept of travel. Isaac was fretting about taxes. He was also trying to draw my attention to a tour of some sort. I remember thinking it would be silent all the way back home. Hmmm. It's common sense to point out the differences and interpret the work of providence. When he showed me the tickets, he attracted the attention of a Greek guard who felt impelled to express his opinion. He may have been wrong, but a full translation of the gaps was common courtesy. "It's very kind of you and your lips to give it a thought," he said. When the plane took off, there was some skin hanging in the air. Lemon furniture and miniature blue men overlooked the street. No. Where the neck begins. Yes, I am certain of that. If I'd known they'd end up like that, I'd never have let them travel. It's so sad when a young couple are found in pieces. It's the opposite of good. Yes. OK, I will. Thank you, officer. Goodbye.'

xvii

ND REBEKAH lifted up her eyes, and when she saw Isaac, she lighted off the camel."

LIFE.EXE

i

I MET BETTY outside the train station at nine o'clock on Monday morning. She was leaning against the wall with a generous helping of fresh darkness behind her as I discoursed crudely with my heavy suitcase.

'Have you got enough clothing in there?' she asked.

'Yes. . . hopefully,' I replied, my rough words standing up to her gold lettering.

'We'll be away for seven whole days, remember. A sudden stop in front of the eye can be stubborn.'

'I know. Let's just get going.'

We made our way through a naked commotion and found a summer crop of seats just in time. The train pulled out the auspices near the door, creating a morning of good conscience for two lovely girls.

'I'm really looking forward to our trip to the country,' Betty pearled.

'Me too. It's been ages since I saw grass between the stones.'

'Are you talking about the r-word, Sally?'

'The r-word? I'm not sure. . .'

'Never mind. I booked us a lovely little cottage with a nice head of hair on top. There's a ball of grass in the corner and a huge column at the rear for us to enjoy—but if the weather's good, we'll probably do most of our work outdoors.'

Betty, my business partner, had insisted that a transmutation of the scenery was required as we planned our future strategy. She thought that our office in the city had become a waterlogged colony, and I agreed. She said we would come up with our best ideas if we bowed to hot flowers in the frame of fresh air, and since I had recently been having recurring nightmares about being defiled by a larger-than-life Excel spreadsheet, I was more than happy to welcome the decorative gravel stages leading to Ash Cottage.

'What are your plans for the future of the business?' I cupsized my companion.

'That will become clear over the next seven days,' Betty answered with a string of off-white remarks that conducted my eye down to the dark pink fault line of her bosom. 'You just need to focus on the big, bouncy road in front of you.'

'But where does it lead?'

'To a strange joy at the top of a pyramid.'

I sat comfortably in the carriage and watched in shy happiness as the melting ruins of oast houses flew by the window, making me feel like kissing a brochure. I had expected to see a great deal of visual beauty, but the kind that promoted itself to me on the train was so thick on the imagination that I had a full stocking hanging overhead.

Around the halfway point of our journey, Betty suddenly took me in a fierce hug of fingers, and I turned to see old mahogany falling on her face.

'I hope everything goes to plan,' she soundwaved deeply. 'I enjoy my own strength, but I need you to enjoy it too.'

'*Is* there a plan? I thought we were going on this trip to try to come up with one.'

'Yes, Sally. There's a plan. A big, big plan. It was signed for in the crash. Excuse me—I'm going to laugh now.'

Betty sat back in her seat and, somewhat unnervingly for me, began laughing a crazy laugh of the sugar-dead, which continued for the remainder of the journey.

'Agh-hagh-agh-hagh-agh-hagh-agh. . .'

ii

S WE APPROACHED the cottage, I had a strong opinion in my soul: it seemed as if the UK went on in Paradise forever.

'It's beautiful,' I said.

'Yes,' Betty replied. 'The doors are open to a week of temptation.'

The sound of my suitcase crumbling along the path wasn't enough to break the tough loaf of golden girl silence baked in the summer sun. We entered the building in one piece, expertly placing the bread of our presence into the thatched oven like the well-rounded dough mongers we almost were.

'You can have the biggest room, Sally. There's a lovely view of the garden from there.'

'Thanks, Betty.'

I unpacked my things with no loss of life, politely asking the curtains to satisfy the needs of the window and checking beneath the bed for faulty coronation stones. All in all, the room was decorated with my satisfaction.

Betty already had brunch prepared by the time I emerged from the enclosure with a few special welcome effects.

'It's not too steep for you, is it?' she asked, placing a plate of bread on the table.

'No, it's fine.'

'Good. We don't want to hit on a cousin.'

We sat down to a good episode of food and drink in which the butter was generous and the tea was brutally slaughtered. A subtle sign of youth with rosy cheeks was installed in the crossbeams to watch over us as we ate and drank, occasionally smiling a mouth of foam, exactly as the brochure described.

'We should get down to business soon,' Betty said from behind a beard of crumbs.

'OK. What should we start with?'

'Education. It's a drug we can invest in.'

'That sounds interesting,' I tiptoed. 'If the publishing industry were to. . .'

'Wait!' she interrupted, slanting an eye at the cherub above. 'It's much better if we discuss this while out walking.'

'Yes, yes. Of course.'

'So finish off those seeds and get your boots on. I'll be back in a minute to give you a "007" view of things.'

'OK.'

As I finished my food, I watched Betty rapidly expanding in her room. She removed a huge amount of papers and folders from her suitcase and threw them on the bed before frantically searching through the blackprints and pulling out her phone to text someone. Since she didn't know she was being observed, she allowed a serious eye of violence to slide forward and reveal a harsh tomboy on multiple levels.

As soon as she looked up and saw me staring at her, the second impression burned down.

'How long have you been watching me?' she laughed.

'A minute or so.'

'We're friends, aren't we?'

'Of course,' I tendered.

'In that case, you won't mind if I close this,' Betty pounded back, slamming the door affirmatively in my face and shaking a small avalanche of relations.

iii

I HAD BEEN FEELING increasingly worn down and clichéd in the city, my thoughts divided by a sarcastic clap at the end of a sculpture. Every day at the office was an uphill battle to keep saltwater from my cheek, and the inevitable drips and drops soon created an ocean reflecting an alien sunset at me. The atmosphere at home with John, my boyfriend, was hardly charitable either.

Walking through the woods and breathing the chitzum air with my business partner was a transformational experience which made me feel like an entire nation smacked calm by a cattle hand. We walked and talked until my saloon door was wide open, but unfortunately a couple of unwelcome visitors took advantage of this and activated traces of the eternal enemy inside.

Firstly, my ankle began to play the trumpet of pain, sounding a long, hot toot of fire through my skeleton and putting me completely out of business. I tried to inform Betty of my problem, but she seemed determined to plough on with her monologue in hard black and white.

'It's probably just a temporary spasm,' she said. 'Anyway, I was talking about our products. . .'

'No, it's serious. The old injury John gave me has come back. It's a violent partner all over again.'

'Oh, you'll live. We need to discuss targets too—even software needs something to aim for, after all. And I'm sure you'll agree that there's no better sign than youth. We can plant the language seeds there, but how do we convince the parents that their kids should be cleverer than them? Maturity drives a pretty hard bargain.'

The other problem that affected me was a feeling of dizziness caused by clouds being imported through a small seed-shaped hole that had opened up in my forehead. I suspected it was a reaction to the food Betty had prepared for me earlier, but I bowed to all possibilities. After a few minutes of suffering, the fever above and the pain below managed to combined forces in my centre, creating a cross on which to crucify the green girl.

'The pages in kids' books only need to be small, like kids themselves. It's just a matter of passing through a rectangle. We could easily get them to read about British monarchs, US presidents or any other type of cold-blooded creature, but small brains have one foot in the etheric and one foot in the physical, so they won't view Ancient Egypt or the French Revolution the same way their parents do.'

The grass beneath my feet felt forced. It was a terrifying wakeup call that I was unable to act on.

'Betty, I. . .'

'Most libraries contain more pictures than words, you know. It's just that most people can't see them.'

'I think I'm going to. . .'

'Jane's coming to the cottage tomorrow, by the way. There'll be an interview in the living room.'

My body was being looked at by a pair of eyes in a piece of meat waiting at a tomb. The clouds inside my head were pounding out a series of oppressive code symbols that the environment insisted I wore. With indescribable feelings, I sank down inside the ring of trees that surrounded me, and let my own narration slip away.

'I think I'm going to lie down at the foot of this tree and count my lucky stars in the darkness of unconsciousness,' I groaned in decline.

As I made a home for myself among the moss and rocks, the last thing I heard was Betty whispering by my hand.

'Gravity is a reflection of its audience,' she said, almost twice.

iv

LIFTING ME INTO a sitting position, Betty helped me to grow up and become accepted by the world I found myself in. My surroundings had changed, but the familiar sight of my business partner helped to bring the others to light.

I was in bed, heading up a pillow, or was it a holiday? It was night and a candle burning sheepishly on the dashboard slowly kindled my senses, leading me to notice a dark-haired gentleman in a peculiar uniform crouching at the foot of the bed. As I watched him washing a black substance from his hands in a small porcelain basin, I felt the inexpressible security and relief of knowing there was a complete stranger in the room.

I stared at the face of the gentlemen and felt bumpy.

'Well? Am I?' he asked.

I tried to answer, but I ended up offering him my hand instead.

'You're doing very well,' he declared, stroking my fingers and smiling. 'But be particularly careful at night: that's when people usually get violated.'

He gave me guidance and sucktoote like a documentary on terrorism narrated by someone who didn't know what terrorism was. All my fears seemed to evaporate like holograms, leaving me in a cottage, miles away from John, as the dark gentleman moved in and leaned his arm on my pillow.

He seemed to weigh more than a human being.

'I suppose you wish to know my name,' he said softly. 'Well, I am known as the Chairman.'

His name whooshed around the dark room and caused a cheque to be written by my trembling heart.

'Maybe you should go back to sleep,' said Betty.

'No,' I hushed. 'I . . .'

'Do you want a drink?'

'No.'

'Something to eat?'

'No thanks, Betty.'

'The writing on your heart's cheque is faint,' the gentleman said. 'I can barely make it out. But your goodness is a thick band in the world's body. I can see that clearly. I can rely on you not to give in to the temptation of darkness, can't I?'

'Yes, of course. I'd refuse anything for you. I'd. . .'

'Great civilisation!' he cried suddenly. 'It is past ten and I am due back at Mansion 28 tonight!'

Inexpressible sorrow assailed me as the man jumped to his feet and shimmied towards the door.

'Will I see you again?' I called.

'To encourage the idea, you must question it,' he answered before disappearing from view.

Perhaps I was still voting with a feverish ticket, but I couldn't help thinking that the issue of men could finally be resolved.

'Who is he, Betty?' I asked. 'I'm going to think of Mansion 28 and cry now. Can we invite him back?'

'You're sick,' my colleague said, placing a hand on my brow. 'You have to go back to sleep. You'll get better that way. "Sleep is the thing for me," you need to repeat to yourself.'

'Is it really the thing for me, Betty?'

'Yes, it is.'

'Is it *really*, though?'

'Yes.'

'How do you know?'

'I just do.'

'Are you sure?'

'Positive.'

'Sleep's the best thing?'

'Yes.'

'OK, then. Goodnight.'

v

HE FOLLOWING MORNING, I opened my eyes to see the pane of my bedroom window modelling a huge crack and the wooden floorboards trotting out a fragmented tale about a teacup that had fallen from the chest of drawers and smashed into pieces.

Too excited to dress properly, I rushed from the room wearing only a t-shirt with a picture of a half-naked woman on it.

'Good morning,' said Betty, who was rifling through her papers in the living room. 'You've come to give me ideas, haven't you?'

'No, I've come to get ideas from you, Betty. There's a crack in the window that I don't understand. I don't remember seeing that yesterday. And a porcelain object has had an accident I just can't sympathise with. What's going on?'

'Oh, yes,' my colleague said nonchalantly. 'There was an earthquake last night. The cottage was shaking catacombs, but you slept through the whole thing.'

'An earthquake? In England? How unusual!'

Betty stared at my bare legs and made me feel like an hour-long prayer in the cold. Time underwent a change, and a Bible reading finally ended, allowing me to look at myself in the mirror.

'I saved you some porridge, by the way, Sally.'

'Thanks,' I stirred.

'But hurry up with your breakfast—Jane will be here for the interview soon.'

Jane was a freelancer who helped us sponge out from the employment field from time to time, and on the few occasions that she had visited the office, the woman struck me as a good term. I was told that she mainly worked as an actress, and that her experience of performing educational shows for young children, of teaching wet lessons from the heart, meant she had something valuable to offer us. Her full potential was only just beginning to be realised, according to those in the knowledge pool. . .

I bubbled my eyes up from the cold porridge and attempted to ask Betty about Jane but found myself enquiring about the gentleman from the previous night instead. My business partner's response was simply to raise her hand without turning to look at me and let it hover indifferently around itself until I took it as a sign to suspend my speech.

After breakfast, I washed and dressed at a modern speed in order to be ready in time for Jane's arrival. When I opened the door to the knock of the educational actress, the woman behind it seemed surprised to see me, and I thought she looked different somehow.

'Would you like a drink?' I asked.

'To all intents and purposes, no,' she said, pushing past me and bagging it straight to the living room to see my colleague.

'Shut the door!' Betty commanded as I followed the unconventional wisdom of Jane's steps. 'Hurry up!'

I placed myself in the room and did as she said, only to be given a look of dirty fingernails.

'With you on the other side, please.'

My nerves were suddenly as shot as Sisyphus' fag, but I did as I was told. I closed the door and retreated to the classical environment of the kitchen, where I stood and stared intently at a china plate with a bugger of blackbirds painted on it. While baking the feathered creatures into a pie with my eyes, I eavesdropped on the conversation between the two women in the living room, Lord's supper 'n' all.

'A class of kids is in my hand when I read. . . everything is quiet. . . you start every lesson with British history, then move onto American. . . one uses such phrases to remain top of the class. . . explosive command prompts. . . there's hidden software in language. . . you can see how the world is created. . . most of them seem to respond, but with a few errors in pronunciation. . .'

Although I struggled to hear entire sentences, I was able to glean from the snippets of speech that Jane's experience of influencing the thoughts of children was the main topic. After about 15 minutes of straining my ears, I made an unwanted breakthrough when a loud academy of laughter issued from the room, making the china plate vibrate and causing the blackbirds to escape. The sound became even louder as the door was flung open by a cackling Jane, who was now wearing new jewellery and carrying what appeared to be a number of legal documents in her hand.

'Jane's got the job,' announced Betty.

'What job? I thought Jane was already employed by us.'

'The new job, silly. Our business is changing. Our roles are changing. The whole world's changing. See Jane out, please.'

I had been rearranging things in the kitchen so as not to arouse suspicion, but it didn't seem to matter. I put the china plate back on the shelf and walked an awkward vacuum with Jane to the front door.

Just as I was about to do something desperate, the actress turned to me and spoke in a hushed tone: 'This company is destined for great things, you know.'

'I certainly hope so,' I said, fiddling with a button on my blouse.

'And I see important things in your future too. A tall, dark stranger will pay you a visit and make your heart want to blow its life savings on him. You'll be bursting with emotion.'

I was about to say that her prediction had already come true, but Jane was halfway down the garden path before I was able to roll my words out.

vi

ETTY AND I spent the rest of the day walking in the surrounding countryside as she described the millimetres of evolution to me. Despite my bad ankle and recent dizzy spell, it felt good to be outdoors, to be walked through nature and disappear in the present tense. I went pretty hard on mineral resources and ancient words as my companion informed me of the new rules and tasks related to our changing business.

'Fear of failure will hold you back more than physical difficulties,' she said.

'Yes.'

A shocking pair of zuzoks, we reached the site where I collapsed dramatically into a bundle of code symbols the day before. Our return seemed to prompt Betty to place my arm in a Hugh Hefner hold with her right hand while pointing to the ground with her left, as if trying to make me melt.

'You slipped in and out of consciousness right there, Sally. I spent a whole hour trying to keep you alive. I removed some of your clothing and rubbed my hands over your body to warm you up. It was like rubbing cold meat at first, but eventually I worked up a good heat with a few herbs and spices. Your skin became soft and moist as the cold wind went blowing backwards in search of corporeal fruit. I had half a cup of coffee to get you back to the cottage safely, Sally. And do you know what I did? I called for help. Long, deep and hard, beyond the walls of the forest. And that's when the gentleman from Mansion 28 came.'

'The Chairman!' I exclaimed through an eye-shaped window.

'Yes. He was all stiff fingers and thin sheets at first, but things were ungloved in time. We possessed either end before carrying you through the trees and back to the cottage. When you were safely tucked up in bed like an auspicious bun in an oven, he seasoned you with a little French kiss on the neck.'

I was sure that the Chairman's caress would have provided a canopy of wide-pegged time had I been awake to receive it. He even formed a bell-shaped curve on my bed, down which all the hot tears in the shower with John could trickle away.

'Will we see this mystery-eyed man again?' I asked.

Instead of replying, Betty held out her hand in broad daylight. I shook it instinctively, although what it symbolised was beyond me.

'We're partners,' she said, gripping my paw like a whore-handler. 'Business partners. You remember when I went to the trade fair in Paris?'

I nodded physically.

'I met someone there. I never told you—but I'm telling you now. I had to endure a week of excruciating pain, just as you will have to. Success is related to effort, after all. He's a powerful man with a strong voice in many countries. It helps to separate the cherries from the pearls.'

The relationship between Betty and the Chairman was clearly not to be spat at. I wanted her to tell me more but I knew she couldn't. I simply went on smelling a flower that emitted the breath of the Chairman on a dreamy night, and praying for a resolution to the issue of men.

After a few minutes, I looked down and noticed that Betty still had my hand held firmly in a madam clamp as if trying to keep me permanently restrained in a den of vice.

vii

'**Y**OUR DEPARTURE has plunged me into chaos,' John said over the phone. 'I've been acting badly of late. I've realised that, and I want you to know that I'm deeply and wobbly sorry.'

'Your apology means nothing if you're not going to change,' I blared over the note of throbbing pain that sounded in my shoulder as I shifted my position in bed. 'It's cold at night and I hope for something better.'

'I figured. I know I'm not as fun as I used to be, but I'm not a complete waste of time either. You can't just bladder away eight years.'

'You're the one bladdering away eight years,' I retorted. '*Violently.*'

John spent the next hour trying to convince me that things would be different when I returned. I would know freedom and excitement again, history would be sweeter, and a deep note of satisfaction, like the one struck on our first night together, would be heard once again. I knew it was all possible, but the half-thoughts undrew themselves almost instantly in the presence of the old faces.

'It's always hard at the end, isn't it?'

'Is it?' John responded bitterly.

Although I couldn't see him, I knew he was rubbing his forehead.

'Betty has just hired an assistant,' I said. 'At least that's what I think has happened. All I know for sure is that the business is growing and changing, and people are changing along with it, and I don't want to be left behind. We may need to relocate. . . permanently.'

'Sounds like you've got everything figured out, you cocksure lady boner!' John said angrily before hanging up the phone.

I let my head slowly digest the contents of my heart before swallowing it all back with an inward sigh. Just as I was about to fall back on a reputation for feathers, I noticed that there was a small card on my pillow. It read:

I'M THE CREEPER; CATCH ME IF YOU CAN!

Although I didn't understand what it meant, the card seemed to bend backwards towards my youth, hinting at a childhood before my childhood and reflecting many important events in the sparkling blue facets of an impossible jewel-like object. Feeling like a gravedigger, I regained a lost week each time I read it.

It was necessary to create a link, so I wandered out of my room, clutching the message in the stench of stale water.

My colleague was also head over heels in discussions with someone on the phone, but as soon as I entered the living room, she immediately told the person on the other end of the line that she would have to call them back. This small damsel deed made me smile a spare tyre as it was nice to know that Betty could still make time for me.

'Yes?' she said. 'What is it?'

'Discombobulation, I suppose. I just discovered this curious item on my pillow and I can't expand a sufficient number of horses to hold the reason of it.'

'Oh, that,' she said, glancing at the rectangle of unknowledge in my hand. 'That's just a buckarastano. Nothing to worry about.'

'A buckarastano? What's that?'

'It's like a business card, only it's printed in a special way. I had a few of them made up today. They're useful for organisations like ours. But don't spend too much time thinking about it—you might regain more memories than you can handle.'

I was decomposed by the investigation. Usually it was poor quality food or seawater that produced the effect, but I was a victim of a powerful magnetic impulse right there in the cottage.

'When did you get these buckarastanos made up?' I asked Betty. 'We've been together pretty much all day and night. There aren't any shops for miles—only trees.'

'You've just answered your question, dear,' she said with a missing smile. 'Now go back to your room and stop thinking like a witch. Tomorrow we'll be walking through the woods and forming a business plan, so you should rest now.'

'OK, Betty. But what shall I do with this buckarastano?'

'Put it in your handbag and wait for a new age to begin. Now go to sleep—sleep is free, after all.'

'Yes, sleep *is* free. Goodnight, Betty.'

'Goodnight, my eyes.'

viii

I AWOKE the following morning to the sound of the building flapping its wings to a severe Jack Skellington scenario.

As the cottage was landing back in the garden after a dream flight, I exited the bed and peered out of the window to see Betty turning ecstatic circles in the garden. She was grinning a particularly serious dervish with a pincushioned personality, seeming to vanish up her own wounds in the vegetable patch.

When she saw me at the window, she laughed and staggered towards the house, apparently not noticing that she was trampling all the greens beneath her feet. As she came closer, I could see that her eyes were glazed like two pane-smashing rocks that would land her in jail.

Mouthing the words 'I am the night' over and over again, she stopped before the window and began slowly touching her legs. Betty seemed so unsteady that I initially thought she was rubbing herself in order to stave off numbness and remain upright, but the rubbing was so slow and sensual it suggested she was longing for a pleasurable expansion of some sort.

She was wearing only a thin t-shirt, which she suddenly lifted up to reveal an image of an extremely interested woman showing a hairy path through a garden of flesh to me.

I turned my face away in embarrassment but a sudden movement seen from the corner of my eye made me turn back: Betty had toppled over and was technically shutting down on the grass, school rules to the outside world.

'Betty!'

I rushed out to find my business partner on the lawn, breathing heavily and doing the short-term body disaster routine.

'Are you OK?' I asked, stroking her forehead.

'You've given me ideas,' came the reply.

'What's wrong?'

'I've fallen, Sally. I touched you when you fell; now it's your turn. I'm a woman. Sing, waltz and be fascinated by me.'

Her chest was heaving berrily and her cheeks were flushed. She continued rubbing herself despite seeming only half conscious. I had to keep pulling her t-shirt back down as she persisted in showing me the graphic image on its underside.

'Play with me!'

'I'm not able to play, Betty. I need to get you inside. You're sick.'

'Rub my fruit. Make a picture for the kind director.'

'No, no. You're delirious.'

'I'm soaking wet.'

'Betty!'

I searched for an answer in my head, for anything that made sense quickly. A pulse was pounding in my temples, but I completed my initial work by peering around a pillar in my brain and watching a star shoot in through my nose.

'I'm streaming the sweetest juice inside my clothes!'

'Betty, please!'

'I was appointed to drive near Robert Smith fans—a different species after five minutes.'

'Good gracious!'

I stood up and called for help, my voice the only true sound in the hard freedom of the surroundings.

'Help! Help! There's a fallen woman here! Can somebody come? Mr Chairman? Can you hear me, strong Mr Chairman?'

I imagined the Chairman arriving in his strange uniform like a Moon Man, with tight gloves and goggles, a figure desired eternally through a telescope. My imagination suddenly took off and I felt I was the Chairman and Betty was me, being swept up and carried back to the cottage to be French-kissed all over the neck and face.

I could almost hear him whispering softly in my ear as he laid me on the bed, instructing me to be happy and relaxed while he administered sucktoote.

'Mr Chairman?'

I called out for the Chairman with all my fairy stories and movie screens but there was no response, so I had no choice but to carry Betty indoors myself. I helped the murmuring woman to her feet and allowed her to use my body as a crutch despite the pain it caused me.

'That's it, Betty. Small steps.'

By the time we reached the door, pain had embedded itself in Alps around me. My shoulder was ice, my ankle rock, and I still blamed John for the injuries. I was thinking of deadly snowslides for centuries as we stumbled into the cottage, knee-deep in vortices.

Shouting blanks at the agony, I eased Betty onto the bed. She was no longer talking and her eyes were closed as if she didn't exist.

'Can you hear me, Betty? I'm worried. This does nothing for my happiness. What the dog is going on?'

Feeling increasingly concerned for her welfare, I shook her furiously until her eyelids flicked open. To my horror, I realised her eyes had become parentheses to herself and it was impossible to explain what she was made of.

'Speak to me, Betty! Say something!'

'Ur. . .'

An echo was writing back to me at last, from a place where a million people longed to be heard. Lost tribes working together to find their place on earth, standing stiff and making pudding, laughing and condemning to a pulp.

'Listen to me, Sally,' she finally said, grabbing me by the blouse button and pulling me closer. 'Who's to blame for this? Me? I've got a vision, I've got goals. I've got a whole fucking world to motivate me. I've had all the luck and you've had none—well, that's about to change. If you do as I say, you'll see more. You'll see that I'm above morality. Don't ask questions that are longer than a syllable. Are you ready for the truth?'

'Yes,' I said, rubbing my chin, my ears and other family members.

'Are you totally fucking sure?'

'Yes! Yes!'

'Here it comes. . .'

'Yes?'

'Grtash!' she screamed at the top of her pulmonary organs.

ix

I SPENT the rest of the day looking after Betty, salmoning between her bedroom and the kitchen with water and towels. She wanted to stick to our original plan of strolling through the woods and discussing business but I insisted she remained horizontal to recuperate.

To tell the truth, I was so shaken by the earlier incident that I felt unable to keep my mind focused on professional matters. I felt as if my personality was owned by a clump of hazel.

'Sally?'

'Yes, dear Betty?'

'If I died,' she said, sitting up in bed, 'would you be sad?'

'Of course! I'd be devastated.'

'Would you rush out and burn the sacred circle of trees to a black disc?'

'Probably,' I answered.

'Then I'd like you to promise me something. . .'

'OK.'

'If I die, you need to return to my old school and destroy something for me. It's a painting of a black snake which you'll find on the wall of one of the art rooms. It's my work, but it was painted with poison. Will you destroy it for me? It's extremely dangerous.'

'I promise to destroy the snake for you.'

'Thanksss.'

For some reason I was reminded of my first meeting with Betty. I was at a friend's apartment when my future business partner turned up, knocking on the door and shouting gritty rectangles through the letterbox. After being let in, she slammed a wad of papers onto the coffee table with the power and speed of a finely chopped signal, claiming all sorts of complex reasons for it. It soon came down to talking, however, as that was part of the job.

'It's time for wine,' she announced, pulling a half-empty bottle from her bag. 'I would offer you some, but that would require a change of clothes.'

'How did your meeting with the publishers go?' my friend asked, wearing a large portion of the evening.

'Meh!' Betty responded with a wave of her hand. 'Publishers these days are so unwise. I'd rather do business with a pressure valve. I was left waiting in the restaurant for an hour, and when the guy finally turned up he suggested I had a corpse buried in my portfolio.'

She leaned forward and spread the papers out across the table with her strong hands, revealing a collection of unusual ink drawings.

'Take a look,' she said to me, 'and tell me if you see any corpses in there.'

I could make out images of birds with dirty wings, fish angrily blowing bubbles, and cats peering out from behind piles of stones. They all streamed a darkness that said no shore, but I saw nothing that resembled a corpse.

'No deadies there,' I declared.

'Thank you, my dear. At least someone's on my side. What's your name, by the way? I'm Betty.'

'I'm Sally. Sally Air.'

'Very nice to meet you, Sally,' she said, not interrupting. 'If only there were more people like you in my industry.'

'Funny you should say that. I'm thinking about starting a company. . .'

And that was how it all began. It was bright colours and gold bracelets rolling over the land within a matter of months. Pictures of two lovely girls on a morning of good conscience quickly emerged from a self-reflexive pop-up book, eclipsing the scenery in semi-relief in the cold light of day.

I presently cast my arms down into the sparkling waters and, to my astonishment, brought up what felt like the pitch-heavy remains of a drug-addicted woman.

Sitting on the edge of Betty's bed in the cottage, I couldn't help letting the body drip on the political faction of duvet between us, sprinkling some of the burden among the crowd to see where the doldrums were born.

'Something you want to ask me?' the patient willowed.

'Um. . . yes. Was there a picture of a woman in your portfolio?'

'A woman? Oh, I don't know. There were all sorts of things in there. Anything's possible, I suppose.'

'What about a dead woman? Is that possible?'

'I'm not a line in a film,' Betty said curtly.

'Yes, I know. I'm talking about your paintings and drawings. Is it possible that I saw the corpse of a woman in there when I first looked, her body covered in needle holes?'

'Sally, dear, you said yourself that you saw no deadies in there, didn't you?'

'Yes, yes, I did. You're right. Sorry. I shouldn't doubt you, or myself. It's just that. . .'

'What?'

'Why do some people oppose our books?'

'Because they don't understand them, Sally. It's as simple as that. People want to destroy what they can't explain.'

'That's very true. . . but there's more to it in our case, isn't there? There's something about your illustrations being too deep to look at. How can an image be so graphic that it becomes dangerous for a person to take it in?'

'That will become clear in a day or two, my dear. For now, all I can say is that there's a special ingredient in the ink, something that takes the pictures to a great, black abyss, but which makes my pen brighter, if you know what I mean. If I were in my own pictures, I'd see a child's face looking at me.'

'And what would the child's expression be?'

'I don't know because I've never been inside my pictures—my head's too big to fit.'

'But can't you guess?' I candled.

'What do you want me to say, Sally? That the child's expression would be one of horror? Is that what you want?'

302

'No, I don't want that. I really don't. I just need to know whether. . .'

'Excuse me,' Betty interrupted. 'But I'm going to laugh now. I'm going to laugh the sickly laugh of the sugar-dead for the remainder of the journey, so I'm afraid you'll have to chat to yourself.'

'But we're not on a journey now. We're. . .'

'Agh-hagh-agh-hagh-agh-hagh-agh. . .'

Betty did just as she said she would, falling back on a feathery headrest as the noisy star on her neck tore bright holes. I sat and waited for the laughter to stop but there seemed to be no large or small endings in sight, so I eventually stood up, patted my business partner where the clavicle met the scapula, and left the room.

Several hours later, once calm had descended on the house like bony fingers brushing the carriage roof, and I was seated in a dark blue moment on the sofa, attempting to make sense of Betty's work and the future of our business, I heard the rising and falling of childish energy from across the gulf of meaning.

I followed the sound of a woman's shape yo-yoing in the air and found myself back in Betty's bedroom, staring in disbelief at the patient, who was now bouncing up and down on her bed. Munupalupt was on the wind, a few leaves at an angle.

'What are you doing?' I asked.

'I'm jumping to your defence, Sally!'

'Be careful! You'll do yourself a mischief.'

'Mischief is my middle name,' Betty M. Mason snorted as her head hit the lampshade for the twentieth time. 'And I've no need to be careful–I've got nothing to lose.'

'Nothing to lose? What about your career?'

'Ha! That's not real. . . It's just a load of old wireless guidelines.'

'I've always admired your work,' I said. 'You're not going to die, are you? That's not what all this is about, is it?'

'We're all going to die, Sally. It shouldn't come as a surprise. You've already seen the old mahogany falling on my face. I'll be back on the bench one day.'

The dark ink seemed to be spreading and the picture had failed to connect, so I decided to grab the woman by the solid performance and attempt to forcibly stop her bouncing. As I pulled her down from the atmosphere, I noticed that there was white powder all over her face and every item of jewellery she was wearing had a bright, shiny wheel spinning inside it.

'What's going on with you?' I asked.

'Om nom nom nom.'

'Can you elaborate on that?'

'Hissssssssssssss.'

Betty fell back with glazed eyes and went completely polar ice on me, causing each particle of faith in my blood to come to a halt. Just as I was beginning to freeze along with my female medical problem, I saw a tiny glimmer of something even more miniscule than faith, like the crumb of a crumb inside a slaughtered loaf of bread, and somehow it gave me the strength to keep both of us alive.

I baked the pair of us into an emergency hot cross bun of temporary care—Betty horizontal, me vertical—in order to ensure that we made it out of the evening in one piece. By the end of the process, I was very, very small.

X

THE FOLLOWING DAY, after the culinary crucifixion of my faith, I felt just about ready to apply a mental leavening agent to my time in the country and quit the cottage. I was raising a very heavy question mark in the dough of my mind when Betty, suddenly full of the currants and raisins of life, rushed into my bedroom to deliver sweet spice.

'Get your best frock ready,' she announced. 'We're going to Mansion 28 tonight!'

'What?' The news was so ear-catching that I barely even registered the fact that its deliverer was wearing only a loose gown to cover the raw flurry of her body.

'You heard me, Sally. We're going to see the Chairman.'

'The Chairman! Oh, Betty! Bola Bola Saka Lo Bis So!' I was so happy, I was shouting silver.

'Yes, we've got a date with the half-French kissing-healer.'

'Oh, viscoelastic materials! How wonderful!'

The status of the media could have changed completely in that moment, but it would have made absolutely no difference to me because the news I had received was so exciting. I was Gandhi on the cover of *Time* magazine, thin but proud.

'How did he get in touch?' I asked. 'A handwritten invitation? Will he be dressed in his uniform like before? Maybe he'll be wearing a suit of purple velvet and a pair of tight leather gloves. Oh, the fast basket! Will he swirl a depiction of sucktoote in a glass tube for me? Will he write a description of ecstasy on a wax tablet?'

'Frost yourself down, Sally. You're getting far too excited. All will be revealed in time.'

'Yes, Betty. I'm sorry. I'm just a bit triangled by the idea. . . We're really going?'

'Yes. Now take a deep breath.'

'OK.'

From that point onwards, it seemed I could depend utterly on my tides and hear the contents of an alternate existence in minute detail. I no longer needed the window of the modern world in order to see myself pressed pleasantly against a sofa by a figure who weighed more than a human being; I was cushioned adequately by a pair of mysterious eyes and thick lips.

Later on, as I was spreading a tube of grey-green makeup over my face and thinking about which dress to wear, my mobile phone was suddenly incited to violence, picking up an audioknife and holding it against my ear in response to the call of John.

'What is it?' I asked my troublesome partner, feeling like an old dog-and-bone model.

'It's eight years,' he said. 'Eight years unsweetened. I've been thinking things over and there's going to be a serious shortage of me if you don't come home immediately.'

'What are you talking about?' I had a pretty good idea what he was talking about, but I didn't want to pull a hamstring on a porcelain bowl without even needing to urinate, so I tried to remain outside the John.

'I'm talking about suicide, Sally. . . I'm going to do it if you don't come home tonight.'

'Don't be so unintelligent, John. I'm here with Betty until the end of the week and we've got important work to do. What are you trying to achieve?'

'Um. . . maybe a bitter taste.'

It became obvious that he had been drinking and was expressing himself in squiggly horizontal lines.

'I think I'm tough enough to become Honourary President of the Unknown,' he slurred. 'You made me realise that there's a solid block of poison where the honey should be. If you don't come back, it's official.'

'Please don't do this, John. I can't come back now.'

'Why not? What are you doing tonight?'

'Tonight? Oh, er. . . nothing,' I rubber-balled him. 'Well, it's something. . . Betty and I are doing something. . . but it's nothing, really.'

'Then you can cut your trip short and see me. Standing in this forehead is stroking me to disaster!'

'No. You're being unfair. I'm not a nun!'

'It's up to you, you smelly woman,' he said before hanging up.

I remained seated on the bed with the now blunt audioknife against my ear for some time, rubbing the cracks in the road in an attempt to clear my conscience.

It seemed John always had to harm someone. I was constantly afraid that he might jump off a lighthouse or commit overkill on pills, and I was tired of painfully dragging the wondercup up the stairs every time he got drunk. For the first time in my life, I decided to let the wondercup, the wonderspoon and the wonderplate all remain on the ground floor.

As I applied the last of the grey-green paste to my face and wrapped my body in blind materials, I was reminded of a book I once read about a guy who apologised all the time for being in love. He seemed like a sweet, sweet man—exactly the kind of person I hoped in vain that John would become.

'Ready?'

'Ready.'

Stepping out in my new dress as the time to visit Mansion 28 arrived, I realised that, for the first time in years, there was wild fruit growing on my body.

'You look delicious,' said Betty as I emerged from my room.

'Thank you,' I replied as I felt a tiny strawberry pop on each of my breasts. 'But I feel nervous.'

'Nervous about meeting the Chairman again or nervous about John doing something stupid?'

'How do you know about John?' I asked with an unconscious approach.

'I read a lot. These things happen in books all the time. Anyway, you needn't worry about John or the Chairman—the story is always agreed upon before anything else.'

Just as I was about to bung up another question, I felt something fall down my front from above. I looked up to see the rosy face of youth in the crossbeams grinning with the satisfaction of being able to see right down my top. The foam generated by the cherub's mouth was bubbling over and dripping down like blobs of cream all over my strawberries.

'We've dealt with business,' Betty queened with an eye up the angel. 'Now it's time for pleasure. . .'

xi

O MY SURPRISE, we were taken to Mansion 28 by a horse-drawn carriage which pulled up outside the cottage as soon as Betty mentioned it. The coachman had cheeks like a trumpeter and a wind in his mouth with which he blew the horses forward.

Beneath the lightest of touches from a set of bony fingers, we climbed into the carriage and attended to our freedom.

'You've got a purple arse,' Betty remarked with a giggle as she entered after me.

'Thanks.'

The shakes and fibres of the journey increased in length until a steep compromise gave way to a view of the nesting sites of the dark forest population. One by one, the meditation barriers were overcome in the moonlight, and the stockings hanging overhead were filled with the legs of mystery.

'Everything's whizzing so nicely,' I said, placing my heart in the centre of it all.

As demonstrated, you can see a place of beauty after a few days of growing in the countryside. You can spread yourself through a cloud and start again, turning on the same living hills throughout your career without disturbing your position beneath the stars.

'Hey, is that an oak tree?' I asked the man in front.

He pulled up his collar and shrugged.

The shittr of the West sank behind the treetops and blushed in silence, clearly liver to the deep flow of the near future.

'We're here!'

Upon arrival at Mansion 28, I could feel the pleasure of opera music vibrating along the songlines; passion and elegance were buffed at a glance, and my mind felt a long way from the Big Stubborn One and his squiggly excuses for music.

Betty and I quickly got our acts together, passing on a 'thank pharaoh' to the carman as we disembarked and headed for the outdoor kitchen, from which thick brown plumes of chocolate smoke could be seen rising in the night air.

'Bonbon?' asked a man dressed like an Arab.

'No thanks,' I said, content to suck on all the tiny chocolate particles that entered my mouth as I inhaled.

'Kill her!' shouted the Arab.

'What? But I, I. . .'

'Only joking,' he smiled. 'Enjoy your evening.'

'Oh, thanks.'

'By the way, it's froth for noise here,' Betty whispered conspiratorially. 'I'd bop out from the ears if I were you.'

'OK.'

We reached the outdoor kitchen and feasted our eyes on the sweet technicalities of the scene: cigars made of liquorice, ice-cream snowmen and a huge map of Europe made from Rocky Road. In addition to the Arabs, there were smaller men dressed as gnomes serving food to the guests.

'Gostak?' one of the little bearded helpers asked me, holding out a plate of what looked like wisdom teeth covered in hundreds and thousands.

Betty gave a nod to indicate that I should take one; but before I had a chance, a figure with a very big idea suddenly appeared on the balcony above us.

'The Chairman!'

'Welcome to the higher dimensional party at Mansion 28!' he shouted to the excited crowds of people below, spreading his arms and smiling groundbreakingly.

The magnetic man then unzipped his trousers and let a flock of black feathered creatures fly out from them over our heads. With biceps buttered, he announced at the summit of his voice: 'I'm an old wooden crow that loves everything!'

This drew huge cheers from the garden of guests, who were rolling ecstatically in their cashmeres and spoonies.

I barely had time to turn to Betty and remark upon the irrelevance of the history of the world before the Chairman appeared next to me in his bulbing suit of purple velvet.

'Do you know *Labyrinth*?' he asked. 'The film starring David Bowie?'

'Er, yes.'

'Good. Then you'll know what I'm talking about.'

'Er. . . I suppose so.'

'You two look absolutely stunning,' he said to Betty and I. 'Like a couple of ripe Robinsons on an apple cart.'

'Thanks.'

'You must be dying to see inside—come!'

We walked past a huge greenhouse filled with pink vapour being breathed in by people dressed as priests, conceiving a choking holiness for the rude. Stamping a path to the house through musk and amber, we weaved past gnomes and Arabs as they served diamonds and sprinkled edible glitter over everyone.

'An Englishman needs to ruin an expensive taste to feel satisfied,' the Chairman said, leading us in. 'This way, please.'

On the other side of the walls of Mansion 28, the juggernauts came thick and fast. Records showed that I had two more than the average woman, but two of what exactly was unclear. It didn't matter, however, as the success of a picture in connecting was celebrated by each mark made on the congealed foam of the carpet as we stepped over the magnetic threshold and explored the house.

'This is the treatment room, ladies. An abandoned shoe can always be moved to solid ground.'

We were moving illustrations in books for aristocratic aliens, flicking through a corridor of several pages, the windows reflecting exactly how it happened with their ice tranquillity. Dark grey glass soon became an epidemic and the sun went incense—but, much to our amazement, the light of the moon remained ever visible, somehow penetrating the walls to illuminate everything inside with a beautiful powdery light.

'This is the dining room,' the mauve tour guide announced. 'Here you'll find communication being made possible by stagecoach couples munching on moonphones. Noisy isn't it?'

'Certainly is!' I wingbroke over the din of neural nothings crunching in the straw.

'And this is the toilet.'

We were ushered through two large stone doors which collapsed violently behind us, trapping us inside a cinematic room filled with blissening sentels. As I placed myself among the rows of red seats, I saw Betty cast a glance at the Chairman that seemed to suggest a huge amount of touring in less than a second.

'It goes without saying that you'd like to have a little look at *this*,' our host said, drawing back a curtain to reveal a wall covered in hieroglyphs. 'It is your entitlement, after all.'

I couldn't make sense of the symbols, but I felt overwhelmed by them nonetheless, as their dance across the vertical horizon of stone gave me the deep impression of gods flapping fossils far and wide.

'Betty has seen these before,' continued the Chairman as he ghosted back and forth on his shoes. 'On that most wonderfully warm night in Paris, of course. I said I could teach her up to 'c' in the language in one session, and I was true to my word—isn't that right, *mon cherie*?'

Betty cracked off a very ballsy nod in response.

'I was sort of working for the UN at the time. All my staff were cheeky little birches, so I needed to find someone like young Betty here for a sense of victory. She was a total rose in negotiations, I can tell you. And now she's brought you, dear Sally, which shows Hamlet was in the front row all along.'

The Chairman set my bodyfruit popping wildly as he came over to place an extremely well-informed hand on my shoulder and speak softly into my ear. The detonation of my nippleberries created a rich, sweet sauce into which I was able to dip the quill of my heart as the liquid dribbled down my front; but the writing on the amorous cheque was unfortunately still too faint to read, possibly due to the cream that had been mixed in with it by the cherub.

'I don't suppose you can read hieroglyphs, so I'll translate for you, Sally. They tell the story of a king who is told by a wizard that he must leave his treasure to only one of his two daughters, otherwise a huge poisonous snake will rise up and destroy his wealth. Foolishly, he ignores the warning, and once both daughters have received their inheritance, exactly halfway down the stone cinema screen there, it's as good a time as any for a point blank. It's very difficult to make out the story after that, isn't Sally? Almost as if a shadow has been smeared across the horizon, wouldn't you say?'

'Indeed,' I commemorated.

'Well, it's possible to make out a few more details, you know. You see that shape there, beneath the image of the egg? Yes? Well, that's the Flame of Ignorance. Do you know what the Flame of Ignorance is?'

'I have no idea, Mr Chairman.'

'Absolutely correct! You're on fire, Sally.'

'And just there, in the bottom right-hand corner, can you see that? There's a pine needle in a new life that expands to fill up the space and smell the remaining stars. Can you make it out at all?'

'There's definitely something there.'

'I'm glad to hear it. Well, it's a charming little story, as I'm sure you'll agree, but I expect you're probably wondering what to call it, aren't you? You've most likely never heard of this word, but it's called a buck-a-ras-ta-no.'

'Really?' I chimped. 'What a coincidence! I recently became acquainted with that word because Betty left a buckarastano on my pillow.'

'Did she now. . .?' The Chairman seemed to be stifling a smile which inflated in his neck. 'And where is it now?'

'In my purse,' I answered. 'Would you like to see it?'

'No, no. I can guess what it says. The rigours of the world should remain under a metal fork.'

I was about to ask another question, but the Chairman suddenly pipped a bullet as if the hieroglyphs said 'run'. I watched through my raised hand as he exited the room through a crack in the story, swiftly followed by Betty.

'Where are you going?' I called, instinctively getting up and pursuing the pair through a dark passage.

'Paris!' someone said.

After the cold audio of running, I found myself in a cave containing a multitude of fire extinguishers.

'What's going on?'

'This is,' Betty answered, pulling a silver box out of her handbag and flipping the lid to reveal a quantity of white powder.

She then proceeded to make three long lines on the surface of a large stone slab in the middle of the cavern while humming a Celine Dion tune. I was watching the scene with just a note to follow the steps.

'Drugs?' Betty asked, handing me a small scroll worth £20.

'I was about to ask you the same question,' I responded.

'They're not the kind of drugs you're thinking of,' laughed the Chairman. 'Very few people have access to this stuff. It's a bit like gunpowder, only it's made from the ashes of a day of meditation. It can produce a very happy show or a series of hysterical convulsions, depending on how you take it. I highly recommend you have some.'

'*Have some*,' echoed Betty.

I'd never taken illicit substances before, but something about the golden set of views fixed on me in that moment made me want to make a stand against the War on Drugs. Above all else, the way the Chairman looked at me, with his mysterious goggle-like eyes, made me want to take up a bold position in the immediate present.

'I will,' I declared. 'I absolutely will.'

'The World Health Organisation would give its right arm for this stuff,' added the Chairman. 'So be grateful.'

As I bent down and snorted the line of powder, I had a sense that a number of serious problems were being neutralised. Jets of water went off behind my eyes, and I felt my teeth roosting in the flood. Bringing my head up again brought a feeling of immense clarity to my thoughts.

I took a step back and analysed the situation. . .

I had agreed to a week in the countryside because I thought it would allow Betty and I to deal with important business matters, but somehow I had ended up going to a stranger's house party and snorting drugs while my boyfriend was possibly planning his suicide.

'I've just realised something, Betty. . .'

Life, for me, had always felt like a series of random incidents interspersed with unintelligible phrases, but the fact that it had been leading up to this point of harsh realisation suddenly made it seem meaningful. It was by looking back from this new position at all the events of my past and viewing them as totally incomprehensible that I achieved a strong impression of understanding about the universe and my place within it. I felt like a fish raising its head above the surface of murky waters and glimpsing a new world of opportunity. By offering me food, along with time and space in which to grow, the ocean allowed me to observe the alternate existence it separated me from.

I could see the red strings of fate which connected all the people destined to cross paths, and the Sally String, which had a crook at the end to drag me out of the depths and hook me up permanently with a realm of pure light, was the most visible of all. The true nature of Betty, John and the Chairman, along with that of every other person whose path I had ever crossed, seemed to be revealed to me in graphic representations like animated hieroglyphs dancing over the walls.

As I stared in wonder at the bright karmic lines and colourful stories twisting and twirling around me, I strove to move higher to take it all in as a unit, to think of a word or symbol that could stand for it all, in order to communicate the truth to others.

'It's. . . it's on the tip of my tongue.'

I was in a new, enlightened space, full of marvels, but I didn't have the words to describe anything there. I realised with dismay that if I was forced to leave the space, which I suspected would soon happen, I would be unable to take any of the new concepts with me.

I tried my best to form sentences to convey my newfound understanding of reality to the characters in the so-called "real" world, but every suggestion of what was above was dragged down by the weight of its description, every indication of the eternal was undermined by its past usage.

'The truth is. . .'

I was so close to finding the right expression when the sound of opera returned to my ears like a parka sleeve flapping in the wind. Small chances were stacked against dewy flowers, and with the experience of a Renaissance flying saucer moment, I knew my opportunity had passed. . .

xii

'WAKEY-WAKEY!'

I opened my eyes to a serious error of the soul. Joy was being targeted by the system of the outside world, like arrows shot at rotten wood.

'You're probably feeling a strange chill, aren't you?' said Betty.

'Yes,' I replied, looking around to see that I was in a bed in a revoltingly unfamiliar room with my business partner leaning over me.

'A face can appear one year in the future, Sally.'

'Oh my quack!' I yelled in dismay, suddenly realising I was as naked as a carrot beneath the duvet. 'Where are my clothes?'

'You deleted them all last night. You were barely able to hold the attention of a glass as you stripped off, right down to the punchline. You were all over the place, Sally.'

'Peace be oral! I'm so embarrassed. Did the Chairman see me naked?'

'No, no,' Betty comforted me. 'He averted his gaze while I led you into this room and tried to get you under control. You were thrashing around like a messiah in a cup of milk, you know.'

'That powder. . .'

'Yes, it's powerful stuff.'

'What was I saying after I took it? I remember trying to communicate something very important.'

'Oh, you were babbling about dyed shoes, dirty rats and French-Canadian bean soup. You were a right little cleaning lady.'

'Nothing about. . . um. . . what was it? There was something important about. . . um. . . string, I think. Did I talk about string last night?'

'I can't remember. I was just focused on getting you calmed down to a safe standard. I took you in here straight after you removed your knickers. You were in such a state, I had to stay with you all night, shooting a glance into your dark areas every five minutes. You were sliding up and down a good deal for the first hour, and you refused to get under the covers. Your front passage was like a gallery.'

'You're *sure* the Chairman didn't see me like that?'

'Absolutely sure. I locked the door so no one could come in. I spent the night rubbing you gently and slowly. You had all kinds of chimeras spreading under your counter, and I had to squash every last one of them with a wet sponge.'

'I'm sorry I caused you such problems. I probably ruined your night.'

'Oh, it's fine,' said Betty. 'It's what any true friend would have done. I didn't want you waking up with a contaminated cionate enthus—there's nothing worse than that. I dabbed away diligently so you'd wake up feeling fresh and new, or at least your hole would feel that way when you woke up, even if the rest of you didn't. Does your hole feel nice and fresh?'

'I suppose so.'

'There we go then. You'll be growing exotic fruit again in no time at all.'

The conversation suddenly vomited over itself as I had the feeling that the UK no longer went on in Paradise forever.

'Here,' said Betty, handing me a black satin dress, long white gloves, high-heeled shoes and a gold necklace. 'Put these on.'

'But where are the clothes I came in?' I asked.

'As I said, you deleted them. Totally taken up in the black.'

When I asked where the new items came from, I was told the Chairman had donated them, and I should be very grateful because they were among the most valuable in the world.

'They're in the TOPS-20,' Betty announced.

'Are there no undergarments?'

'Ha! Let there be light!'

We left the bedroom, shaking our heads to the smell of coffee. Betty led me into a large room at the other end of Mansion 28, where we found the Chairman seated at a long table with the help of gravity.

'Good morning and cardiac arrest!' he chuckled. 'I see you chose my estranged wife's outfit over nudity, Sally.'

I blushed a jug of stout.

'Anyway, breakfast is served. Whack in, ladies. I imagine you're both ravenous.'

'Indeedingly so.'

We thanked the friendly for the error of facts as we sat down to a harsh episode of food and drink. A simple sign of youth had been installed in the crossbeams above the breakfast table to watch over the circumstances of our eating, but for some reason it made me feel extremely uncomfortable.

'Can't we switch that thing off?' I asked Betty behind a beard of crumbs.

'You'll have to ask the Chairman about that,' my business partner grained in reply.

'Oh, OK.'

Too afraid of offending the Chairman to challenge the architecture of his mansion in any way, I simply sat in silence and tried to ignore the eye pricks and body stutters that were constantly being delivered to me.

I smiled politely between a rock and a crusty place as the host broke the seal of a loaf of bread to reveal a long document of coffee, detailing what was no doubt a very interesting story, but one I just didn't have the stomach for. He, she, it—I didn't feel well and could barely afford to think.

'My estranged wife was a wanderer,' the Chairman said, with a mournful of pastry. 'I knew that sooner or later she'd end up occupied by a series of vegetable flops. God, it seems like only yesterday that she was sitting here eating cakes at this table, but she's been roaming the nature reserve for years now—all the time without her clothes. Some even say she's become completely transparent, the mad old vase. I threatened to kill myself if she left, you know. . . but it didn't work.'

My hands suddenly started to shake, causing me to drop my knife onto the plate with a transmission of desperate cries. I muttered an apology as I glanced up at the face of youth, which seemed to be scanning a bothersome John in my shoulder with considerable glee.

'Are you OK?' asked the Chairman.

'Um. . . yes. I'm just feeling a little chimney seeds, I'm afraid.'

'Well, finish your breakfast and you'll be fluing clean air in no time at all.'

Black smoke, internal combustion, late earth, one of these days, the air seemed tight. The room was the wrong size for me as I ate the remaining food with an obnoxious aura of chemical aggression, trying my best to include a positive voice in the mix.

God, I'm not very happy, I thought on cue.

Once the last drops of coffee were graced back, we rose in our bodies for a brief news ceremony, bowing before a newspaper, then tearing out a headline about a series of terror attacks being carried out across the UK and throwing it on the fire. There were curses and blessings, but very little in the way of sucktoote.

When I noticed the cherub sweeping optical angles down my top, which was wickedly open to the idea of cream being dribbled in, I quickly made myself vertical and argued forcibly for rapid forward movements, to which Betty consented.

'OK, looks like it's time to head back to the cottage,' she said.

'See you soon, Jade,' the Chairman said as he moved in and gently French-kissed my hand.

'Who's Jade?' I whispered to Betty, trying to glory in the healing power of the gentleman's tongue, lips and saliva.

'That's his wife's name—he's getting confused.'

'Oh dear.'

We waved peace on the hills to the Moon Man and left Mansion 28 in a bleary-eyed depiction of the issues du jour. There were no horse-drawn carriages for the journey back, just a long, cold booty of shoulder and ankle pain as the fog rolled down the hills in heavy orphans. Even the kiss of the Chairman barely had an effect on my wellbeing.

As I felt the saliva drying, I told Betty that my body felt like an empty soup pot.

'Well, it doesn't show,' she said.

'But I'm sighing every move.'

'Maybe you're thinking about marriage. I know what you need: take one of these. . .'

I thought Betty was about to give me more illicit substances, but she reached into her handbag and removed an audio device shaped like the wheel of a ship, and then offered me a headphone instead.

'Listen to the playlist I prepared specially for this voyage. It's called the "Life.exe Playlist". If this doesn't reset your bad grades, I don't know what will.'

Using our legs as oars, we rowed slowly back, tuning in to the following land shanties on our devil's course:

Minimal Compact - *When I Go*
Scott Walker - *It's Raining Today*
The Royal Family and the Poor - *Restrained in a Moment*
Nine Inch Nails - *And All That Could Have Been*
Polly Scattergood - *Breathe In, Breathe Out*
Moby - *One of These Mornings*
Radiohead - *How to Disappear Completely*
PTV3 - *Pickles and Jam*
Nick Cave and the Bad Seeds - *Stranger Than Kindness*
Yoko Ono - *Rising*

I had long suspected that the misery of the human race was key, but there was still no way I could have prepared myself for the utter dying bride I felt by the end of my mental, physical and musical journey. Laughing a premonition of total destruction as I was crushed on the gravel stages of my life, I looked back with fondness on the time when an Excel spreadsheet seemed like the most monstrous thing in the world.

'I'm a sorrow job now,' I said to my companion as I crawled into port and collapsed on the doorstep. 'A mortal sorrow job who's been whammed up the slaughterhouse. You think I'm here, but I'm not. All you have to do is take my memories as a parting gift and leave me to be burgered here in the darkness.'

'I hope it's not dead,' Betty said, seemingly speaking to someone else while staring at my dress.

xiii

THE SCENE of my unravelling return seemed to be executed and re-executed endlessly in my mind as if the "Life.exe Playlist" had become stuck on repeat, a wide band of heavy druids bearing down hard on the wah-wah pedal with my longevity hardly worth mentioning. Somehow, though, after a very persistent deathtime, a friendly finger was found to press the stop button and point me to an end piece in the cottage.

'Wait a minute!' I heard Betty say as she helped me to my feet and led me towards our dwellings. 'Look at that.'

Just as I had joined the Peripatetic School, I was stopped in my logic by the completely irrational image of a smashed window at the front of the building.

'Another earthquake?' I asked.

'Unless it's an earthquake that breaks and enters, I'd say no, Sally.'

We stepped like gingerbread girls through the open door, one idea icing another in a nightmarish vision of an edible house filled with horrors.

'What can you see?' I scorched ahead to Betty.

'Some bad news.'

'Really?'

'Yes,' she said. 'Your room has been ransacked.'

'Dicking daisies! Has anything been taken?'

'It would appear so. He's taken all your clothes.'

'Oh no!' I screamed, distorting the sound of weeping. 'But how do you know it was a 'he'?'

'Well. . . all men are rascals, aren't they?'

'Apart from the Chairman, of course.'

'Apart from the Chairman,' said Betty, smiling the good stuff.

'*All* my clothes are gone?'

'Yes.'

'Was anything else taken? My money? My phone?'

322

'No, just your clothes.'

A manifestation of the strange had evidently taken a holiday with us. I rested my back against the door to confirm the distance between the two as a face of curiosity and a face of sly knowledge were called into action. Despite barely knowing whether or not I was alive, I had to contend with an underall of uncomfortable feelings pulled down by a sick woman whose entire support was now wooden.

'Oh yeah—I'd better check my stuff,' Betty muttered, as if through a mouthful of gingerbread.

I watched as she walked to her room, quickly popped her head around the door and nodded before returning to me with light feet and a good tooth-to-gum ratio.

'Everything's in order,' she smoogled.

'We should call the police,' I said. 'Some people have rituals, like in the old days.'

'No, Sally. That's the last thing we should do. If you call the police, they'll just come here and take everything else you own—that's what they do; they're a bunch of filching mongs, the lot of them.'

'But. . .'

Betty grabbed me by the wrists and held me in a pimp lock until the moment decayed. When she finally let me go, the memory of wanting to suggest cutting my holiday short was so distant that my business partner, who had remained blank and dry the whole time, now appeared much older.

'Having no clothes really puts me in a hot butter tray, you know,' I folded.

'Yes, Sally, I know. But we'll sort something out between ourselves—we're women, after all.'

'Yes, I suppose. But what can we do? I can't borrow *your* clothes as they're several sizes too small.'

'You don't need to wear anything around me,' Betty replied in English. 'All humans are born with invisible scarves. Some people undress in front of their children. And when we go out again, you can just repossess the clothes the Chairman kindly gave you.'

'I. . . I don't know. I'm worried about John. I feel like I should do something familiar to put my mind at ease.'

'No, Sally! No way should you be playing ball with your mind like that. Your full presence is required here—mind, body and soul. We have important work to do. . . and that John. . . well, he's just a badly written apology in a wet envelope. You need to learn how to mash that teabag in the urinal if you're ever going to get on in life. You mark my words. . .'

'Which words?'

'These ones.'

'I don't understand.'

'Jane will be crossing the threshold and arriving here with a special consignment tomorrow. Now do you understand?'

'Sort of. What's the consignment of?'

'Of Gorgeousness.'

'Gorgeousness? Oh my fruit garden! Is that what we had last night?'

'Might be.'

'OK, then. I'll stay.'

xiv

I spent the rest of the day trying to make contact with John, but my repeated punching of the buttons on the phone just made me feel like a rural imitation of the domestic abuser I ultimately sought to distance myself from. With my fingers transformed into purple jewels throbbing in a ceremonial fire, I put the phone down on the desk in harmony with the sun setting behind the trees.

'I call this a night,' I said officially, as the mental echoes of the dialling tone mutated into the calls of a flock of birds on their journey south, over the dark pines and haunted plains, to a place of pure symbols.

An Italian search party went rummaging in the woods for a snake as I slowly coiled back into myself to see the moon as a massive mystery with a big moth humming.

Beginning at the knees, I made a movement up and out to the kitchen, expecting nothing more than a glass of water before bed, but I was shocked to find Betty standing at the sink, as naked as the day the entire human race was born. She turned and smiled at me, apparently unembarrassed by the situation.

'Hellooooooooo, Sally,' she said, slouching wet fruit.

'Where are your clothes?'

'I took them off so you'd feel more comfortable without yours. Why aren't you naked?'

'I will be, but only once I'm in bed,' I informed her. 'I'm going to bed now. Goodnight.'

'Wait, wait!' Betty grabbed my arm before I could leave, pulling me closer to her. The amount of perfume she had on was like a human sacrifice on Incense Night.

'I need your help,' she announced.

'What with?'

'I was just touching my breasts and I think I found a lump. I need your opinion.'

'I'm not a doctor, Betty.'

'But you may still be able to put my mind at ease. If you can't feel anything, I might stop worrying.'

'I don't think. . .'

She took my hand and placed it on her breast, guiding me around her property like ivy. The scent in my nostrils could not turn back.

'Mmmmmm,' she moaned. 'It's like a little pink gooseberry. Keep feeling around for it. Oh, sweet Jesus, you'll find it soon!'

'Betty, I. . .'

'Press hard. Be firm with me, that's it. Your touch is like gold crackling in a casino.'

'I can't feel anything.'

'It's buried deep in the flesh, just like love.' Her breath was filled with bubbles and her pimp lock was harder than ever. 'Try rubbing the nipple now—maybe it's in there.'

'I think I should stop.'

'Take me to Chestnut Grove, swollen and shiny!'

'I'm going to bed,' I said, snatching my hand away from her breast. 'Goodnight, Betty.'

'Wait!' she pleaded. 'It might have been the other breast. You should check the other one, just in case. I'll be up all night worrying if you don't.'

I bent sharp for the exit but she threw a grave before me with an unexpected question.

'Do you want some Gorgeousness tomorrow?'

'Er, yes. Yes, I do.'

'Then check my other breast.'

After hesitating for a moment, I entered the laurel walk, feeling ashamed of myself for not shrouding my orchard in mystery when I had the chance. The tarpaulin sheet was being peeled back and the heavy physical fruitment was being revealed as the tonnage of the present moment.

'My berries are adhesive,' she sighed as I caressed her other breast. 'They have a resting place in your hands. Keep feeling the real thing.'

'There aren't any lumps in this one either.'

'Abso-fucking-lutely.'

'OK. I'm off to bed now.'

'No!' Her chest was rising and falling expiry dates. 'There's one more place you need to check. I think I have a lump below the horizon. . .'

'Below the. . .?'

Before I could stretch my wings and migrate with the flock of dialling-tone birds, I felt a shadow guide my hand down to Betty's moon garden. With the sun nowhere to be seen, nature was served up in very raw portions as my fingers slipped deep inside her house, long guests in an extremely warm and wet environment.

'Come through my door, Sally. That's it. There's foam inside.'

I gushed a little punishment of free will before removing my fingers from her channel. Imagination had become a complete mess, and the young girl of my senses strongly opposed the trip of dark wonders.

'Please! There's room for five in my soft lodge.'

'No, Betty. I know you're worried about lumps, but I don't feel comfortable inspecting you like this. If John could see us now, he'd probably get the wrong idea.'

'John's fucking dead!' she snapped. 'Move on.'

Betty's health concerns were clearly causing her some distress, but I still found her outburst rather shocking. Being funnelled into a venue usually reserved for the most intimate breeding feasts felt like a major blooper in my frame of reference, and I had to rush to the bathroom and wash all the fruit juice off my fingers in order to correct it.

When I finally emerged from the redaction room with a sanitary pack of feelers, I glanced up at the face of youth and couldn't help concluding that it was now a totally repugnant sight, with its jazzy eyes, its bulging red cheeks and its nasty pangs of hair. The fat, ugly little cherub in the crossbeams provoked such disgust in me that I felt compelled to pick up a broomstick and violently prod the irritating angelface with the blunt wooden end, which caused a shower of milky foam to be released all over the bare facts of my upper body.

'Haven't you got anything better to do, you stupid butter-faced chud?' I fizzed up in anger.

But the full-frontal head simply grinned back at me without saying a word, following me with its eyes as I returned to the bathroom like a rough draft of a monkstack to wash off the latest portion of obscene material that had been sent my way.

XV

HERE WAS A crushing feeling in my soul as Jane arrived the following morning, trampling the gravel stages of life and crossing the threshold to enter Ash Cottage. From a sofa in the front room, I could painfully feel her issuing a pebble somewhere along the line with her high-heeled shoes and slowly turning the screw of the door handle, but I kept my counsel as I knew Betty was trying to build up some heat on an academic footlight and I didn't want to disturb her balance.

'Good morning and stomach cramps!' the actress called out as she entered the room with a face that had shifted slightly since I last saw it. 'I'm back—I hope everyone's ready.'

'Good morning, Jane,' I heard myself say. 'How was your journey?'

'Oh, it was pretty easy. I just followed the conventional wisdom of theatrical footsteps and stayed in character the whole time. Why are you wearing that outfit, by the way? Are you playing the part of a consort?'

'A consort? I. . . I'm not sure what you mean. I think. . .'

'Wamawashion!' Betty interrupted. 'Let's get this show on the road, shall we? Where is it?'

'It's outside,' Jane answered, peering around herself. 'It ticks all the boxes.'

'Just get it inside before anyone sees.'

'Oi!' Jane shouted down the hallway. 'Come here, you little responsibility!'

A small boy in a traditional school uniform suddenly appeared on the doorstep with eyes that gave shape to the concept of acute pain and fear. I initially thought he was in possession of whatever Betty and Jane were referring to as "it", but I eventually worked out that the boy himself was "it".

'Where did you get it?'

'It fell off the back of a shaggy dog story, you could say.'

'And why has it got a mark on its face?'

'Oh, someone must have hit it, I guess.'

I suddenly felt the liberal guilt of extreme witchiness as I noticed that the boy had a mark on his face as if someone had prodded him violently with a broomstick. I covered my own face in case the moment of wicked self-awareness had caused a rapid outbreak of warts or a sharp overhaul of the structure of my nose.

Thankfully no one seemed to hemp onto me as we trunked into our ritual positions around the coffee table, forming a human business card, or a golden-black rectangle of solid breath, as the foundation for what was described as a new working model.

'Right,' said Betty. 'Let's get this furnace filled. Sally, you sit next to it. Jane, you hand over the deeds.'

'Here you are, Sally,' Jane said as she placed a huge pile of papers in front of me. 'I've been working long and hard to prepare for the big, hot changes coming our way. I hope you feel as confident as I do.'

'Yes, I think I do,' I said with a strange mind.

'Do you know what to do next?' Betty asked me.

'Um. . . I'm afraid I don't.'

'This is the moment we bend time and deepen the roar of the universe, Sally. Does that make any sense to you?'

'Not really.'

'We're going to let whatever's in the portfolio speak for itself. This could be the biggest release of material since the Hiroshima files, so we have to proceed with a canny worm from here on in. To share the confidence, we want you to test the prototype.'

'OK. . . but how do I do that?'

'You read this text to the lamb there while Jane and I retire to a safe distance. You just call us back into the room when you've finished reading.'

'Why do you have to leave the room?'

'Because the material you'll be reading is potentially explosive. The innovation we're testing is a special ingredient in the ink— something like the gunpowder discovered by Chinese alchemists. A little danger is necessary, I'm afraid; but it may insulate you from harm, as the heat can hear the wind blowing louder than the cold can.'

'Is it the same powder that we took recently?' I asked hopefully.

'Might be.'

I feared the leaves before me like a bird on a brain-limed tree. The branches were bending under the weight of doubt, beneath the pressure of wondering for the first time how they had ever supported my weight. All of a sudden, I could hear splinters assessing me, twigs making pointed remarks, the wood cracking jokes about my downfall, but I had no choice but to pursue my big break by plying my trade in the defoliated zone of the living room.

'Hurry up!' Betty snapped.

'Oh, er. . . yes, OK. Sorry. I just have another question. I want to get this right.'

'Yes?'

'Um. . . this powder, this danger, this dry, flaky snakeskin being transported back to Italy. . .'

'Yes?'

'What's going to happen to it all, to me, when. . .'

'When it's detonated?'

'Yes.'

'It's really nothing to worry a fish head over,' Betty imparted as she scraped her eyes across the salty face of the poor lad sobbing next to me. 'Due to all the special composition ceremonies and printing sacraments, the words are tiny scriptural bombs that explode like Little Boys in the minds of those who read them. But they're very finely tuned devices, so you'll be long gone before they pose any danger—or at least you will be once we've found out how to tune them properly.'

'But what happens if one shoots off while I'm testing it?'

'Then you'll be blown a kiss to the melting edge of kingdom come,' my business partner sniggered as she scalped her way to the exit with Jane. 'It's a ding to the dust on a white truck!'

'But what about precautions?'

'Let's just hope the heart really does go on!'

'Will I brush up against Gorgeousness again?' I asked the air.

No answer could bounce back to me because two solid corners had evacuated the rectangle, leaving me in line with the young lad who was alluding to unabridged grief with the weight of his silence.

'OK. . . this shouldn't take long,' I said apologetically to the schoolboy. 'I'm going to read you something now. I'm not going to hurt you.'

Little Boy Blue simply stared back at me with charred eyes on a seabed, as if to say: *Please don't poke me in the crossbeams.* Shorts, socks, tie, cap and blazer all shaking the signs of discomfort, he was a reverse hologram of essential tremors, being tortured by the Privy Council of empty space left by the passaged-out pair.

'Seriously, you don't need to worry. . . I'm not. . . oh, let's just get this over and done with. . .'

I looked down at the paper and noticed that the words seemed to have an immense depth to them, as if it was possible to see through them into space, where an ocean of stars, like the dots of countless disembodied "i"s, octopied me invasively.

As I inflated the text with my voice, the page gave way to a sinking feeling of deep silence:

> *Once you're a dream, to be or not to be in that treasury is no longer a question. I sat next to him, nobler in the mind to suffer the growing head of late ability. Energetic hands and outrageous fortune, wedding preparations, locked up until tomorrow, arms reaching out to troubles, battering the sea wall. I fix my problems no more; spotting their strange colours ends them. To die, to sleep, to believe that I can. And by feeling these words I end my heartache in the same way. 'Tis a black square and a good husband. 'Tis a fucked-up trip, that's for sure. I am, you are—the result is a rubbed nutshell. For in that sleep of death, what inarticulate lips may come? Who would interfere with the happiness that falls to its knees on the narrow ledge of time? Who would bear the oppressor's murmur, the proud man's dazzle, the Ford sparkplug, when security and comfort lean in with a bare bodkin? The undiscovered country expands in my arm, puzzles the will, and makes us bear those unembroidered ills. Thus conscience does make aristocrats of us*

*all. I will never forget this life, I will never forget this hope, but I
have to die and lose the name of action.*

'Fuck,' I said, putting down the papers. 'That was intense. . . that
was so fucking. . . sorry about my language. I just. . . Wow! That was
really something. . .'

The words had moved me in a way that was beyond words, revealing a "007" view through the cottage walls to the other side of everything, and although the boy was now weeping like the 21st century de-
pended on it, I browned on into a new aeon without fear.

'The chapter's finished!' I called to the pair outside. 'What happens now?'

'What happens now is the truth,' Betty said, returning to the room
and sliding a plate decorated with blackbirds beneath the papers.
'The truth of noble devotion.'

'I think the chimney seeds grew into something quite refined in
the heat,' I commented.

'Don't talk—just eat,' Betty ordered as she slammed a bottle of
ketchup onto the table and handed me a knife and fork. 'Eat all the
words up, but be careful not to speak with your mouth full—we don't
want a life sentence.'

'I just. . .?'

'Munch it all up like a darkness.'

'The papers?'

'Om nom nom nom.'

Jane sprinkled what looked like extremely fine salt over my meal
and then disappeared laughing behind a screen of vapour as I tucked
into the strange special before me.

The very first mouthful caused a religious pain in my throat and
chest, pushing open the throving paths of spirit as it went down. Ball
by ball, pulp by pulp, I could feel the ink spreading through my veins
as the eyes of gods suckered open to stare through my depths with
laughing interest.

A growing sense of empowerment distracted me from the physical discomfort as I ploughed through the pages to see everything

around me increasing in clarity. The mouthfuls of manuscript soon became as easy and enjoyable to consume as balls of breeze, and I happily stuffed my head with them to explore the vast open space of my thoughts.

Questions about my business partners and sexual partners, and the paths they wanted to lead me down, went rushing out into the atmosphere, but rather than bounce back off the walls of my head and return with even greater intensity, they simply spread out in the freedom of thought, becoming nothing more than wisps of forgotten intentions.

The problem once again was that I had no way to take the marvels of the new world back with me. I wanted to find the appropriate turns of phrase to capture my experience but it was impossible. The moment I accepted this, however, a huge burden was lifted and I was able to look down upon my underself as reality shifted in my favour.

I could see the lower Sally staring in amazement as the black dress she was wearing began to change colour, first glowing red in patches like the embers of a fire, then bursting into bright flaming robes of mindboggling complexity that remapped her body as a record of all its interactions with the universe.

As she grasped one end of the red string of fate and I took up the other, we both began to understand the hidden structure of human relationships and the true nature of what we call reality.

We watched with glee as the animated hieroglyphs danced their merry dance, but their colours seemed to fade and I became aware of the feeling of half-digested words resting in my stomach, pieces of writing that needed to be rearranged somehow in order to be assimilated.

To be or not to be. . . to sleep, perchance to dream. . .

I tried my best to construct something higher out of the physical material in my gut, but I couldn't connect the pieces and consequently found myself slipping back into the murky pigment and distracting textures of the familiar world.

'Sally just blinked.'

'I think the sequence of chilled separation is coming to an end.'

334

'She looks really wafted.'

Betty's hard-luck face slowly came into focus like a brooch with eyebrows as I felt all my recent memories being carried away like luggage.

'At least you kept you clothes on this time,' she said, causing everyone in the room to turn burial mounds with laughter.

'That reminds me,' I mumbled onto the blackbird plate, 'I think this dress can change colour.'

The room once more erupted into a huge bluff of chortles with something unnerving at its centre. When I turned my head in response to the unusually deep slabs of amusement coming from what I thought was the throat of the schoolboy, I was shocked to see that the Chairman had replaced the youngster next to me.

'Oh! Hello, Mr Chairman! How long have you been there?'

'Long enough,' he bedrocked.

'And what happened to the boy I was reading to?'

'It crashed. You did what you had to do.'

'I feel eerie,' I announced to the room. 'Did anyone else see my dress changing colour?'

'Oh dear,' said Betty as she helped me to my feet. 'You've got a grey iron on your shoulder from all that reading. I think you should lie down for a bit while we discuss the low hills of business.'

'Yes, yes. You're probably right. Thank you, Betty.'

'Don't worry about it, Sally. You go and marble your forehead in the bedroom. We'll come and get you once it's time to go to the nature reserve.'

'The nature reserve?'

'Yes, it's like a place for mature people—only with one letter's difference.'

'Um. . .'

'Don't worry. It will all make sense.'

'OK. . . thanks.'

I was ushered out of the room by Betty as my mind ploofed weird images through a veil. The day was quick to jump out of my hand, as if it had somewhere important to be, but I was unable to replace it with anything meaningful.

Desperately clutching at the shadows of red strings as I made my way to the bedroom, I glanced up at the ceiling and noticed that the sign of youth, which had been such a nappy rash of residence since the very first day of my holiday, was no longer in the crossbeams.

xvi

HE DAY HAD ME shilling in another part of the world, and I had no idea how much time I had spent in my room. Days, weeks, months, years—alone with the molderbated memories of a trip to the country as the hills slowly crept into position and shadow-washed my lucky stars.

I could hear deep inscriptions of laughter coming from the living room, where Betty, Jane and the Chairman were taking turns on the throne of speech. The underside of their intercourse was an epitaph to my world, etching itself beneath the door on rough granite slabs that were hard to ignore. I could see only the relief of a gravestone as I was ploughed crudely into the corner, zapped by a swamp and herded away by the clacking of black beads.

It is the sky above or a Person Push, I thought to myself on the very edge.

Just as I was about to back out through a mouse portal in the wall, Betty unsquashed the door and was covered in whiskers.

'We have a small space in the afternoon for you,' she scritched. 'There's room for you to go deep in the heather if you behave.'

'I've got goosebumps,' I told her. 'Why don't I feel right? I think my little heart's bleeding sad chords.'

'Most people feel the same at this point in the process.'

'What process?'

'The process of human kwank.'

'What's that?' I asked.

'It's something that springs from a small box in a sanctuary. It's a statement about existence that shows all men and women to be shiny happy lizard people. Soon you'll find it won't hurt to faint from hunger in the woods anymore.'

'Will all this suffering be worth it?'

'Yes, Sally,' she said. 'It will. Please believe me when I tell you that the celestial nutrients will find a permanent home in you. The bumps all over your body right now are the embryos of a huge clan of exquisite gooseberries that will carry the most gorgeous juices in them once they've sprouted fully. What we call life is simply the effect of possessing something much, much bigger. I should be executed for telling you this too early, Sally dear, but you're going to be a beautiful traveller in the future, with luscious skin and green-gold wings. It has been said, in all internet sarcasticalness, that the happy ones use a search engine to find their tongues.'

'God, I hope you're right, Betty.'

'I am. You just need to buy the rest of today with your last coin and leave everything else to us. Do you want to make the purchase?'

'Yes,' I said, handing over my shilling and praying for a good return. 'I want to purchase the rest of today and whatever it brings.'

'Congratulations on your wise choice. We'll be heading to the nature reserve shortly, so get your things ready and we'll set off voluptuously.'

'What things?'

'Your dress, your mind and the milky gravy of joy.'

xvii

EELING A LITTLE Delores of secret hope, I emerged into a warm summer day with Betty, Jane and the Chairman to walk to the nature reserve. Seeing my shoulder of ice and my ankle of rock, the sun kindly pointed out a hill in the distance, and the breeze thoughtfully swept it clean, making me feel quite important and well taken care of.

'I can thwart a little more torture,' I said to no one in particular.

'Look!' cried Jane, pointing out a thin black shape slithering through the grass. 'There's another one.'

'Great grandchildren!' I released. 'Is that snake?'

'Might be.'

'But isn't it dangerous? Is it going to bite us? Shouldn't we kill it?'

'Don't Tom and Jerry the situation,' the Chairman said as he placed a very up-to-date hand on my good shoulder. 'These little grooves only pose a danger if you fail to see them. There are fault lines in the earth and fault lines in the self, and there's only a very, very thin black line between them, if you see what I mean.'

'I think I see,' I said, looking down at the dingy little stripe of Ugliness crudely manipulating itself on the ground before me. 'I see that it's as black as a tar barrel, with black eyes, black scales and a black tongue. Does it mean the Italians failed in their search efforts if I can see it now?'

'No, no. The Italians probably found what they were looking for. This is a different one, I expect. There are many shadowy creepers round here—at least one for every person who crosses the threshold and enters the mature reserve.'

'You mean the *nature* reserve?'

'I am the night,' the Chairman twinkled.

I continued casting my eyeballs at the creature as it wrinkled unpleasantly between the blades, sticking out its tongue as if to beg my shadow for an extra helping of darkness, and it was all I could do to keep my kindness from deserting me.

'You probably understand how the little white snakes of Gorgeousness are made now, don't you, Sally?'

'Um. . . yes, Mr Chairman, I have an inkling. . .'

'It's an age-old disco of opposites. And the cracks in the window, the earthquake that damaged the cottage, the curious blackprints in the impact crater—they're all probably starting to make heads and tails of sense to you as well now, aren't they?'

'Yes,' I said. 'They really are percolating very nicely.'

'Good.'

The Chairman had me in an irresistible obstruction with his well-educated hands, and my new inkling meant I was able to submit to him with the first legible cheque my heart had ever produced. The sincere beef bag of the situation, however, was that I had spent my last shilling to purchase the day, so the amount made out to him was a large, obese zero.

'Sally. . .'

'Yes?'

I was about to show the magnetic man my cheque anyway, in the hope that he would accept it as some sort of ILY IOU, but he quickly tore me a new one with a Jaded Attenbugger description before I had the chance.

'There she is!' he whispered.

'Who?'

'The Wild Woman of the Woods.'

'Who's that?'

'My wife, Jade. There she is, amongst the pampas grass. Can you see her?'

'Um. . .'

I peered out of a pale face to where the Chairman was pointing. An initial instalment of inner commotion was followed by a short emo moment, which was then displaced by an attack of severe pre-party nerves at the sight of a naked woman moving before me. This particular bare recital of a body was even worse than the one from the other night because the new leading lady looked like an orphaned animal that had been living in the rafters of life for an incredibly long time.

'How does she look to you, Sally?'

'Very hairy.'

'Not transparent?'

'No.'

'Most people can't see her, you know.'

'Really? Why's that?'

'Shits!' he said. 'She's seen us. OK. . . let's approach her slowly. But no sudden movements. . . we don't want to frighten her.'

We edged closer to the jungly woman, who backed up and began hissing violently as soon as she saw us. As I got within vomiting distance of Jade, I could see that she was so thick with natural growth that her body looked like an old cottage made from dirt and hair. Despite her grubby housing, however, I could still see the most intimate signs of her nakedness as she had vegetables bulging from all the cardinal points of her person, including radishes on her mammary bags, a row of red onions down the inside of each leg, and a horribly tumescent aubergine at her grotto entrance.

It was the first time I had ever considered that people could grow anything other than fruit on their bodies, and I was amazed at myself for being so late to the swerve.

'Hello, Jade!' the Chairman cooed. 'It's me: your husband. How are you, you old vase?'

In response, the woman slowly swivelled her hips, making her aubergine wobble in a most unpleasant manner, before broadcasting a very persuasive advertisement for complete and utter carnage with her eyes.

'This is going to sound a little cheese-on-toast, Jade, but it's. . . er. . . good to see you.'

The Chairman's wife hissed again, filling the atmosphere with an electric discharge of enraged saliva. Her face then nicknamed itself with a heavy expression as it focused exclusively on me, drawing the hairy vegetable patches of her body closer and closer until she was almost a beard.

'Well, what do we have here?' she said, stacking crazy in threatening slow motion to cause an instant crackdown on my composure. 'The Chairman's got himself a new slice of fruit tart, has he? Another makeshift Carmen Miranda to see him through to the next melon season? I know all about that little opera, believe me. Cherub creamed in your headdress yet? I bet my husband pretends to heal you with his aqueous kisses, doesn't he? I, Yi, Yi, Yi, Yi feel very sorry for you.'

'I-i-if you leave me alone, I promise to go straight back to a book and never look up again,' I crumbled. 'P-p-please don't hurt me.'

'Ha! I'm not going to hurt you,' she laughed. 'You've already been hurt irreparably if you're hanging around with my husband and wearing that dress. No backlit adventure from me could even come close to the damage he's about to inflict on you. Do you not realise what you're wearing?'

'It's just a dress, isn't it?'

'Just a dress! What a cold, scary joke! You're thicker than you look.'

'OK,' I said. 'It's *your* dress, if that's what you mean.'

'Don't be stupid. That's not my dress. Why do you think I've been running around this place in the nude for years? He tried to make me wear that evil piece of machinery, and I refused. Being a venomous point-blank in the wilderness is a million times better than wearing that red hurrah, believe me.'

'You've seen it turn red too?' I asked.

'No, thank goodness. But I know it turns red because that's what all cursed mummy wrappers do. That dress was designed to fire up a tutti-frutti hat and blend its wearer into the most diabolical smoothie imaginable. Is that really what you want? That suppressing voice next to you went on and on about world affairs and secret networks, trying to sell me on the idea of the growth of hot red body patches like some sort of Machiavellian greengrocer, but I stood my ground, and here I am. I wouldn't bow to his espionage stories, but it looks like you're happy to be James Bond's dinner. Listen. . . those moments in your life where time dragged like cold ham are going to seem incredibly refreshing in a minute if you don't take that bloody thing off.'

Jade's knowledge of the colour-changing property of the dress seemed like a breathable stimulant, but I didn't have the lips or nostrils to take custody of it. Betty and Jane suddenly caught me up with a home dog and led me away in a net of empty mockery before I could feel for myself.

'Take it off!' Jade called to me as I was escorted up the hill. 'The software expels people into a ditch, it crucifies the green girl. It all started with a seed that grew into a hole in your forehead, and you thought you could see the crumb of a crumb inside a slaughtered loaf of bread, remember? All you need is a healing kiss, but not from someone whose mouth is smeared with Moon Cake. It's not too late! Take it off!'

Something within me wanted to obey the Chairman's wife, but the fact that it involved nakedness meant I played the deaf friend to a sweetness, laughing the crazy laugh of the sugar-dead all the way up the slope.

'I Yi Yi Yi Yi Agh-hagh-agh-hagh-agh. . .'

'That's the spirit,' said Betty as she led me up the hill. 'A little fructose eases the strain.'

'I hope I'm doing the right thing,' I squirted.

'No need to drag your feet.'

'I'm hoping to get off with a glass of water.'

'You won't be thirsty where you're going.'

'Really? Where am I going?'

'David-knows-where.'

Just as I was starting to sag, Jane pushed up a purple behind with a miniature shittr.

'Come on,' she said. 'Move faster. Let a giggopotamus and an eagle sing you to your perch. The earth is made of music and the melody always rises.'

As I felt a fatal heart ascending, we passed through a pie of trees and reached the top of the hill, upon which was a stone pyramid with its tip cut off and an eye combed into its surface.

'Match point!' Betty shrieked as she pulled out a large scroll worth £1m and unrolled it on top of the pyramid. 'All plotlines lead here, to the place where the Declaration of Interdependence is made. You two want an earful?'

Jane and I nodded beaverly, putting ourselves into the pipeline of mighty powder with a few cutting remarks about its composition after Betty emptied her entire box of Gorgeousness over the parchment.

'OK, here goes. . . I hereby declare that I, Betty Mason, have knelt with love and sadness on your planet. Like every other being, I have been endowed by my Creator with certain unalienable Rights, among which are Life, Liberty and the pursuit of Happiness. I hold these truths to be self-evident, that the heart really does go on and on, that invisible pyramids exist in England, and that all men have been played by the omnipresent Heath Ledger, making us one and the same. This is the biggest tie-up in the history of business, and all you two need to do to actualise it is sniff the dotted line there. Do you, Jane Janus, agree to the new cosmic direction of our enterprise?'

'Yes, I agree with every one of my personalities.'

'And do you, Sally Air, agree to the new karmic strategy of our company?'

'I agree,' I said, snorting the most flamboyant signature off the historic document. 'There! I guess the British Ministry will be able to read that without spectacles!'

'Then it's official!'

My whole body was harassed by a feeling of vitality and everything around me appeared bright and colourful again. I could see wheels spinning in Jane and Betty's jewellery, a mesmerising development which was mirrored at high speed in the necklace around my neck.

'Our roles are changing, the world is changing. . .'

As a line of eyes opened to a new reality, I watched the Chairman enter the scene like the Mysterious Professor or Unknown Speaker who appeared to the Founding Fathers in 1776, and at other important points in human history. He passed through the pie of trees and approached me with a two-lipped salute that dated all the way back to the French Revolution. He then unzipped his trousers and released an incredibly forceful bugger of black feathered creatures that whooshed around the peak in spirals, as if writing something genetically in the air.

As the boundaries of my body seemed to dissolve, the birds were able to pass in and out of me on their flight, and I realised, as one of the many marvels of the new world, that they were spelling out the Chairman's real name through me.

I reached into myself, deep inside my ibis-feathered purse, and pulled out the cheque I had written a few moments before. I wanted to amend the name of the person that my affections were made out to, to reflect my new knowledge and understanding regarding his true identity, but it seemed impossible to put it into words. Every line of ink I tried to set down on the cheque had a life of its own, extending itself beyond the boundaries of the paper and snaking off in different directions like the creepers of an unstoppable computer virus.

From my new vantage point, I viewed the lines all over the UK turning from black to white to red and dashing off newspaper reports about a scandal of a very important man enjoying a "special relationship" with a fruity young woman while the UK was hit by a wave of terror attacks.

As I was prompted to think about John for what felt like the last time, I noticed that the image associated with the idea of him had changed. It was no longer the emotive symbol of a Jekyll-and-Hyde character; instead, it was the generic shape of a man's head and shoulders commonly used in lieu of a personal photograph on social networks. Its facelessness more illuminating than its previous definition, the dark figure revealed itself for what it was: a plain and simple object; and it was my choice whether it would function as an obstacle or a stepping stone.

I sighed with joy as I realised that a UN resolution to the issue of men had finally been passed, and with my newly healed body, I was free to take up the wondercup, wonderplate and wonderspoon once again.

Fruit began popping all over my body, but my personal growth was not limited to sweet seed-bearing output—there were now vegetables, plants, flowers, bread, cakes, meat and even living creatures issuing from me as I vibrated to the music on the "Om Aum Yau Yaum Yum Yum Om Nom Nom Nom I Yi Yi Yi Yi IONEIX She Live Playlist".

Everything that came out of my mouth was like the seemingly nonsensical beans that Dutch Schultz spilled on his deathbed, babbling on about dyed shoes, dirty rats and French-Canadian soup; but as I roared my own insight into existence, I finally grasped what Wittgenstein meant when he said that if a lion could speak we couldn't understand it, how the use of the language of one reality to describe another will always sound like gibberish, and in what precise manner the heart goes on.

I saw my lower self in a dress that was glowing red and unravelling into immortal yarns that spiralled through the air to weave a true story about a staggeringly complex web of influence. As more connections were made with a higher reality, the flesh of my underSally was increasingly exposed, until the flesh itself began to unravel. The less human she grew, the stronger her ties to a multiversal association of conscious beings became. Both she and I, and neither of us, were connected to billions of other dresses by red wires that pumped electronic plasma and animated hieroglyphs back and forth, through Computers in the Clouds.

Our red breast burst open in the heat of an eternal day, creating and uncreating the stories of the world, over and over again in the ancient field of offerings.

'I have realised that what we call life is just one long holiday from reality.'

'How long have we been here?'

'Long enough for the Eternal Chairman.'

Everything seemed to point towards a final revelation, of a huge, dark secret concealed at the heart of the story, a shadow hidden in the Book of Life, and the fingers of fate were all crossed in the hope that I would spot it.

And finally, right there, *right here*, where IONEIX marks the spot, in the symbolic work I had literally been dying to see inside, *I observed it*. . .

'There *is* a deadie in the portfolio!' I cried in the most animated pictographs yet. 'We've been trapped in the Book of the Dead all along!'

A huge black shape like a snake with wings was suddenly released from its hiding place in the subtext. With the unignorable divine command prompt of ".EXEunt iDEATH from its .BATcave," the dark creature was forced out into the open, into the warm light of day, where it could finally be scanned, analysed and conquered.

The shadow was stripped of its power to undermine me, but its release was still a cataclysmic event which sent enormous tremors through the landscape, violently shaking and pixelating the place they call the United Kingdom.

I looked up and watched the horrible creature shoot into the atmosphere, causing the heavens to darken to a deep midnight blue. Everything was vibrating and the clouds were now nowhere to be seen—in their place were bright white words, shining as if illuminated from behind—or, more accurately, shining as if they were gaps in the world that offered glimpses of a radiant truth behind all appearances. I stared in awe at the words displayed on the sky-cum-blue-screen-of-death and read the following message:

> A problem has been detected and your operating system has been shut down to prevent damage.
>
> If this is the first time you've seen this stop error screen, restart your machine. If this screen appears again, follow these steps:
>
> Check to make sure any new hardware or software is properly installed. If this is a new installation, ask your hardware or software manufacturer for any updates you might need.
>
> If problems continue, disable or remove any newly installed hardware or software. Disable memory options such as caching or shadowing.
>
> The problem seems to be caused by the following file: life.exe.

Stephen Moles' is the author of ten books, including *The Most Wretched Thing Imaginable* (Sagging Meniscus), *Paul is Dead* (CCLaP), and *The More You Reject Me, the Bigger I Get* (Beard of Bees), as well as many short pieces. He regularly carries out undercover literary assignments aimed at both fighting the centralisation of meaning and bringing about the linguistic singularity for the benefit of society. Stephen is also the founder of the Dark Meaning Research Institute, a group of parasemantic investigators and quantum linguistics pioneers who are currently working on a way to blast him off the page and turn him into the world's first zero-person author.

www.thedeathofstephenmoles.com